Eight Nights in Four Corners

A Novel by

Spencer Deering

Eight Nights in Four Corners

Copyright© 2003 by Spencer Deering

ISBN: 0-9740030-4-2

TurnKey
press·

2525 W Anderson Lane, Suite 540
Austin, Texas 78757

Tel: 512.407.8876
Fax: 512.478.2117

E-mail: info@turnkeypress.com
Web: www.turnkeypress.com

For my editor, my partner, my friend,
my love, my life, Sandra.

Prologue

Apromising cab just off Sixth Street caught Luke Stahl's attention—a purple Cavalier parked curbside, boasting chrome rims and dark curtains hung across the back window. Luke opened the door and threw himself into the back seat.

The driver, a stocky Mexican in a ravaged leather jacket, turned around, then grunted. "Where to?" His breath smelled like fish sticks and Listerine.

Luke, in serious need of a fix, let out a breath. "You know Dre, right?"

The driver looked him over. "Who are you?"

Holding up his hands, Luke said, "I'm nobody. I've been trying to get in touch with Dre ... " He considered whether to bolster the cabby's confidence by dropping another dealer's name. "Or Paul. Neither one's around, and I'm looking."

The cabby turned to the front, but Luke saw his frown in the rearview mirror above the hanging crucifix. "For what?"

"Chop."

The cabby looked out his tinted window to the left. "How you know Dre?"

"I met him through Marshall."

"The frat boy?"

Surprised Marshall's reputation had traveled so far, Luke said, "Yeah. I'm his brother. Dre's hooked us up before."

The cabby seemed satisfied. "Dre's gone, but Paul's around." He looked at Luke through the rearview. "How much do you want?"

"A gram."

"Cost you a hundred."

"Why?"

"'Cause it's a pain for me to get it."

"I'll go with you. Paul knows me."

"Fuck no! I'm going alone." His eyes, still appearing in the rearview, dared Luke to resist. "You want it or not?"

Luke had no choice. He was lucky enough to find this guy; another chance at coke would need a miracle. "Fine."

"Give me ten minutes. Meet me at The Skull and Snatch."

Luke nodded. "I'll be out front."

The cabby grunted again. "You got the money on you right now?"

Luke slid across the backseat, stirring a stench like low tide. "Yeah," he said, breathing through his mouth.

Left jonesin' for an hour and a half on Sixth Street, Luke tried to distract himself with the energy of Texas' music mecca. Never too far from The Skull and Snatch and always on lookout for the cabby, he drifted from club to club, listening to the beats thrusting from open doors and outdoor bars. The range in music matched the variety of faces and styles on the street: from hard-core punk to rock, from country to college. Luke admired the fact that preppy UT students, Latinos, and blacks coexisted peacefully on the carless strip. Though he'd already spent a year in Austin, the "multicultural vibe," as one travel brochure put it, still impressed Luke. A part of him appreciated the chance to participate in the Texan anomaly.

But every time he stopped in front of a club, Luke didn't enjoy the music or cultural harmony for long. Too desperate for the cabby to meet him with the cocaine, he couldn't stay still. His mind repeatedly told him to quit and go home. When a deal took this long to come through, it was surely a bust. But he couldn't give up, and figuring the night was too hot for anything but hanging around Sixth Street anyway, he continued walking in circles.

Finally, Luke spied the cabby by Taco Bell, limping toward The Skull and Snatch. Approaching Luke and nodding toward the alley, the cabby, his lips tight, looked pissed.

Luke followed him, turning his nose away from the cabby's stench that trailed him like a slug's slime. In silent exchange for his hundred bucks, Luke received only a tiny, folded piece of foil that held what looked and tasted like a mix of flower, petrol and pixie dust. He almost kept quiet, but he figured he had nothing to lose except a little face; the cabby wouldn't make a scene so close to a crowd. As the cabby turned to walk away, Luke cleared his throat and grabbed the cabby's shoulder. "What's this?" Luke asked, trying to sound tough.

When he turned to face Luke, the cabby's eyes opened wide, but his surprised expression soon gave way to contempt, forcing Luke to reconsider his approach. The cabby narrowed his black eyes and whispered through closed teeth, "What the fuck you talking about? That's good shit."

"This is crap." Noticing his declaration was too loud, Luke lowered his voice. "It's all white and grainy. I need Dre's usual—the yellow tar."

The cabby knocked Luke's hand off his shoulder and stepped into him, his face an inch away from Luke's. Clearly, he wanted no part of a suspicious conversation with a college kid while his cab sat unguarded around the corner. Luke, finally realizing how shady they looked, began to glance at the passersby.

"Listen, *cabron*," the cabby said, his breath now reeking more of fish than Listerine, "you better take that shit and be happy." He then screwed up his face and added, "You think I can't get my man to come back here, find your preppy ass, take this shit back *plus* the money you're holdin', and then knock your cock in the dirt?" Still facing Luke, he backed away and turned to walk down the alley. Luke made a move toward him, but the cabby thrust his right hand into his leather jacket and glared at Luke, who froze. Without breaking his stare, the cabby growled, "Just walk away." Then he disappeared into the alley.

Probably a good idea, Luke thought, and did as the cabby suggested. Discreetly, he stood in the alley's shadow and re-examined the powder in the foil. Then he ambled past the huge, thumping speakers, through the daunting iron gates of The Skull and Snatch.

Calling the noise that boomed from the amps music would be an overstatement; it was merely asynchronous, slammed guitar chords accompanied by an impossibly loud, guttural roar. Luke assumed there couldn't be many people in a venue that played such crap, so it probably had an empty bathroom.

Though the club wasn't packed, a startling number of patrons, mostly underage kids, danced on the center floor, trying to take Gothic cues from the few legal customers trapped in their juvenile infatuation with blood and makeup. Black draped everyone and everything inside. The only color in the place came from green, purple and pink ropes of hair that swung from the dancers' spinning and bobbing heads. The crowd had as much rhythm as the music coming from the stage, so the colored frenzy against the black backdrop resembled a whirl of too many broken disco lights in a black-lit basement.

Even though he couldn't have looked any less Gothic, no one was concerned with Luke in the least. He bypassed a bald bouncer, a man the size of a bull moose, whose eyes rolled back in his head in an apparent attempt to look at his own brain.

In the bathroom stall, Luke took out the foil and his key, then shoveled the majority of the coke up his nose. Because he was sure the stuff was weak, he took little time between hits, thinking he'd have to snort it all to feel even the slightest buzz.

He was wrong.

In a moment, his heart began to gallop and his chin and neck fired out, like a turtle trying to escape its shell. He took the biggest breath he could, but it wasn't enough; he felt like his body would implode if he didn't deliver it more oxygen. But his breaths weren't satisfying and he began to reel. Involuntarily, his hands shot out to the side, bracing Luke against the stall's vinyl walls. His arms felt stiff as iron. He tried to bring his head back to its normal position, but it resisted his pull.

His short breaths failed his body. "Oh Christ, Luke. Oh Christ," he whispered to himself. It felt like his arms and head were fleeing his body and he had no recourse. He did what he always did when he felt out of control and on death's door: he repeated pitiful pleas to a God he otherwise never spoke to, and he thought of his mother, devastated, looking over his casket. "Oh Christ. Oh Jesus Christ." Because his extremities rebelled, he thought it a cruel joke that he had remained conscious. He felt hyper-aware of his incapacity and his lungs' shrinkage. Soon, his mind joined his body's insurrection, and his mother's devastated countenance peeled into other images: the cabby, Luke's father, his house's broad oak door with its gleaming glass, his dead brother's wounded neck, his high school's football stadium, and finally nothing. Whiteness.

In time, a black shadow slowly drew over his line of sight and soon extinguished the final blade of the bathroom's fluorescent light. He collapsed, his head coming to rest under the toilet bowl. Before he lost consciousness, Luke felt his head slam and then settle between a peculiar temperature contradiction. The coolness of the toilet's slimy ceramic base overran one cheek, while the warmth of the wet concrete floor seeped into the other.

"What the hell are you doing?"

Luke came to and looked up to see the face of the massive bald bouncer, whose eyes had reverted to their normal position. He pulled Luke up by his collar.

"Oh my God," Luke whispered. He looked the bouncer full in the face as if he was a long-lost friend. "I'm alive."

"What?" the bouncer snapped. "Are you fucked up?" He shook Luke vigorously, then asked, "What are you on?" Obviously Luke was no threat, because the bouncer relaxed his grip and helped Luke up. He then softened his tone, "Besides the sun's coming up. It's time to go home." He paused and looked into Luke's eyes. "You need the rest."

Luke's neck still felt like steel, but he had regained control. He mustered a nod toward the bouncer and slid out of the stall. But on his way to the bathroom door, he felt very peculiar, noticing he leaned to the right as he walked. His attempt to balance himself was to no avail, and he slipped on the thick, black bar sludge that coated the floor. He fell facedown.

The floor of a punk club's bathroom is not the place to be at 5:30 in the morning; he threw up as soon his face landed in another's bile. He looked up, silently pleading for assistance, but the bouncer only winced, pulling his face back into his thick neck. "Goddamn!" the bouncer coughed. Again his tone turned aggressive. "You *are* fucked up." He yanked Luke to his feet and yelled, "Get out of here!" Shoving Luke repeatedly toward the exit, the bouncer kicked him twice in the ass.

Though it was early, the sun's glare almost knocked Luke off his feet. He shut his eyes and brought up his hand to shield his face. It took every bit of energy he could gather to walk to the Blue Moon Café's canopied doorway and find some protection from the light.

He dragged himself to the counter and ordered dry toast and tea. Thankfully, he turned and saw a fraternity brother at the other end of the counter, who looked no healthier than Luke.

"You look like shit," he said to Luke.

"You too."

The young man threw down a piece of bacon. "I'm going back to the house. Need a ride?"

Luke nodded. Silently, he put two dollars on the counter and followed his friend out. They rode home in silence.

Part 1

"I'm on a night train ... "
Guns and Roses

1

The first weekend Alex had his license—when Luke was seven—he took Luke to the desert. They drove well into the evening. When nothing but sand and dried shrubs surrounded them, Alex pulled his truck over to the side of the road. He turned off the lights but left his radio on, playing "Black Magic Woman."

Alex got out of his truck. "C'mon!" he yelled to Luke, darting into the darkness.

Nervous, but sure his big brother would let nothing happen to him, Luke followed Alex's waving flannel shirt. But Luke's short legs had difficulty leaping even the smallest shrubs. He started to trot, looking down to avoid the next hazard. When he looked up again, his brother was gone. Luke felt his heart drop to his stomach, his throat tighten.

In the pitch black of the desert, something tripped his ankle and Luke went down. His young mind couldn't fathom whether he'd been attacked by a bush, a hyena or a ghost. Fear pieced his heart. His eyes saw only black; his hands felt only sand. Instinctively, he rolled onto his back and fired his legs like pistons, trying to dissuade the would-be attacker.

As he fought his faceless, shapeless enemy, questions spun through his mind: Why did Alex make me run into the desert? God, where is he? Did this "thing" get to him, too?

"Got you," Alex said. His slow words fell from not more than five feet away, but Luke still couldn't see his brother.

"Alex!" Luke could feel his relief well up in tears. "Don't do that!" His frustration then released them. Shuddering with sobs, Luke shrieked, "Where are you?"

"I'm sorry, Luke. I'm sorry. I'm down here." Luke got up and put his hands in front of him as he shuffled toward his brother's slow words. "A little bit more." Luke

felt Alex's wide hand take his and yank him down to the cool desert floor. Luke landed on his back as his brother fell next to him.

"I didn't mean to scare you, bro. Swear. I was just playing."

Alex never meant any harm, and Luke quickly forgave him as his eyes adjusted to the stars. He realized what his brother was sharing with him: a secret in the night. Luke's breathing and heartbeat slowed as he stared at the glittering show.

Without his heart thundering in his ears, he could hear Santana in the distance. Typically when he was alone with his brother, he'd be preoccupied with what he should do or say, but laying on the desert floor with no one around, nothing stirring, Santana in the background and the stars above, Luke felt at peace.

Alex's voice spread into the night, "Beautiful, isn't it?"

Luke stared at the Big Dipper, its outline so clear he had no trouble connecting the dots. "Yeah."

"We can always come out here if we want. Just us. Whenever we want."

"Everyday?"

Alex laughed. "Not everyday. Most days, though. Long as Dad lets us."

Luke shivered. The mention of his dad broke his peace.

His brother patted him on the shoulder and added, "Even if he doesn't."

The cool desert seemed to move Luke to speak. "I think we can fix him."

"Dad?"

"Make him nicer."

His brother squeezed his shoulder.

"I mean," Luke continued, "you've done a lot, but I can help. Stay out of his way more. Don't talk to mom around him so much. Stop doing stuff he hates."

"Luke, listen to me." Alex slowed his voice even further. "It's not your fault."

Luke nodded in the darkness.

"Hear me?" Alex's regular voice came back to him. "Let me handle Dad. You worry about yourself." Silently, Luke reached up to take Alex's thick hand.

And the two brothers stayed bound in the quiet darkness—on their backs, hand in hand, looking at the stars.

2

I miss Alex, thought Luke as he looked at his glass house glowing in the sun. For a long moment, he stood on his gravel driveway thinking of his dead brother. He sighed from ache of absence. Then he pulled his swollen duffle bag out of his roommate's trunk and slammed it shut.

The air outside, as dry and hot as it was, felt refreshing after the pummeling he'd taken from Josh's relentless air conditioning. Earlier, when they reached the outskirts of Lubbock, the AC's vicious chill wrestled Luke out of his much-needed nap. He woke with a line of drool on his shoulder and every goose bump on his body standing at full attention. Josh's parents gave him the Mustang for having a terrific first year, and he insisted on shutting the windows to use every feature at full power. Though Luke despised this habit—especially when he needed some fresh air after the abuse his body endured last night—he couldn't complain. Josh was generous to offer him a morning ride back home and Luke took it. He had no other options; he had put off going home after the semester ended and there were few kids around, let alone anyone willing to give him a ride to Lubbock.

With Alex in mind, Luke looked over the Mustang's hood, scanning his scorched backyard. The lawn had always been green from all the irrigation and fertilizers his father dumped on it, but the surprising change in color matched the landscape Luke noticed since he and Josh left school. Heading west they had traversed the hills outside of Austin, then the land sloped into the familiar, topographical monotony of the West Texas flats. The area had suffered a hot, rainless spring and with each mile marker they passed, the grass turned a lighter shade of yellow. And now, Luke's own backyard was white-blond. He circled toward the front of the car.

Josh rolled down his window and looked back to his friend. "What are you gonna tell them?"

Luke walked up to the Mustang's driver-side door and rested his crossed arms in the open window frame. "Jesus, I don't know," he replied, not wanting to let go of the car. "Maybe I'll just go in and tell them everything." He looked inside Josh's console and a devious thought came to him. "Here, give me that napkin—I'll write it all down in black and white." He scribbled down his semester grades.

Josh looked at the grades and raised his eyebrows.

"I know. I crushed my GPA," Luke admitted.

"You'll get it back up." Josh paused then asked, "Did they ask why it took you so long to come home?"

Luke shook his head. "I just told them I had some cleaning up to do at the house, after post-exam night turned into a week. My dad didn't care. He loves that shit."

Josh laughed uneasily, passing his eyes over Luke's ashen face. "He *was* pretty fired up after the Oklahoma game. He loved telling stories about being a Beta." He paused, looking down at his console. "Is he gonna make you quit the house?"

"Shit, I don't even think he'll let me go back to school." Luke then added, "I don't know if the *school* will let me come back to school."

"They won't kick you out for one bad semester." Josh grabbed the steering wheel to pull himself forward, then fell back into his seat. "All right, brother, good luck. If it gets hairy, give me a call—I can come pick you up and you can stay at my place. My old man would love to see you; he thinks you're a legend."

"After this semester everyone thinks I'm a legend." He dropped his head and looked at the asphalt below. "Jesus Christ, what a fucking daze."

"Maybe you should ease into it a little bit, don't hit them with it right when you walk in the door."

"Maybe, I don't know." He picked up his head and looked at Josh. "Listen, I really appreciate it."

"No sweat, it's not far out of my way."

Looking back at the ground Luke said, "I also mean for this semester. I know you tried to help me get my shit together. Thank you."

"Welcome. Look, I'm sure I'll see you this summer. And if you're comin' through Midland, give me a call."

"I will." Luke patted the door, turned from the car, and dragged himself over the white grass toward his shimmering house.

"Jesus Christ!" his father boomed, shaking the napkin in Luke's face. "What the hell have you been doing all semester? We sent you back with your word that you'd do well, and then you spit in our face with this!" He began to pace around the living room. It was noon, and even though it was Saturday, Luke was surprised to see his father still wearing his robe and slippers. "Are these even your real grades?"

Though his eyes remained down, concentrating on his feet, Luke muttered his first word, "What?" His focus hadn't shifted from his toes since he had entered the dark living room, its minimal light slicing through the closed Venetian blinds. With two grilled cheese sandwiches in hand, he had kissed his mother on the couch and silently crossed the room to hand his father the napkin. Since then, he had kept his eyes lowered to absorb his father's invective.

"Are these your true grades?" his father repeated, scanning the letters on the ragged napkin.

"Why would I lie about *those* grades?"

"Shit if I know—I'm just wondering why you passed chemistry, but failed Spanish?" He paused. "Why *did* you fail Spanish?"

"Yes," Luke's mother said, "and why, for heaven's sake, did you fail creative writing? You love to write—and you're so good at it." Opposed to the sadness Luke had anticipated in his mother's face, she offered only a mask of wonder.

Luke sat down next to her on the over-stuffed couch, its hunter green fabric cut into thirds by wide, vertical gold stripes. He remembered when he and Alex had constructed make-believe forts, using the couch's backrest along with the dark blue pillows and colorful afghans his mother kept in the room. It was on this couch, too, where Luke used to lie down, resting his head on his mother's soft lap, while his brother played football with his older friends outside.

Luke took a breath before responding to his mother's question, but his father cut him off. "Luke," he said, trying to sound restrained. Still, he spoke too loudly, as if he wore headphones. "I know last fall was tough. It was a tough time for all of us, but my God, we've said it a million times … we have to move on. You told us you agreed, and that you'd do fine in the spring. But Luke, getting grades like this takes as much effort as getting all As." He tightened his face as it crimsoned. "Goddamnit!" He looked at his wife. "I knew we shouldn't have sent him back, but you said, 'No, no, he can do it. He needs it.' Well, look what happened." He tossed the napkin into her lap.

"Steven," she said calmly, "there's no need to be nasty."

"We've been too lenient with him, Martha. Look what's happened."

She looked to the napkin in her lap. "Luke can do well, we know he can." She turned to Luke. "But why ... how did you get these grades?"

"I don't know. It was so hard to concentrate on anything. I would sit in class and try to listen, and then I'd try to get some work done in my room or at the library, but my mind would wander, and then... " He didn't know how to finish his thought without sounding weak to his father, so he rerouted his response, "I especially couldn't read. I haven't read anything straight through in months. My mind can't focus. I just—"

His father cut him off again, "Well, maybe you can't read, but what about writing? You don't need to read to write, do you?"

Even in the midst of his shame, Luke wanted to yell out when his father asked such foolish questions. But he was in no position to refute, so he dropped his head again and spoke slowly through clenched teeth, "It's the same thing. Either way, I just can't concentrate." After a long pause, he looked into his father's bewildered face then his mother's concerned one. He'd seen neither expression since the previous fall. "I ... I ... I don't know why. It was just really hard."

"Goddamnit! I know it's hard. It's hard for all of us. We all have to deal with it— Alex is dead. But Jesus, I'm back at work, and I can't tell you how hard it is to focus on reading draft after draft of all those freakin' contracts, but I do it." His father went to the bay window, picked up a forgotten cup of coffee, finished it, and then came back to where Luke and his mother sat. "Your mom comes home every night and grades until midnight. You think that's easy? We don't want to do it, we don't like to do it, and it's *really hard* ... but we have to do it!" He took a deep breath. After looking at his wife, Mr. Stahl softened his voice, "We want to help you get through this, but we don't know what to do. We'd love to—"

"Yes, Luke, we want to help you," his mother added, "but we don't know how. We thought going back to school would help, but clearly... " She trailed off and looked at her hands. Fury he could handle, but her disappointment flattened him.

Though he couldn't tell his parents the truth behind his failure, he wanted desperately to offer them some truth about his life, even if it had nothing to do with his performance in school; something they could sense was real. But he couldn't tell them about his exploits over the past months, so he decided to focus on the future.

He picked up his head and rubbing his temples said, "I want to go somewhere. I don't know where, but away. I don't even know why; I just feel like I should go. Maybe to the desert." He started to speak more quickly, "I feel awful. I don't know what it is. But—" He stopped, then continued, "Don't you ever—" Again, he stopped. He thought he sounded foolish, and his parents' puzzled expressions confirmed it. He looked back at the carpet.

Finally, his father yelled, "Run away? What the hell have you been doing for the past semester? You obviously haven't been doing anything—isn't that running away?"

"No."

Seething, his father bent over and shouted at the back of Luke's lowered head, "Well, what is it then?"

The burn of tears rose in Luke's throat. He could let his mother see him cry, but not his father. Cooling his tears, he said, "I don't know, but it's not running away."

"Jesus, Luke. Well, when you know what it is, you tell us." His father stood and went back to the window, his breadth filling the frame. "But until that time comes, you need to figure out how you're going to earn your way in this house." Quietly he added, "You can live here if you're taking advantage of school, but you're not going to freeload."

Luke picked his head up and looked at his father.

With a newfound conviction, his father finished the talk by raising his thick finger in Luke's direction. "You will pay your way." After looking from Luke to his wife and back again, he dropped his hand and walked into the kitchen. Hearing ice cubes tumble into a glass and the spin of a bottle cap, Luke and his mother exchanged a knowing glance. They sat in heavy silence, only broken by his father's slippers padding their way up the tiled steps.

Finally, Luke said, "Mom, do you know what I mean?" Miserably, he bit into his sandwich.

"Yes, Luke. Of course I do—everyone feels like that at some point." She stood up as though she was going to retrace his father's pacing, but she sat back down. "I'm sure there were times when even your dad wanted to run away, but he didn't. As an adult you can't just leave. That's a luxury of youth ... " She continued, "You know how much he wants you to do well in school. It's everything to him."

"I know, I know." Luke stood up and said, "It's not like I'm some stupid kid who doesn't know how important it is—like I'd be happy getting a job collecting trash. It's just that I can't do it right now." He went to sit on the matching green love seat across from the couch and looked into his mother's narrow eyes. "And I can't talk to him about it. I know he's tried to be ... nicer ... since Alex died, but I still can't talk to him."

Desperately, he wanted to put his head in her lap, encouraging her to run her hand through his hair or over his cheeks. Yet, after his brother's death last November, the bond they'd shared disappeared. He knew she tried to care, but her touch had grown chilly, felt forced. He grabbed a blue pillow with gold tassels and clutched it to his chest. "How do you get through school?"

"I don't know." She sat on the edge of the couch with her legs sealed together, held at an angle. As she spoke, she began to work an invisible cream into her hands. "I— I'm just numb; I don't think I've felt anything real for months. I go to school and execute the same lesson plans I've had forever, then I come home and grade papers. But I only check for errors, line by line; I can't ever comment on the whole." She drew in a long breath. "I know what you mean about reading and writing: I haven't read a book for months. Right after everything happened I could read. God, I must've read fifty books." She shook her head at the marvel. "But now I can't do any of it." She sighed, looking at the same spot on the carpet that had earlier demanded Luke's attention. "There's a part of me that would like to escape from it all too, but I can't."

"So you know the feeling—just wanting to take off?" She nodded, lifting her sad eyes to meet his, and Luke began to cry. "I hate getting you and Dad upset, and every time I got a bad grade, I'd tell myself that I had to do better so I wouldn't disappoint you, but—" He began to sob and could barely utter his next sentence. "But I just couldn't get anything done." He groaned, wiped his nose with his sleeve, then bent over, sandwiching the thick pillow between his chest and legs.

After a time, he lifted his face and saw that his mother, though concerned, looked doubtful. "Luke, I know there's more to failing than simply not doing your reading."

"I know, I know," he said. A post-sob shudder ripped through him. "I didn't go to a lot of classes. Sometimes I just didn't get up."

His mother's voice lost its doubt. "Did you sleep a lot during the day?"

"Sometimes. I felt terrible. I *feel* terrible—all the time. And I'm sick of it! It's been seven months and I still feel like shit."

"Seven months is not a long time, Luke. You're not just going to get better. It—"

"I should."

"No."

"A little."

She started to cry. "It's too soon, Luke. Too soon."

Luke stood up and screamed, "I need to feel better!" He took three steps in a tight circle and sat back on the couch. "I just can't figure out how. Maybe I should go to the desert, like Alex and I used to."

Dubious, she studied the bags under his eyes. "Do you think it would help to speak to someone who has experience in these types of things, someone a bit more objective?"

A bolt of energy shot through Luke. He wanted to run out the door. Without any idea why, the thought of a shrink terrified him. But he subdued the inclination to take off when he looked back at his mother. Sadness rested in a cloud around her; its intensity matched only by his desire to rip it away from such an undeserving victim. He got up to touch her thin shoulder. "Sure, maybe that would help. I don't know." Trying to think of something to say as he rubbed her small bones, he stammered out a few syllables, but, as had often happened in the last months, he found his mind to be slower, unable to retrieve the soothing words.

His mother reached up to touch his hand, but he backed away, leaving her hand alone on her shoulder. "Mom, I'm really tired. And I guess I need to start thinking about a job." He knew this suggestion was empty, but he searched for anything to smooth his exit. "I'm going up to my room, to get things settled."

She turned to face him, her moist face compelling Luke to grimace. "I know something's wrong with you," she said softly. "Something more than Alex. But I can't help—or try to help—if I don't know what it is."

An urge of complete honesty rose in Luke. He wanted to blurt out how often he'd seen night peel into day from the roof of the Beta house, and how he'd spent each of those days trying to force his amphetamine-filled body to go to sleep, usually with little success. School was perpetually the last thing on his mind; getting high, or avoiding the next crash, had been his sole focus.

At least he would be reaching out with the whole truth for once, telling her everything. But he couldn't. It would crush her to admit to his drug use.

"Mom," he said as he went back to touch her hand, "I'm sorry. I'm so sorry." His remembrance of college brought back the vivid memory of earlier that morning, feeling like death, riding back from Sixth Street to the Beta house. His head began to hurt.

For a long moment he stood next to her debating whether to kneel down and bury himself in her lap. But he couldn't. Instead, he stepped away and walked out of the room.

Luke slammed his bedroom door behind him, hoping his parents would hear. He threw down his duffel bag and unbuttoned his madras shirt. His room was just as filthy as he had left it in January; his mother had made a point of not cleaning it up if he insisted on being such a pig.

Why he had met his parents with the news of his grades puzzled him. Inside, he had known his father would explode, and his mother would've done better with a bit of preparation. Yet, he didn't have the patience to analyze the reasoning behind his immediate disclosure. He did it and it was out.

"I didn't fail on purpose," he mumbled as he fell into bed.

It was this thought he picked at like a scab as he flopped on his bed, and as his tears dried and head cooled, sleep took over his weary body. It was this same thought that gave him unconscious fits during the night.

Suddenly awake before dawn, Luke got out of bed and shuffled from his room, down the dark hall, and into Alex's room. But after he flipped the familiar light switch, he regretted his decision. A cheap, blue Ikea headboard along with a matching nightstand and desk—all unmoved since Luke had insisted Alex's room be converted to a guestroom—stood around the sterile room.

Next to the desk, Luke slid open the closet's mirrored door, engaging the automatic light. In the back of the vacant closet, under the bare clothes rack, sat a large cardboard box marked 'Alex.' Luke opened it, seeing only a few loose items at the bottom. He didn't find trophies, jerseys, playbooks, pictures or anything he'd expected; rather, he pulled out one blue teddy bear with a dial in its belly, a ratty baby's blanket, a small cut-off cast, and an award from Alex's sixth grade year, which read, *For Excellence in Arithmetic.* He dropped the award back into the box. Holding the open side of the cast to his nose, Luke ran his fingers along its texture. Letting the cast fall, he put his head in his hands.

Luke turned the knob on the bear, and the teddy's stomach emitted the sound of a soft, human heartbeat. He remembered when he had asked his mother about the sound. She said, "When little babies are fussy, the heartbeat comforts them. It gives them a sense of being safe, like being inside Mommy's tummy."

Luke pulled the blanket to his nose and inhaled, but he smelled only laundry detergent. For a time he sat there, listening to the heartbeat puncture the stillness. Then the bear's heartbeat slowed, and finally stopped. Again, he pulled the blanket back to his nose.

No smell. No noise. Nothing.

Luke replaced the bear, the blanket and the cast. He grabbed the box with both hands, carrying it out of the closet and out of the room, shutting off the light. He brought the box down to the garage. There he placed it on the highest shelf above his father's Tahoe, between an ancient badminton set and a set of rusted hand breaks from the dirt bike Luke received on his tenth birthday.

3

*A*lex died on a windy day, four years after he wrecked his ankle and returned home, two years after he started coaching. Luke didn't see his brother the afternoon he died, but he felt the wind. He remembered it shrieking and surging as he drove home from school, almost shoving his car into the oncoming lane. It came out of nowhere in quick, violent bursts. Even for West Texas, the wind was vicious.

As assistant coach, Alex was sent that day to the off-campus practice field to tell players the head coach had moved practice into the stadium to avoid the whipping wind. Alone in the parking lot waiting for stragglers, Alex stayed in his truck to avoid the gusts. He started to chew his favorite mix of gum, tobacco and sunflower seeds. Luke had chewed it with him a couple times. It was nasty and it made you spit more than you can imagine, but Alex loved it. He had spit outside his pickup truck as he waited in the lot—they'd discovered the puddle of brown juice next to his body.

Alex must've gotten sick of opening and closing the door to spit, so he just left it open. He then started to play a game of spitting at certain targets on the ground, leaving juice-covered inconsistencies on the asphalt. Luke bet he got sick of that, too. Probably, he was in no rush to go stand in the wind back at practice but he also didn't want to feel bad about it, so he had to come up with a game that took all his attention.

He started spitting through the rolled down window of his open door, but the challenge wasn't there. So he rolled up the window and started to spit between the top of the door and the truck's frame. It was a demanding shot, especially with the wind. He tried at least once and ended up spitting on the window, which he didn't wipe off all the way. The police figured he had to lean into it in order to get the spit out and over the door, so he *grabbed the handle on the top of the driver's side opening and hoisted himself up when he spat.*

Luke tried to do it once just to see. It was an awkward position to hold for more than a second. But Alex was strong and must've held himself in place.

Alex tried a couple of times because there was spit splattered on the other side of the door, where the wind blew it back. He probably wanted to clear the entire door to land the spit on the other side, so he braced himself with his right hand on the steering wheel and pulled with his left on the handle, launching himself up as he spat. He extended his head out of the car, but his body and hands remained inside.

At that moment, a blast of wind slammed the door, the top of the frame impeded by his neck.

What wrung Luke's soul every time he thought about it was that the first blow did not kill his brother. It only knocked him out. His limp body fell back into the seat, but then slid over so that his head hung out of the car. The wind continued to blow and the frame repeatedly slammed on his head, like a loose screen door in the breeze. The police thought another twelve to fifteen times. They found him that evening when someone drove by the stadium and saw the open door of his truck.

4

uke began to pace around his room, kicking random articles that had rested on his floor for the better part of a year—an ancient clock radio, a fraternity paddle, a creased cummerbund. Stowing the box had done nothing for Luke's despair. It still clogged his chest, pushing against his ribs.

He tried to focus on his frustration with his parents. After pacing made no inroads into his empty feeling, he grew furious with himself for not finding the remedy to his paradoxical situation: his selfishness got him into this mess, but he didn't feel he could be anything *but* self-absorbed until he felt better. In order to get better, you have to focus on yourself, right?

He noticed the madras shirt he'd stripped off the night before, crumpled at the end of his bed. "Christ!" he yelled as he grabbed it, tossing it onto a pile of old pizza boxes that slanted toward the center of the room. The force of his flying shirt straightened the leaning tower of cardboard.

Seeing his preppy uniform hang on the pizza boxes, Luke concluded that he had been right the day before: he did need a change and he needed it now, but it needed to be more than a change of clothes. Luke yanked off his khakis with a zip and pull and replaced them with a pair of cruddy jeans he found under his bed.

As if the jeans brought with them a flash of inspiration, Luke hunted for T-shirts. White T-shirts. He found a few that were a bit too small in the bottom of his closet, slipped one over his head and threw the rest—along with an extra pair of jeans, some soap, a toothbrush and toothpaste—into a gym bag and took it down to the garage. At the door, he paused for a moment considering writing a note to his mother as he'd always done when he went out. But this time he didn't know what to say, so he silently slipped out of the house.

His father's Fat Boy sat in the back of the garage in a cloak of dust, and though speed of departure was important, Luke couldn't go without first bringing out the bike's brilliance with a quick wipe. With a rag in hand, he rubbed the curves of the red and white gas tank and tail, swiftly tapped at the hard-to-reach spots between the handlebars, and stroked the chrome exhaust pipes that flared out in double exuberance. The machine was a thing of majesty—its low-slung heft and formidable engine reeked of power.

After unhooking his father's jet-black, silver-studded saddlebags from the garage wall, Luke tossed his things into one side of the leather satchel and shoved a beat-up tent into the other. He didn't like the look of the tent sticking halfway out of the compartment, but he didn't have time to readjust. His courage was dwindling as the image of his enraged father came to his mind; he knew if he stalled, he wouldn't go at all.

With flawless, speedy activity, Luke ditched the tent and unhooked a bungee cord from the garage wall. He secured a rolled-up sleeping bag to the back seat of the motorcycle. After he hitched the saddlebags onto the back fender, he hit the garage door opener. Luke leaned the bike upright, started the engine and drove out of the garage and onto the road.

From the motorcycle, the earth, and the roads paved upon it, appeared infinite. The incredible sense of freedom riders rave about is no exaggeration: a bike gives new life with every outing and, ironically, it's this rejuvenation that balances out the risk a rider faces each time he climbs on. Luke understood this contradiction, so he breathed in the air's candor and reveled in its unexpected cool dips. This was exactly what he needed. Though his throat still felt swollen from his sobs the day before, he convinced himself he felt better. Soon, the desert air would let him breath easy.

After miles and miles of asphalt had slid under his tires, his nerves settled back in his spine, and he shook off his clinging shame. Since childhood, his father was the only one who could make him feel small, and he hated the shrinking he sensed in himself at home.

Now, as he sped north on Route 385, his back straightened against the rolled-up sleeping bag, his jaw set, and his voice boomed out the first thing that came to mind, "Take me hooome … country roooad … to the plaaace … I belooong!"

A little cheesy, he knew, but on the motorcycle he wasn't concerned with censoring his musical preference. Denver's classic lent itself well to an endless, energetic repetition of its motivating chorus. Plus, his voice was inaudible over the engine's roar and this, combined with the music that played in his mind, convinced Luke that he sounded just like John Denver. So he belted it out.

Because his parents wouldn't worry until nightfall, the early afternoon was his ally. Luke's father had often let him use the Fat Boy, the one generous gesture he'd offered Luke after Alex died. But Luke had never used the bike overnight, let alone the several nights he envisioned. He figured he had some time before the gnaw of guilt would force him to call home; and knowing that call would allow his weak voice and shame to reinvade his body, he decided to enjoy the fleeting indefatigability.

A safe distance from his left-behind gloom, Luke cautiously unwrapped the grimy images of the past semester, even his last night in Austin. In the course of half an hour, he could've died twice: first, at the hand of a cabby with a gun and nothing to lose, and second, inhaling something so toxic that he felt his major organs contract into freeze-dried fruit. He saw himself, half-dead, stumbling out of The Skull and Snatch, protecting his eyes from the sun. Luke shook his head and let out a laugh of disbelief, though he knew not to do anything as foolish as again promise himself that he would stay clean. *Fuck it*, he thought, *I'll live through worse.*

Now the sun felt like a warm friend along for the ride. His blazing companion followed him for a few hours on 385 north, and again as he cruised west on I-40. Luke drew in the invigorating warm air that whipped his face and ears.

Lacking an internal compass, he decided not to take any risks; he simply followed the interstate west, pursuing the sun through the Texas/New Mexico border until someone, something or someplace convinced him to stop.

The sun began to drop and just as suddenly despair hit Luke's chest. He hadn't escaped it as he thought. He realized a run through the desert wasn't enough; he still felt constricted by his pain.

The wind cooled considerably when Luke turned north onto Route 285, toward Santa Fe. He rolled the throttle so that the lone gauge in front of him read 80 mph. Above him the sky was seamless blue, but miles ahead, a blanket of clouds cut the firmament into two distinct worlds. Far enough away so that he could see the sun-light on the top of the cloud blanket, creating an extraordinary juxtaposition to the shadowed world below it, Luke noticed a peculiar effect. The lighted clouds appeared to bend down toward their own shadow on the ground, creating a ramp into the sky. He rolled the throttle further, burying the needle at 120 MPH, disregarding the fact that a loose pebble, darting animal or small pothole would surely mean his death. The threat of his own extinction whined mildly in the back of his mind, but one outrageous thought drove him in the midst of the magical setting: if he could drive fast enough, far enough, he could ride up the ramp into the heavens.

5

In Matilda's Tap Room, Luke felt dreadful. The ride to Santa Fe had only withered his drawn spirit further.

He needed to feel well, and resting his back on the bar's brass rim, he sensed his answer as a familiar need grew in the back of his throat. Some get it when they have a drink or get in their car and want a smoke; others get it when they take a hit of dope and need a cigarette. Luke felt like shit, had swallowed six bourbons and had been playing pool for an hour—he needed coke. The boredom that stared back at him through the faces of bright, white smiles and tan faces only intensified his longing to mend the tear in his soul. *Yes*, he thought, *I need a little blow*.

Luke had heard enough about the tiny city to know that its action was in the central plaza, and earlier, he had located the site quickly. The mountain breeze and mellow atmosphere had beckoned him to park his bike and enter the fray of tourists and squatters on the inviting grass. They crouched in the midst of pastel buildings, housing everything from chic art galleries and restaurants to a Baskin Robbins.

The dirty, squatting kids in the plaza had invited Luke into their circle of chatter and smoke. They identified themselves as part of the "Rainbow Crew," who were on their way to Taos but got hung up in Santa Fe. *Whatever you say*, Luke thought, *as long as you keep passing the pipe*. And they did. The conversation never turned from their potent hatred of everything societal and their youthful dreams of finally finding the legendary Rainbow Commune, where they'd be unequivocally accepted. Unfortunately, none of them knew exactly where it was. But as the nappy crew began to yawn and stretch like children, setting up their various tents under a dark sky, Luke's high wore off, and the breeze brought a chill. He needed to figure out what to do that night, and the crew's liberality with dope hadn't extended to their canvas shelters.

Fortuitously, at that moment, a familiar, gawky young man with long greasy hair tucked neatly behind his ears had walked out of the Baskin Robbins, shoving his uniform visor into his back pocket. It had only taken him and Luke a moment's glance before they'd recognized each other: the young man was the son of Luke's father's ex-partner back when they had lived in Dallas. After exchanging a few pleasantries, the generous new friend invited Luke back to his place and out for the night.

But to his chagrin, his new friend, Jeff, had brought Luke to Matilda's Tap Room. He'd been in Santa Fe for five hours, and he already found himself at a generic pub, drinking weak drinks and shooting pool for two-buck stakes. *Christ, I could be doing this anywhere*, he thought.

Soon, his need for coke grew flagrant and nothing could distract his focus; he glanced around the room for anyone looking the slightest bit suspicious, but all he found was a sea of blemish-free smiles with no discernable flaws indicating the promise of contraband. He was an outsider with no hook-up or special phone number, and the only guys he knew even slightly—Jeff and his roommate, Chief— would be of little assistance.

Cutting off his view of any potential druggies, Chief pulled up to the bar. Though they hadn't been there long, he was clearly drunk. "Want a drink, dude?" he asked. Chief was tall, slightly pudgy, and wore a delicately tied bandanna around his head, pinning otherwise unmanageable hair to his scalp.

"Thanks," Luke said.

"What'll you have?"

"Bourbon on the rocks. Wedge of lime."

"Oh, I'm just having a beer," he said, as if Luke's drink order was a threat.

Chief was self-absorbed, but he was amiable enough to let a guy his roommate barely knew stay in his place indefinitely, and Luke appreciated it. He asked Chief how he got his name.

Chief said he had decided to change his name as he and Jeff drove out to New Mexico earlier that year. Swaying a bit on his stool, he said, "I wanted him to call me Shark. But he wouldn't. He said it was lame. So I picked Chief."

"Why?" Luke asked.

"Better than Samuel."

Luke nodded, he was right.

The local microbrew Chief ordered had the consistency of stew, and though he tried, he struggled to get it down. Then he started in on his life story. Luke discovered that Chief and Jeff were recent prep school grads. They were finding themselves during their "gap" year, a term Luke had heard certain parents borrow from the British in order to make their sons' misguidance more fashionable. "We almost went to Jackson Hole," Chief said, "but we thought Santa Fe was less trendy." Lo and behold they found that a ton of other kids had the exact same idea.

Raising his eyebrows with as much legitimacy as he could muster, Luke said he couldn't believe it. He asked Chief about his plans.

Chief said, "Dude, I just couldn't go right to college. I mean, I've been grinding forever. I needed a break, and my old man was totally supportive of my need to just chill for a while." It was the same response Luke had heard from the myriad of Chips, Tads and Jennifers at the bar to whom Luke had posed the same question. Chief added, "My dad said he and my stepmom, Tiffany, would maybe even come out here to visit." Then he started to complain about his stepmom and how he got screwed trying to get into college, which led him into a tirade against affirmative action. Chief's bemoaning of the system that had clearly given him so much opportunity confirmed Luke's conclusion that the action he looked for was certainly not in Matilda's Tap Room.

Chief and Jeff looked satisfied with what seemed to be their typical exploits: drinking overpriced beer and playing pool with the aforementioned Chips, Tads and Fer-Fers who needed a drink after they worked—or didn't—that day. Most of them, like Chief, enjoyed the fruits of being lucky children of over-indulgent parents. In none of the kids did Luke see a scrap of suffering. There was nothing behind the vacant smiles but vacant lives.

Jesus, I need some blow. He scanned the room for anyone he thought might have a clue as to where to go. Then, like an eagle sent from Tiresias the seer, a glassy-eyed Arab walked briskly into the bar toward the pool table. He lit a cigarette and asked if he could have the next game. "Sure, man," Jeff said, coming around the bar, smiling wide and extending his hand. "We've only got three."

As they waited for the table to open up, Luke could tell Jeff was preparing to engage the Arab in a pseudo-intellectual discussion about the plight of dark-skinned people in America. Jeff fancied himself a highly sensitive individual: he had read about and discussed minority struggle and America's savage inequality in his all-white classes in the hills of New Hampshire, and he could feel this guy's pain. Even in the short time Luke had known him, he saw that Jeff dragged his naïve guilt of privilege around Santa Fe like a sack of potatoes. Whether he shook his head at the destitute "Rainbow Crew," sighed when he passed a Native American hocking turquoise, or gave a dollar to any person of color on the street—sometimes before the surprised tourist even asked—Jeff tried to manage his remorse of opportunity.

Chief, on the other hand, did not intend to give the Arab anything more than a look of mild disgust. He took the other route available to recent prep-school grads— fear and aggression. Luke knew what idea ran behind Chief's drunken, narrowed eyes: I've got what you want. Stay away.

Taking in the very different reactions, Luke laughed to himself then stepped in front of Jeff before he could speak up. "What's up?" Luke asked casually.

"Nothing," the Arab replied, hanging on his pool cue and staring intently at the balls on the table. "You?"

"Nothing," Luke said. He looked over the Arab's shoulder in an effort to seem disinterested. "You from around here?"

The Arab looked into space and took a deep breath. As he did, Luke caught a glimpse of his eyes and felt reassured by his huge pupils. "No. No. I'm visiting friends." He nodded to the door of the bar and said, "Up the hill." He took another deep breath, followed by a huge drag of his cigarette. The players in front of Luke and the Arab finished, and the Arab went over to rack the balls. Luke broke and nothing fell. His opponent surveyed the table.

The pupils like serving plates and the cycles of deep breaths were a dead giveaway that this guy held drugs, but his reticence was a puzzle. This close to a score, Luke's appetite grew uncontrollable. He took another drink. To Luke's relief, the Arab loosened up as he proceeded to kick Luke's ass. Between shots he inhaled half a cigarette, gulped his drink, and commented on the plausibility of the next miraculous shot he had planned.

Before he had ever given up control of the cue ball, the Arab drilled the eight ball into the side pocket in front of Luke and shrieked, "Oh, man! Did you see that shit?" He looked over to the bar and yelled to no one in particular, "Who's next?"

Luke's patience had worn out, so he decided to go for broke. "You partying?" he asked, trying to offer a subtle, knowing nod.

"What do you mean?" the Arab said, a smirk wrapped around his Winston.

To keep the Arab close by, Luke disregarded the next opponents' quarters and started to rack the balls for another game. He looked over at Chief and Jeff who were fumbling with the jukebox in the corner. "You know, *partying*," Luke said.

"Why? You?"

Luke pulled the rack off the table. "I would be, but I don't know anyone." Never taking his eyes off the balls, Luke heard the Arab grunt, then saw the balls rocket out of position as the collision cut into his ears.

"How about those guys?" the Arab asked, nodding to the jukebox.

Luke could taste it; this guy was his in. "They're cool and all, but they don't know anyone. How about you? You know anyone around here?"

The Arab moved more slowly as he lined up his next shot. "Don't know." He paused as he lit another cigarette and then proceeded to bank the five ball in.

"Maybe you should've aimed for the *eight* ball," Luke said.

"Eight ball? Man, you are ready!" He shook his head and lined up and dropped two more balls. "Let's say I know someone to party, and he hooks you up. What's in it for me? I'm happy staying right here." He swept an arm over the table and declared, "Shit, look at these shots I've made!" With that, the Arab missed his attempt to pocket the nine ball.

Luke caught the Arab's eye. "I'll hook you up." After a moment, he broke the stare, grabbed his cue, and studied the table. He tried to sound relaxed as he looked at the balls. "What do you mean you're happy staying here? How far would we have to go?"

"Not far. Out a bit."

Chief and Jeff returned to the table. Chief passed around cigarettes and asked for drink orders, skipping the Arab. "You guys done?" Jeff asked.

Luke's heart leapt; he saw an opening. "I don't know," he said, looking at the Arab. "Are we?"

"Let me just go to the bathroom."

As the Arab turned the corner into the men's room, Chief grabbed Luke's arm. "What the fuck, dude? What are you talking about?" He looked at Jeff and then back at Luke. "I'm not goin' anywhere with that dude."

"Yeah. What were you guys talking about?" Jeff asked.

"You ever do coke?" Luke asked.

Jeff's wide eyes got even wider. "No, have you? Is that what you guys were talking about? Coke? I've never done it. I would do it. Would you?" he asked Chief.

For a moment Chief looked surprised by the suggestion, but he let a pompous mask capture his face and said, "I've done it. It's not that big a deal." *Yeah, sure you have*, Luke thought. He could tell the only thing Chief had tried was sneaking bong hits—probably of oregano—in his dorm room.

Chief dropped his expression back into contempt and poked Luke in the shoulder. "But I'm not goin' anywhere with that freakin' dude."

Any thought that occurred to Jeff sprung into his animated face, and Luke saw his opportunity slipping away as Jeff's eyebrows furrowed and bottom lip stuck out in a half-pout. Luke had to think quickly; he needed Jeff for his car and knew Jeff wouldn't go without his friend. "Look," Luke said, "he's cool. He said he'd hook us up with some guys he knows. He's harmless—he's just looking for a freebie." He looked at Jeff's face to gauge his interest. "C'mon, we could take your car and be back in twenty minutes."

6

While their father sat outside in his truck, packed with Alex's college load, Alex put a bag of ice on Luke's back. "You can't just do whatever feels good, Luke."

"I didn't think I was going to fall off, jeez." At nine years old, Luke had tried to match his brother's prowess on the tire swing.

"I heard you yelling at those kids to push you higher and higher. You need to know when to stop."

"You don't."

"Yes, I do."

"You've never said stop—ever."

Alex made fists with his huge hands that seemed to hang unnaturally from his wrists. He playfully punched Luke on the shoulder. "That's crazy, bro."

"When have you said it?"

Alex thought, letting his chin fall into his fingers. At eighteen his bulk had begun to set, and he looked mannish. Luke shared his brother's broad shoulders, but he forever wished he would some day add the thickness Alex had and he lacked.

Alex said, "Hitting drills, last week. Coach screamed at me to keep popping. It felt great slamming those kids, but after the third round, I said stop because it wasn't worth it."

Holding his own ice bag, Luke sat astonished. "Why?"

"Cause I hurt a kid—Wes Jordan. I didn't injure him or anything, but I hurt him. He started to cry and it wasn't worth it." Alex peered over Luke's shoulder at his back. Then he stood up to leave. "You sure you don't want to come?"

"I don't want to ride back here alone with him."

"It wouldn't be that bad."

"I'll stay with Mom." Silently, Luke followed his brother outside.

Neither spoke for a long moment. Then, looking into the shimmering sun, Alex finally said, "Jesus, it's hot. Three-a-days are gonna be brutal."

Luke looked up into his brother's wide face. "When do you start?"

"Eight o'clock Monday morning. A month of 'em and then classes start."

Luke circled his toe in the gravel. "Mom said I could come to a few games this fall."

"Come to all of them. It's not that far."

Luke pouted. "Maybe. Depends how many Mom'll go to." The idea that his brother was off to college, out of the house for good, was too much. Again he felt the urge he'd felt all day: to jump like a baby into his brother's arms, hoping he wouldn't let go. But Luke was too old. He changed the conversation's direction. "When do they pick the walk-on for the kick-off team?"

Alex laughed. "I don't know. Why?"

Luke shook his head. "It's a good tradition."

"It is."

The truck door opened and Mr. Stahl's voice thundered out, "Alex, let's go! Tahoe's eatin' gas and we need to beat the dorm rush." The door slammed.

Luke's eyelids quivered. He couldn't pin down his sorrow: was he more concerned with Alex's departure or the fact that he'd be alone with his parents for good? "So," he said.

"So ... "

Calling on his wisdom, Luke did what he thought was right for a man in his situation. He extended his hand up to his brother. Alex took it, but yanked Luke to him, lifting him and hugging his head to his shoulder.

"I'll miss you, bro."

"I'll miss you, too."

"We'll talk. All the time."

Luke sniffled in return.

"You take care of Mom now, OK? Keep bringing those little girls over. She loves it."

Luke nodded.

Alex lowered Luke back down to the gravel. "See this?" he asked, revealing a small picture of Luke. "I'm going to have this in my sock—every practice, every game. You'll always be with me." He touched Luke's hair. "Be a good man, all right?"

Wiping his eyes, Luke nodded. "I will."

Alex shoved the picture in his shirt's breast pocket and turned to the car.

Luke watched the truck until it was out of sight, then went inside to find his mother and a small picture of Alex.

7

Outside Matilda's, the four young men packed themselves into Jeff's dad's Saab. Luke and the Arab sat in the back.

After a while the Arab broke the silence, "None of you guys are cops, right?"

Luke wondered why so many pushers would all of a sudden pop this question. What's a cop going to say, Yes?

Jeff, visibly excited, tucked his hair behind his ear as he looked in the rearview mirror. "No dude. No way, dude. We're not fuckin' pigs, dude!"

Chief rolled his eyes and looked at Luke. "Where is this place? We've been in the car forever."

Trying to calm his own nerves, Luke glared at Chief. His attitude didn't help. For half an hour they had been driving on an empty, slim road, which had, miles back, peeled off Camino La Tierra. "Yeah," Jeff said to the Arab, "how far is this place?"

"Chill out," he barked. Clearly, the Arab had come down from his high and was as anxious as Luke and Chief; he leaned back into his seat and stared up at the roof. "It's up here. Keep going up this road."

Luke looked into the deep darkness in front of the car and could only see a few small shanties lit up by the headlights. The heavy silence of the car and its destitute surroundings were almost too much to bear.

"OK, here it is!" the Arab screeched, pushing on the back of Chief's seat. Emphatically, he reached across Luke and banged on the left window. "Make a left! Make a left!"

With the Arab's command, a collective, audible sigh reverberated through the Saab, and Jeff steered the car into a village of tin and cardboard homes. As the headlights' beams swung to the left, illuminating the wretched little buildings that lined the road, Luke saw that the patched roofs looked covered with ancient, multi-colored quilts. Once pointing his car down the road, Jeff slowed and turned his high beams on, which did little to penetrate the blackness in front of them. Three of them looked around expectedly at the dark shanties, but the Arab only said, "Just follow this road."

Chief finally lost it. He slammed his feet down like a child, though he didn't turn around. "What the fuck, dude! You said it was right here. Where is it?"

Unsettling silence was the Arab's response.

On the other side of the shanty village the road dropped down into utter nothingness. "Pull over here," the Arab said.

"What?" Jeff asked. "Why?"

"Because, that's where I'm going," the Arab responded, pointing into the darkness. "Turn off the car."

Luke wondered how in the hell this guy made it all the way into town from this place. "Where?" he asked, peering into the dark. "There's nothing over there."

"Sure there is." The Arab pointed his bony finger toward nothing. "Look."

"Oh, you mean that barn," Chief said. He must have had keen eyes—Luke couldn't see anything. "Jesus, there's no road that leads over there."

"No. I'll just walk through the field." The Arab opened his door, and as if it were an afterthought, said, "How much do you guys want?" With one foot hanging out of the car, he fidgeted like a gerbil.

Luke knew how bad this could be. A part of him wanted to kick the Arab into the dirt and tell Jeff to take off. But the need in the back of his throat wouldn't let him turn back. "You're not going alone."

The Arab looked amazed. "Hell yes, I'm going alone. They don't like surprises, and me showing up with three pretty white boys is a big surprise. So, you give me money, I'll go and come right back."

Jeff and Chief started fishing in their pockets. "How much for an eight ball?" Chief asked.

The Arab and Luke looked at each other, then at Chief. Luke asked, "What the hell do you want an eight ball for?"

Chief looked meek. "I thought that's what you get, an eight ball."

Luke shook his head at Chief, who dropped his. Then Luke looked at the Arab.

"We'll just have a gram and a half. How much?"

"Two hundred bucks."

Jeff quickly extended a wad of bills toward the back seat while Chief went back to fishing.

"Wait a second," Luke said. "Why the fuck is it two hundred bucks?"

"Is what it is." The Arab paused and nodded as he prepared to say something else. Luke knew what was coming. "This is *good* shit." And there it was. Luke had yet to run into a pusher claiming that his was the worst cocaine available.

Knowing Jeff betrayed Luke's leverage by immediately withdrawing a fifty and twenty-dollar bill from his pocket, Luke tried to bargain anyway. "Eighty bucks is plenty. Shit, that's still a fuckin' rip-off. Your boys in there," Luke nodded toward the darkness, "will probably give you a gram for thirty."

The Arab narrowed his eyes and said nothing.

What have I gotten us into? Luke thought. But this was not the time to pull back, so he lowered his tone in an attempt to sound dangerous, "We'll give you two hundred, but that includes your cut. We want a full two grams when you get back. No skimming." The Arab feigned offense as he clutched his chest as if to say, *Moi, skim?* "You can keep whatever you can get on top of that," Luke continued. "And don't try to fuck us. I know what a gram is." Luke's attempted toughness left the car deflated.

The Arab, in apparent agreement with Luke's terms, got out with the money and headed off toward the barn. Jeff went to turn the radio on but Chief grabbed his arm. They waited in silence.

After an eternity, Jeff spoke up. He said what they were all afraid to admit: "Dude, he bolted. I think we should take off. This place gives me the fuckin' creeps. There's, like, nothing out here. There's no sound or light coming from anywhere—even from that village back there. Or whatever that is. We should go." The excitement of the adventure had cooled. This wasn't buying pot from the long-haired trustafarian who dealt out of the Pathfinder he got for his sixteenth birthday, and Jeff finally saw the potential hazard in his present situation.

Luke was devastated. He would've stayed until the sun came up. In general, the closer he got to a score the more desperate he became, and his desperation manifested as passivity. He had done this before, simply waiting for hours. He learned a while ago that if someone said they'd get you drugs and they didn't return soon, 99% of the time they were gone. Still, Luke waited. And now his hope was billowed by the fact that the cabby back in Austin had met him late. "Let's just wait a little bit longer. I'm sure he'll come back. Besides, how's he going to get back to the plaza without us?"

"That fucking bastard. He's not coming back." Chief looked at Luke. "That piece of shit has more money in his pocket right now than he's had in his whole life. I didn't like that guy from the start. Why the fuck did you think some guy you didn't know from Adam would hook you up?" He shook his head and turned toward the direction of the barn. "The only thing keeping me here is the fact that I *saw* him go into that barn. I know he's in there, unless he snuck out another way." Hearing his own voice seemed to harden his mettle. "Fuck it. I'm going in there." He opened his door, jumped out, and ran in the direction of the barn.

Luke and Jeff sat dumbfounded.

Luke leaned forward in between the two front seats and looked into the night to see Chief swallowed up by darkness. Jeff shuddered as the cool air rushed in through Chief's open door. After shutting the door, Luke leaned back and considered the guilt he'd absorb if Chief didn't return. He hit his head against the window. *Christ. Why do I keep getting into this shit?*

Yet again, he swore off drugs.

8

H oly crap!" Jeff yelled.

Luke sat up in time to see Chief slam into the hood of the car and slide over to the passenger side. As he slid he yelled, "Go!" and he continued to scream as he got in the car, "Go! Go! Go!"

Gripped by Chief's terror, Jeff reached for the keys on the steering column. "Fuck!" He started screaming too, "He stole the keys! Shit! He stole the keys!"

"Down there!" Luke yelled, pointing to the keys resting in the ignition between the two front seats. In his fright, Jeff forgot Saab's utmost concern for passenger safety and the unusually placed ignition. "Go!" Jeff reached down, started the engine, stood on the gas, and yanked the car into a U-turn.

The three young men didn't talk. The only noise was Chief's heavy huffing and the whine of the engine as Jeff tried to keep the speeding car on the unlit road. Finally, after looking through the back window for the sixth time, Luke asked, "Jesus Christ, Chief. What did you do?"

Chief took a deep breath. "I went toward the barn—I almost broke my damn leg about nine times on the way over there from all the freakin' holes—but it was a lot closer to the car than it looked. It was like misty, or foggy, you know, so it looked farther away than it was. When I got to the barn, I heard voices inside, but there was no light. Then I got closer, right up to it, and I realized that it was, like, sealed up. Even if there was light in there I wouldn't have been able to see it. So I went around to the side and found a sliding door and—"

"Are you kidding me? Why the hell would you go in there?" Earlier, Jeff had reassured Luke that he had known Chief for seven years, and though he talked a big game, he never acted unexpectedly. He had always played it safe at school, usually hurling cynical comments from the security of the back row.

"I don't know. I mean, it's not like I was fiending for anything. I just wanted to get that fucker. I hate the locals out here—they think we're all such pussies." He looked out the window. "I wanted to get our money back, so I slid this door open and walked in. It was like a frat house—couches and tables everywhere with TVs in the corners. All these, like, what do you call them ... pygmies, were—"

"Pygmies! Where the fuck did they come from?" Jeff shouted.

"No, no. Not pygmies, but what do you call those white guys, you know, with like no color in any part of their body?"

"You mean albinos?" Luke asked.

"Yeah, albinos. But they were all black. You know how you can tell even if they don't have any color? Well, they were black. They were just sitting around, watching TV, but there was this mountain of coke on the table in the middle of the room, and there were these little baggies next to the pile." Chief shook his head. "When I walked in they all froze. I swear to God they must've thought I was a cop. Then *I* froze—almost shit my pants. I'm not joking. But then our friend walked in. He was stirring a drink, and when he saw me, he dropped it. When I saw him I got pissed all over again. I was like, 'You fucker! What are you doing getting a fucking drink?' That asshole was immobilized; he probably thought I was a cop, too. He was like, 'Uhhh, uhhhhh.' So I realized as I looked around the room—I don't know why—but I knew he used us for a ride and stole our two hundred bucks. He did it all under our noses while we waited outside like a bunch of saps. I couldn't believe the balls on this guy. I think he knew that I realized his whole fuckin' ploy. I had no idea what to do, so I ran over to the table, grabbed one of the little baggies and took off."

Luke could've kissed him. "Where is it?"

Jeff spoke up, not completely absorbed by Chief's latest divulgence. "Wait, are you telling me you just grabbed the shit and took off, and they didn't run after you?"

"I don't know. I just took off. They were albinos, dude. They probably can't run."

Clearly upset with the generalization, Jeff yelled, "What the hell are you talking about? Just because they're albinos doesn't mean they can't run. They could—"

"They're not chasing us." Luke could take no more of Jeff's vapid discussion. "Our friend'll take the hit for showing us their hide-out. He'll probably be hung and burned by the end of the night, but those guys aren't going to chase us if they haven't come already. Where's the coke?" He bounced up and down on his seat—the possibility of a score from the dealer's uncut stash was too much.

Chief reached inside his Patagonia jacket and revealed the baggie. The coke, packed into the corner of a large Ziploc freezer bag, looked the size of a racquetball. Luke's eyes bulged. "Oh … my … God."

"What?" Chief asked, sounding afraid.

"This is the most coke I've ever seen. I … I … " He couldn't finish the thought as he eyed the trophy and weighed its heft in his hand. Finally he said, "I thought you said the baggies on the table were little?"

"The ones like these were. They had bigger ones. Why, is that an eight ball?"

"Are you nuts? This is like thirty eight balls. We've got to get home."

"Should I have grabbed the other one?"

"Hell, no." Luke said. He assumed the others to be kilo bags, and he was surprised Chief wouldn't have recognized them as such from the movies. "If you would've grabbed one of those, they definitely would've come after us."

Jeff grew dead serious as he maneuvered the Saab through the back road and once again onto Camino La Tierra. The three remained quiet on the way home, comforted by the light pouring from the streetlamps. While Jeff clung to the steering wheel, Chief looked out the window—probably considering how close to death he had just come—and Luke eyed the cocaine, trying to find blemishes in the powder that might predict a reaction like the one he had in Austin.

Once all of them got through the door and into the light of the tiny apartment Luke got down to business. "Pull down the Coors Light mirror, we can use that. And I need a knife."

Luke took the mirror from Jeff and sat down on the couch as the others took their seats in the chairs across the room. "Jesus," he said, as he poured about two grams on the mirror and realized the girth of the baggie had not changed. "This could last an addict a month."

Jeff and Chief had still not said a word since Chief finished his story. Though Luke was relieved by their silence, he hoped they weren't thinking of backing out. "Let's turn on some music. How about some Allman Brothers? I love 'The Best Of.'" Downright giddy, Luke chopped up the drug as he heard the low voice in the speaker say, "OK, The Allman Brothers Band … " The feeling of perfect anticipation swelled in his chest. An irrepressible glee soared in his soul: he had enough powder to clog a sink and sat in secure comfort with plenty of good music. These few moments, before the first line, as he cut and massaged and rolled the coke, were full of extraordinary expectancy and hope. He began to bob his head in time with the organ riffs in "Statesboro Blues," and he smiled like a shark at Jeff and Chief. Before starting, he reminded himself that he needed to show restraint. Primarily for his hosts, who hadn't a clue. Secondly, for himself. *There's plenty here*, he thought. *No need to rush or hoard.*

The coke was clumpy, a good sign. He collected a share of it under a dollar bill and began swiping over the bill with the blunted steak knife Chief had handed him.

"What's that do?" asked Jeff.

"It smoothes it out and breaks it up, so we can cut it into smooth, sweet lines. See," Luke peeled off the bill and scraped the residual coke into a pile on the mirror. "Now we can carve 'em up." He let out a hoot.

Chief sat silently, staring at the coke.

Jeff spoke up for both of them, "Are you sure this stuff is safe?"

Luke sighed and then laughed to himself as he remembered what he must've looked like in the bathroom stall in Austin. "Yeah, it's perfectly safe. It's like pot, but its just got this undeserved stigma attached to it. I mean people die, I guess, but shit," he took a moment to think of an example, "Len Bias is totally an anomaly." He leaned down to the mirror and added, "Watch me, and then you can decide for yourself."

He showed some sense in the size of his first line, remembering Austin. He rolled up the bill and went to work, making sure he was even as always. Either half the line with one nostril and half with the other, or one line for each. He pressed his index finger onto some dust in the corner of the mirror and rubbed it on his teeth and gums.

"Why'd you do that?" Jeff asked.

"It's a gummer. A little extra. It makes your gums numb, and it feels great when you smoke through it. You can also do this." He packed a single cigarette against the face of his watch to create a small reservoir at the tip. Then he pinched some more dust off the mirror and dropped it into the end of the cigarette. He lit it, leaned back into the couch and inhaled. His sinuses started to burn.

After a moment, Chief reached for the mirror, but Luke sat up. "I'll cut you one."

Chief yanked the mirror off Luke's lap. "No, I can do it." Luke eyed Chief suspiciously, and Chief grew indignant. "What? You don't think I know what I'm doing? Fuck you, I know."

He mimicked Luke's actions to a T, even the balancing act between each nostril and the cigarette, and then he handed the mirror to Jeff. When it passed into Jeff's hands, the mirror began to shake.

The coke hit Luke with full force, and though he noticed Jeff's apprehension he couldn't be bothered. It was like a magic hand that crept up his spine and then, in a second, grabbed him by the base of his neck, sending a thrill into this head. As his eyelids inadvertently recoiled, he inhaled and exhaled loudly through his teeth. Extending all ten fingers, he rolled his head from side to side and sat up on the edge of the couch.

Finally, he felt the relief he'd searched for. "Oh, man, Chief. You're the man! I can't believe you fuckin' hooked us up so hard!" The coke was incredible: only two lines of the stuff propelled Luke into the sky. He reached over and gave Chief an emphatic slap on the knee.

"Yeah." Chief looked a bit puzzled. "I'm feeling a little bit on the roof of my mouth, but not a whole lot."

"How about you Jeff? You gonna try?" The only thing that would bring Luke down, though admittedly not too much, would be Jeff's reluctance. Luke felt he owed it to Jeff to show him the wonder of a cocaine high, its elation and warmth. "I'm telling you, dude, you won't be disappointed."

"Yeah," Chief said, his eyes also wide open. "He's right. Now it's starting to hit me. It's amazing." He nodded awkwardly to the beat of "Southbound."

"Let me help you with that," Luke said. "I'll just cut you a little one."

Soon enough, they had each done a number of lines and the chatter became intense. Luke felt comforted by this talk—the wired discourse about the quality of the coke, the wonder of the drug, the incredible talent of whichever band was on the stereo, and the affection the users had for each other. They leaned forward and back in their seats for hours, putting their nose to the mirror, and only getting up to go to the bathroom or change the music.

The clock read 4 a.m. when Jeff asked, "How's your brother, Luke? I heard he left A&M."

Chopping another line, Luke looked at Jeff and then added more coke to his dose. "He's fine," Luke said, trying to sound casual though the thought of his brother clamped his throat. "Back at home. Coaching." He licked the knife and looked at Chief. "You want some more?"

"Sure," Chief said.

The sun crept into the apartment through the seams between The Grateful

Dead tapestries and the windows they covered, dimly lighting three depressed faces. R.E.M. whined in the background.

Jeff's mention of Alex shook Luke. His high had immediately faded with the rising fear of his returning gloom. Rationally, he knew more coke would do him no good, yet he reached for it anyway.

Jeff, too, seemed to see the futility of any more drug use, but unlike Luke, he decided to quit. "Shit, I'm going to bed," he said. Slowly and with extreme care—never letting his fingers separate from the arms of his chair—Jeff stood up, then wobbled like he'd collapse. He steadied himself and said, "Thanks for the night, boys."

Staring through bleary eyes at the mirror in front of him, Luke called out, "You'll have some trouble getting to sleep, but it'll come."

"I'm headed out, too," Chief declared as he hoisted his big body up and shook his head. He looked sixty-years-old, his face sustaining the far-off look of an Alzheimer's victim.

"Chief, you're the fuckin' man. I'll never forget you yelling and sprinting toward the car and Jeff fumbling around for his keys." Luke heard himself laugh as if his body and senses had divided. "That was hilarious." He leaned down for another line, then picked his head up and pinched his nose. "Are you sure you don't want to stick around and finish off what's here?" Sitting alone with his misery scared him.

Already shuffling into the back room where he slept, Chief huffed over his shoulder, "No. I'm good." He paused before entering his bedroom, grunted and then disappeared behind his door.

Luke looked at the remaining coke and caught a glimpse of himself in the mirror. He was as white as the powder, his eyeballs bulbous. He tried to shrug off the desolation of being the last one standing, but it encased him like a coffin. The crust in his nose, eyes and joints was too thick for him to ignore any longer. He hunched forward and put his head in his hand, feeling his clammy skin against his palm. He wished he had a valium, or at least some Nyquil.

If Alex could see him now.

He got up to change the music. He turned off R.E.M. and began searching for a suitable replacement in the confused mess of CDs around the stereo. Recognizing the cover of a Nirvana import bootleg that rested against the wall, Luke bent down to pick it up.

As his head approached the wall he heard the unmistakable slapping of two humping bodies. He put his ear to the plaster and heard the subtle groans of pleasure escalate as the slapping became more furious. Soon, however, he found the sounds to be less interesting than the music, and after changing to the Nirvana bootleg, he returned to the couch.

With his ear attuned to the sound of their sex, the two lovers were still audible to Luke as he sat down—even over Cobain whining, "My girl, my girl, where have you been?" The slapping and groaning continued, then came to an abrupt stop. Luke cut an enormous line and finished it off with two big snorts, one for each nostril. He hadn't actually felt high for a long while; his intake merely kept the inevitable emotional collapse at bay. But he knew this addition—like any other— would only intensify his devastation when it was all said and done, so he had to stay somewhat sane.

He figured he'd try to reach one last, small peak before falling into the deep valley. But even two more lines had no effect. He felt his eyes brighten, his heart quicken, and his brow moisten, yet his spirit remained an open wound—exposed and defenseless. He knew sleep wasn't in the cards for a long, long time so he decided to take a walk in the dawn to mitigate the impending crash.

9

*A*lex sat at the dinner table with his father while Luke crouched outside the room, behind the closed door. He pulled his tiny knees under his chin and listened to the utensils hit the china. He sat still and barely breathed.

"What are you staring at me like that for?" Luke heard his father ask Alex. Alex made no response. "It's not like I hit him." His father paused. "Goddamn, Alex! The boy's a sissy. You think I'm gonna sit here and let him and his mother giggle and pinch each other under the table and not do anything about it?"

"All they did was talk about a book."

The sound of his brother's slow, patient voice forced Luke to hold his breath. He'd never heard anyone disagree with his father.

His father snorted. Luke heard him swirl his ice cubes. "Fudgy? What the hell kind of book is that?"

"Superfudge, Dad. Luke likes it."

"I don't like how he and your mother make those voices." His father mocked Luke's repetition of the main character's mispronunciation of his brother's name, "'Petah, Petah.' What is that? It's one thing in a book, but Christ ... he sounds like a faggot."

Alex's steady voice didn't change. "He's eight. He likes it."

With his brother's defense—the first he'd ever heard—Luke let go of the breath he held, delighting in Alex's valor. He rose to leave, but his shoulder bumped the kitchen door.

"What's that," his father yelled from behind the door. "Luke?" Again, Luke froze, half a yelp stuck in his throat. "What the hell are you doing?" Luke heard chair legs slowly slide across the wood floor. Then he heard more legs slide, this time quickly.

"I'll check," he heard Alex say.

Luke recoiled from the door but relaxed as his brother's face appeared. Alex made no sound as he looked into Luke's eyes. Luke hoped his brother saw the wonder and admiration he had for him: he'd found his hero.

A smile flashed on Alex's face as he nodded toward the stairs behind Luke. As Alex let the door close, Luke turned to follow the simple direction, but not before he heard his brother's words in the dining room. Patiently, Alex said, "He's upstairs, Dad. Don't worry about it."

10

The commotion of a fresh mountain morning had begun by the time Luke had returned from his walk. Near Jeff and Chief's yellow apartment building, a group of joyful older men—all wearing the same color-coded lycra outfits—sped by on high-tech road bikes, firing their chunky legs and yelling directions to each other. Even though, like most bikers, they were surprisingly out of shape, the riders were doing much better than Luke. They attempted to push off their aging while Luke accelerated his. His soul that soared a few hours ago now felt like the pasty phlegm he repeatedly coughed up and spit out. He had to focus on putting one leg in front of the other just to get across the street.

As he walked up the stairs, Luke saw an attractive couple exit the apartment next to Jeff and Chief's. It took Luke's brain, now running at low capacity, a long moment to grasp they were the couple he had listened to the night before. As they arrived at the top of the stairs, Luke, trying to shield his ghost-like face from their gaze, mumbled, "Morning."

"Hey, man," a cheery voice responded. "Just getting in?"

Luke stopped on the third to last step up and looked at the two fresh faces. The voice came from a tall, blonde young man whose chiseled muscles sprouted from his tight shirt and loose shorts. The smiling girl next to him looked surprisingly similar. As Luke scanned their faces he saw they shared the same thin nose and piercing blue eyes. "Yeah, long night," he sighed.

"I'm sure. Your boys were rockin' way into the night, too," he said, nodding at Chief and Jeff's door. He must've thought Luke was getting in from a night on the town instead of a sluggish walk to organize his mind. "Man, you look beat." The guy looked at the girl for a moment, then back at Luke. "Me and Ilse are heading up to the hot springs. You look like you could use it."

Astounded at the young man's generosity, Luke finally took his hand away from his face to meet the young man's gaze. "That sounds incredible." Luke heaved a sigh of relief at the thought of a day trip. Clearly the antidote for his pain lay elsewhere and this may be it. "When are you heading up?"

"We were just going now, but if you need to get some shit together we can wait." Ilse nodded encouragingly.

"I can go now. Just let me grab something from inside."

He slid by them and into the door of the apartment. Even in mid-morning, only minimal light cut into the dwelling, and smoke still hung in the still, thick air. The place smelled eerily similar to a frat house after an especially raucous night—a mean mixture of urine, body odor, stale smoke and beer. Vomit was the only component missing from the odor cocktail; otherwise it was the perfect frat house reek.

As he ran into the kitchen, he pulled his collar over his nose. Finding the mammoth stash still in the drawer, Luke snatched it and pulled a Ziploc bag out of the garbage, cutting off its bottom corner. He carefully poured some coke out of the stash—still disbelieving how heavy it was—into the small, triangular pouch. Then he poured in some more. He twisted the two ends of the smaller bag and tied them together to seal the opening. Placing his to-go bag in his pocket, he re-covered his nose in preparation for his exit through the living room.

"OK," he said, emerging from the apartment's door. "I'm ready."

They arrived at the springs in the early afternoon. The driver, whose name Luke still didn't know, looked into the backseat to rouse Luke. "Sorry, man," he said with a sheepish look. "I didn't know it would take that long. We had this map and Ilse's sister said it would only take a couple of hours."

Luke could only nod in the driver's direction. He'd spent the trip curled up in the back of the Jetta, concentrating solely on not throwing up. He couldn't believe he made it this long.

Stepping out of the car, the fresh air pushed Luke's vomit back down his throat. After following the driver around the car, he stood on the precipice of a giant crater in the top of the mountain. "We're in the southern part of the Sangre de Cristos," the driver said, looking out on the expanse.

Nodding, Luke barely heard the driver—he'd never before seen such a disarming expanse, and it rendered him literally dumbfounded. His vantage point allowed him to see the entire breadth of the basin, filled only with grass. The absence of any point of reference exaggerated the bowl's vastness, and the overwhelming enormity—plus his inconsequential size in comparison—lowered his jaw. Even in his half-dead state, he weighed his relative insignificance. The flats of his home never offered such a perspective—man and man-made objects were the only breaks in the landscape—and the lack of any topographical diversity allowed him to think his presence was large, consistent, important. But standing over the crater, Luke saw for the first time in his life how deluded he was.

The view breathed some life back into him. A bit of color must have come back to his face, too, because Ilse grabbed him by the arm and said, "Let's go to the springs, shall we?"

Shall we? Luke repeated in his mind. He liked her already.

The hike to the springs was not demanding, but in Luke's condition he needed every ounce of energy to convince himself that his objective was right over the next bunch of jagged rocks. "Have you all been here before?" he shouted ahead in a desperate attempt to gauge how close they were.

The driver stopped and shouted down, "No. But Ilse's sister says they're incredible and well worth the hike." He turned and began up the trail again.

Wholly unsatisfied with the driver's response, Luke began to growl "fuck" each time one of his feet hit the ground. "Fuck … Fuck … Fuck." Soon, even this demanded too much energy, and he quietly paid attention only to the step ahead.

Almost wiping out on a puddle of loose stones, Luke steadied himself against a smooth boulder to his left. He wished he could lay down right there and die. His head spun and the inside of his mouth burned as if it had been scrubbed with sandpaper—each breath tore at his raw insides. If it weren't for the modicum of concern he had for the others he would've stopped and gone back to the car. But he could tell Ilse and the driver, even with what little he knew of them, would never have let him go back alone.

"Hey!" the driver shouted from up the trail. "We made it!"

"Thank the fucking Lord," Luke mumbled.

When Luke reached his guides, a group of ten nudes greeted him, all lounging in and next to a large, steaming spring. Carved out of the black, glistening rock that Luke had clung to on his way up, the spring wasn't alone: at least twelve other hot springs sent up steam pockets from either side of the trail as it continued up the rise.

To the driver Ilse said, "This is my sister, Gwen." She led him to the far side of the spring and pointed to a gorgeous, pale, red-headed woman in the water. Her skin looked like snow under the subtle ripples.

Gwen emerged from the pool with incredible grace, as if something outside her body controlled her movements. Her naked torso pulled effortlessly out of the water, and her right arm rose to extend her hand to the driver. Her left hand slid over her wet red hair, pulling it tight to her head.

"Hello," she said, taking his hand in hers.

In his younger days, Luke had seen a few old porn pictures of women with tall, yet round figures. But recently, the nude women he'd seen, whether in person, in print or on the screen, had sculpted, angled bodies with little flesh to speak of.

Gwen was the antithesis of these modern models. She was full of ideal round-ness—a consummate balance of firmness and softness. Her face and shoulders were perfect spheres that gave way to incredibly supple breasts and plump nipples. Her sides extended charitably out at her hips, then in before rounding out twice more at her thighs and calves. Even her pubic hair formed a rounded maze that could not have been more inviting.

For some, the nude body in natural surroundings—no matter how enticing—would be divorced from the sensual and become simply expected. But for Luke, the desire to hold and squeeze every part of her only intensified as he scanned her bare body.

"Hi. I'm John," the driver said.

John, Luke noted. "And I'm Luke," he said as he walked over to take her hand. She didn't seem to care in the least that he was clothed and she was not.

"Hello." She nodded when he took her moist hand. "Gwen," she said with a grin. "You look like you could use a go in the spring."

What he could use was "a go" with her and a bump from the satchel in his pocket, but he had no interest in breaking out the bag in unknown company. Whenever he didn't have coke, he rarely thought about it during the day. But when it was on him, it was always in the back of his mind: when he could do more, how much was left, who would be lucky enough to get some, how much he should save for later, etc. Even the words of a gorgeous, naked woman standing in front of him brought his mind to the drug in his pocket.

"I sure could." Luke grimaced—he could've hit himself for such a golly-gee comment.

Gwen sneered at the group in and around the spring, then turned back to the newcomers. She announced, "Well, it's great to see you three." After glaring at a gray-

haired man with a wide jaw and deep tan who sat at the far end of the spring, she
added, "Why don't we head to a higher one? This one's a bit crowded." She gathered
her clothes and led Ilse, John and Luke farther up the trail.

Not far up, they found a small spring with only two naked people enjoying its
steam. Sitting next to the water was an older, pear-shaped man with his eyes closed.
He rhythmically hit a silver goblet with a matching silver mallet, creating a calming
chime. A girl, who looked to be thirteen, sat in the water and smoked pot from a corn
pipe. As the four newcomers appeared, the girl jumped out and darted off into the
higher rocks, startling the older man out of his trance. He looked the four up and
down.

After apparently recognizing Gwen, he said, "Sorry about her. Scares easy."

"No problem," Ilse said. "She your daughter?"

Gwen dug her elbow into Ilse's ribs and shook her head, looking at the ground.
The man turned to Ilse, and was about to say something when Gwen asked him,
"How you been, Joe?" She dropped her clothes at her feet and hopped into the
spring.

The man gazed down at Gwen's perfect body, clearly unable to control his stare.
"Been all right."

"This is my sister, Ilse, and her friends, John and … " she paused, then offered,
"Luke." He was touched and heartened that she remembered his name.

Unlocking his eyes from Gwen's shape, Joe turned back to Ilse, and with
irritation said, "No, t'aint my daughter! Shoot, you sure know how to shame a man."
He contemplated his goblet for a moment. "I've got to go find her." He hoisted his
naked body up and trotted after the girl, his flabby ass cheeks quivering in pursuit of
his legs.

Gwen frowned at Ilse, then yelled goodbye to Joe. She settled back against the
moist, rocky edge and closed her eyes. Luke liked this pattern: if a person left the
spring every minute it would leave him and Gwen alone in no time.

Before he knew it, John and Ilse stripped and eased into the water. "Damn! It's
hot!" John said.

"Oh, shut up you wuss. It's perfect," Ilse replied. She reached over and grabbed
Joe's goblet and began hitting it steadily.

As he watched John jump into the spring, Luke noticed his uncircumcised
penis and all of a sudden felt nervous that he would be the odd man out. But he had
no choice in the matter—he'd come this far and he couldn't let a little thing like that
get in the way of his intention. He peeled off his pants and shirt, turning his nose

away from the stench that emanated from his crispy garments. He threw the clothes up onto the rocks, slid into the spring, and submerged himself in the hot water.

He stayed under for a while, letting the hot water loosen his tight skin. He scrubbed his body all over, and as he resurfaced, feeling fairly refreshed, he looked into Gwen's green eyes. They reflected the undulating water. She met his stare and looked as though she was going to say something to him, but Ilse chirped up. "Does anyone have any buds?" she asked.

"I don't, but that girl did," John said. "Check that guy's shit, I bet it's in there somewhere."

Luke chuckled at the bravado of those who favored the communal existence: they figured anyone worth their salt was a participant in their lifestyle, even if the one providing didn't know it. Ilse started digging around Joe's bag, and sure enough, revealed a bag of dope. "Throw me my pants," she said to John. "I've got a pipe in the back pocket." She found her pipe, packed it with pot, fired it up, and passed it on.

Luke felt better but he knew he'd pass out as soon as he smoked pot. He momentarily considered how great it would feel to sleep in the spring, but he didn't want to seem like a bore to Gwen, so he waved off the burning pipe. It went to Gwen, who closed her eyes and shuddered as she drew in the smoke.

As her eyes reopened, Luke's eyes closed and his mind glided into fantasy. Images of their bodies swam in his thoughts: her tight, round legs wrapped around him, slowly kissing her neck, moving down to her breasts, and taking her nipple into his mouth. His fantasy intensified until he imagined pulling her out of the water and resting her rear on the side of the spring, their eyes meeting as she raised her hips and he entered her.

His vision had gone too far, and Luke's eyes flung open, but not quickly enough to subdue his arousal. He stirred the water in front of him to hide his growing erection. Wanting to take everyone's attention from the small whirlpool above his crotch, he turned to John and Ilse. "So, how long have you guys been going out?"

John raised his eyebrows and Ilse giggled. "We met two nights ago, silly," she said. "Why do you think we've been going out?" She looked at him impishly. "Just 'cause we've been hiding out in John's apartment?"

"I don't know. You guys just seemed like a couple."

John grinned at Ilse. "He's probably been hearing us through the wall for the past few days."

As John spoke, Ilse took another hit, and her eyes went from the burning pot at the end of the pipe to meet his. Her lips curved into a mischievous grin while maintaining a seal on the pipe. She finished her pull and slowly exhaled. Silently, she grabbed John's hand under the water and led him out of the steaming pool and up the trail to an even higher spring.

Gwen looked at Luke without saying a word. He hadn't been this nervous since his first junior high dance. His family had just moved to Dallas from their farm outside Lubbock, and after a rural childhood, Luke arrived at the unfamiliar, sweltering gym. He knew no kids, no dance moves, and no cool Dallas phrases. He stood against the wall watching the pretty, refined girls in designer jeans and styled hair on the other side of the gym, hoping desperately for a chance to be alone with one of them. But when a cute girl with curly black bangs asked him to dance, he could only jam his hands further in his pockets and silently look at his shoes until she walked off. After moving back to Lubbock, however, he changed back into a suave character, appealing young prospects. His honed skills continued to work well with the country girls at UT, but with mysterious, gorgeous Gwen he felt as ill prepared as he had when he was twelve.

He asked, "So, do you come here a lot?" He shut his eyes at the stupidity of the question—his second dumb remark.

Her eyebrows furrowed, then she smiled and drew herself to the middle of the pool. She raised herself up out of the water—her generous breasts elevated above the film of steam on the spring's surface, leaving a few lucky droplets to cling to her pink, erect nipples. She arched her spine and tilted her head back so her rope of wet hair broke the pool's surface. Then, as if pulled into the water by her hair, she slowly submerged.

Luke had no idea what to do. Should he wait for her to come to him? Dip under and meet her? What? And then a new terror shot through his mind: *Can she see my hard-on from down there?* He was sure the pulse he felt in his penis was sending waves through the water, and his efforts to swirl the water had no effect under its surface. *Shit*, he thought, *I'm done for.*

Grinning, Gwen surfaced and returned to her place at the other side of the spring. Unconsciously, Luke started nodding his head as if he were privy to some rhythm in the air, but suddenly he realized how stupid he must've looked. He froze his head and sat as rigidly as his dick.

Gwen looked at him. He felt like he had been splayed and pinned to a dissection board. He wanted to say something, but he knew if he opened his mouth he'd sound moronic, so he just sat there and absorbed her inspection. At last, she asked, "A little excited?"

He thought this may be an opening—possibly the only opening he'd get—so he tried to sound as sexy as possible. "Yes." He eagerly leaned forward in anticipation of her response. Still, she furnished no answer. "Are you offended?" he asked, taking some water in his mouth as if that's why he leaned forward.

"No."

"This doesn't happen a lot. In fact, I think the last time was in my sixth grade French class." His words reduced his discomfort and he let them roll. "We had this smokin' substitute, because our teacher went away to France with her husband—he was, like, a wine taster or something. Anyway, this sub was hot and she knew it. I would sit there and fantasize about her, and every time I'd have a boner she would call me up to the board to conjugate some fucking verb. I tried to tuck it under my waist band, but it sometimes popped out. Brutal. I think she knew, and she liked making me look like an idiot." He shook his head. "She probably loved that we all lusted after her."

After exhaling the lightest, most peaceful laugh, Gwen said, "Well, *I* won't make you get up."

"Thanks."

She continued her inspection of him, but appeared to enjoy her study. "I'm going to a farm party tonight," she said, tilting her head from side to side.

Luke shifted under her stare. "A 'farm party?'"

"It's like a rave, but out on some farm. It's in Magdalena. I was thinking of asking John and Ilse if they wanted to come. You can come as well."

"I'd love to go," he said. "Where's Magdalena?" he asked. But satisfied by his acceptance, Gwen had allowed her ears to submerge as she rested her head back against the rim of the spring and closed her eyes. With nothing else to do but anticipate the night's possibilities, and no one stirring around them, Luke, too, closed his eyes, allowing the remarkable warmth of the spring's water to lull him into much needed rest.

Back at Jeff and Chief's apartment, Luke took a shower and did a line of cocaine as thick as his pinky. *If you're gonna be a bear, be a grizzly,* he thought. He left a note for his two hosts:

Thank you for everything … I'll never forget it. Good luck with all.

He also left a hundred bucks for the coke he was not about to split with. It took all of a minute to pack up his stuff—and five more to load his bike—before he snorted one more line and headed out to meet his new friends from the hot springs.

When he reached the meeting place outside of Baskin Robbins—in the same plaza where he had met Jeff the night before—he took in the sun-drenched square. The mosaic of the plaza floor reflected the unique medley of rich as well as reduced locals, artists, tourists, Krishnas and hippies that traveled across it. When he'd look back on his time in Santa Fe, this is the picture that would most quickly spring to his mind. Before the Arab's hideout, before his hosts' smoky, dank apartment, even before Gwen's body in the springs. The sheer joy and energy of this place was incredible. It had taken him until this moment to slow his pace and pick his head up to look around.

"Luke!" John hung out of his car's window, startling Luke out of his daydream. "We've got Gwen, and she says it's a straight, easy shot. Just follow us."

Luke nodded to him, took one last view of the electric plaza, and made a mental note to keep the picture in his mind, unchanged forever. He kicked his bike into gear and fell in behind John's Jetta.

Humming "Thunder Road's" first verse without growing tired of the screen door slamming, Mary's dress waving, or Roy Orbison singing for the lonely, Luke delighted in riding through pockets of cold and moist air. He knew his mates in the car ahead couldn't feel the air as he did on the bike, and he reveled in his more favorable position. The coke had long worn off, and if he hadn't been following their car he would have pulled over for more, but the ride moderated the crash. Plus, he took much comfort in the fact that he had plenty left and Gwen would be meeting him at the party.

11

*T*he Stahls had dessert on their screened-in porch, celebrating Alex's return home. For his first winter vacation from A&M, Mrs. Stahl had made pecan pie. The meal had been a civilized one, Alex telling mildly dangerous stories about the football team's late night binges. They had decided to move to the porch, allowing Mr. Stahl the chance to refill his drink.

With Alex at home, everything was less tense. His wide smile and slow laugh put Luke and his family at ease. On the porch he continued one of his stories, "We get to the hotel and coach gives out room assignments."

"You stay at a Marriott?" Mr. Stahl asked.

"I think," Alex said. "I got stuck with Tony, the self-proclaimed 'Animal from Abilene,' and—"

"What's he, Mexican?" Mr. Stahl shifted in his chair, propping his pie plate on his belly.

Luke felt his chest stiffen, but Alex didn't flinch. Without looking at his father, Alex said, "I don't know what he is." Mr. Stahl shrugged and gazed at his oldest son. "Anyway," Alex continued, "all he did was eat chili dogs. He ran to the Quik Shop and got ten of 'em. In our room, he just ate one after another. Mom," he said, turning to face her, "I swear, when I woke up the next morning the place smelled like a monkey house."

Mrs. Stahl laughed. "Oh, Alex, I'm sorry." She took a bite of pecan pie. "That must have been awful."

Laughing at the imagined smell, Luke asked, "Why didn't you change rooms?"

"It wasn't that bad." Luke's brother looked at him and smiled. "Plus, it gave me a good story."

"Maybe," Mr. Stahl said, "you should've corked his ass. He might have woke up bloated, but you'd been better off." Laughing heartily at his own joke, he leaned back in his chair and put his glass to his mouth, but the ice had stuck. He tapped the bottom of his glass, and all of a sudden the ice released its hold and gave way. Scotch gushed out onto his shirt. "Shit!" He patted his shirt with a napkin. "Martha, what's wrong with these glasses? My God." He looked up, and Luke, Alex and Mrs. Stahl stifled a giggle. Luke and his mother looked at each other with barely a smile between them.

Mr. Stahl's face fell. "What's wrong with you two?" He threw down his fork on the tile floor. "Alex isn't home for three hours and you two are back to your tricks."

Luke said nothing. Long ago, he'd abandoned his juvenile plan to fix his father; now all he tried to do was make it through the meal without an explosion.

Mrs. Stahl put down her plate and reached for Mr. Stahl's fork. "Steven, we aren't doing a thing," she said. "Come on, now. Take my fork and eat your pie."

"No." He threw down her fork as well, the metal clanging on the porch's tile. "I'm sick of you two, always snickering." He turned to Alex. "See what I deal with since you're gone?"

Luke looked at his mother and then his brother, silently pleading Alex to do something. Alex said, "Dad, it's all right." Barely pausing, he asked his father, "See the all-state team?" Raising his huge frame from the chair, he reached his hand across to his father, silently offering him a fork.

Like a toddler who sulked from the loss of a lollipop, but was distracted with a replacement cookie, Mr. Stahl said, "Yeah. Said that linebacker from Caldwell's gonna be an Aggie."

Thank God, Luke thought. If Alex had been gone, the situation would've turned ugly, as it had at least four times since Alex had been at school. Mr. Stahl would've screamed and thrown every fork on the floor. Mrs. Stahl would've cried and run around to pick them up, and Luke would've stayed still with his head bowed, lacking the heart to leave—praying for it all to end.

"Supposedly," Alex continued, reeling in his father, "he's the real deal. We'll see when he gets there."

Mr. Stahl snorted. "Another nigger linebacker's just what you need. Maybe next year you'll make it to a bowl."

"Please, Steven. I don't want to hear that word."

"It's the truth, Martha."

Luke stood up. He could take no more. "Thanks for the pie, Mom, but I need to do some homework." Avoiding his father's sneer, he looked at his brother. "Goin' out tonight?"

Alex nodded. "But I'll be back pretty early. I'll check in on you." He smiled.

It's good to have you back, *Luke thought. His mother was relaxed, his father soothed, and Luke was freed from attention.*

Turning to leave the porch, a moment's anxiety rose in Luke as he thought of Alex's inevitable departure in three weeks, but he repressed it. Instead, he thought of the calm that had settled on his home, and he breathed easily as he shut the screen door behind him.

12

I t was desert dark when they arrived at the farm's entry, the stars crisp against the black sky. John had traversed the dirt driveway at a good clip, and the profound darkness—plus the dust from the tires—forced Luke to follow close behind. Without warning, John's brake lights expanded in Luke's vision, and he scarcely had time to grab his own brake, stopping just inches from John's bumper. Luke stood to see that they had pulled up to a haphazard, open gate that looked constructed by ten-year-old boys wielding some two-by-fours, a few bolts and a massive hinge. Then Luke saw why they hadn't poured through the gate: it carried a half-naked boy dressed like an Indian, his face painted blue and yellow.

The boy kicked the dirt below him and rode the closing gate like a horse into the path of John's car. "Twenty bucks a head," he shouted, as the gate locked uneasily into its equally ramshackle catch.

Gwen leaned out from the back of the driver side and yelled back, "We're with Marco."

"Oh," the boy replied, disappointed. "Come on in." He kicked on the lock between his feet and rode the gate open again, his arm extending a welcome.

Luke followed close to John's bumper as they meandered into a huge pasture that served as a makeshift parking lot. John threw his Jetta into a space between two Jeeps with enormous tires and spotlights adorning their roll bars. As he motored by, Luke pointed to the far side of the field. "Meet you guys back here. I'm gonna park my bike under the trees over there."

When he returned to the Jetta, Luke found no one. He fingered the baggie he still kept in his pocket and headed in the direction of the concentrated beat beyond the parking lot, picking his way through random paths between hundreds of unsystematically parked cars. There were no buildings to speak of on the farm, and besides the headlights of the cars coming into the entrance behind him, Luke saw only a dim light in the distance. It seemed to identify the source of the heavy, pulsing beat.

Luke finally made it to the edge of the parking lot and realized why the light was so dim and why the music, though loud at its source, sounded so far away until he reached this point. He stood overlooking a monstrous pit filled with swirling, multicolored lights and hundreds of shirtless, wet bodies writhing to the beat that pumped out in all directions from a DJ booth in the center of it all. Before entering the pit, he reached into his right pocket to grab a key and the cocaine. Four times he dug the key into the powder then lifted it to his nose. While debating on whether to give this first kick a serious boost with another cycle he felt hands on his hips.

"What are you doing, Snow White?" Luke turned to see Gwen's green eyes reflecting the lights of the rave that raged below.

"I'm glad I found you." He smiled. "Or I guess you found me. You want?" he asked, offering the bag. Though sharing with Gwen was not a problem, an inkling of trepidation rose in Luke and he looked around for possible interlopers.

She revealed a small pill with Papa Smurf stamped on the front. "No. I'm going to be Smurfette for the night. That stuff," she nodded at his baggie, "cuts right through and ruins it. Want one?"

"I'll stick with this for now," he said. Then he snatched the pill. "I'll take it when the blow wears off."

"Let's take it together. It takes a while to kick in; your coke'll have worn off by then. Come Luke," she said, as she lowered her head while keeping her gaze on him. "Down the hatch." She threw back her head the way she did in the hot spring, opened her mouth, dropped the pill in as if it was a pinch of sugar, and then followed it with a swig of beer. He took the beer out of her hand and aped her process.

The fear that she was merely playing with him flew into his mind, but he shook it off quickly. He hoped if he got high enough he wouldn't worry about how she perceived him. Plus, it was a good sign that she gave him a precious pill.

"Now, we must meet Marco," she said. She grabbed his hand and began to lead him into the pit, but halted and turned. "Which Smurf do you want to be?"

Luke paused and gave some thought to the seemingly mundane question. Should he try to be cool and make a pick that could be mistaken as tasteless, or offer something like Dopey and hope she sensed his adorable allure? Finally, the perfect compromise came to him—one that, if she wanted to pursue it, could also shed some light on his personality. He squeezed her hand and said, "Dreamy."

She whispered, "Superb." Her wet breath gave him goose bumps.

Hand in hand, they spilled down the rocky slope into the pit. The coke hit Luke's heart at the same time the reverberating beat plunged into his ears. He inhaled deeply and clenched his teeth.

"Whoa!" he exclaimed, as much to himself as anyone else. "This is fuckin' tremendous." He leaned into Gwen, and for no good reason other than it was his present reality, yelled into her ear, "I'm jacked."

"Good. Hopefully the X'll catch up soon."

Luke grew confident that she wasn't toying with him, but he couldn't figure out why she would be interested in him; the guy who, when he first met her, smelled like death, gave her a line from a scene in "Three's Company," and popped a boner like a twelve-year-old virgin.

Nonetheless, she wouldn't relinquish his hand and led him to the DJ booth. It sat high up on a throne of trembling latticework, which fronted ten foot tall speakers. The leaping beat shook anything and everything around them, including the teeth and bones of nearby dancers. Gwen and Luke had to climb up the treacherous latticework to reach the DJ who furiously mixed the music.

"Marco!" Gwen shrieked when she got to the top.

The second black man Luke had seen in New Mexico, Marco was a bald man with skin so dark he looked purple. When he heard Gwen scream, he looked up and took off his headphones, then leaned over the turntable for a hug.

After he released his grip, he fired off successive questions without leaving time for a response. Luke had to read his lips to get most of what he was saying. "What up, Gwenny? How you been? Sick party, huh? You must have gotten my e-mail, right? But you didn't reply. I didn't know you were gonna come!"

She screamed over the music, "Of course, Marco! I wouldn't miss your show. Besides, this place is incredible." She had to pause, apparently to gather her energy for the next round of yelling. "Whose farm is this anyway?"

"Farm?" He laughed. "That's just something we put in the announcement. This is the back side of some federal land. Their own land is the only land they don't patrol. We never get busted out here."

Gwen smiled. "Well, thanks for the invitation. Your name carries a lot of weight at the door. I—"

"Good, good," he interrupted as he put one of the headphones to his left ear and began mixing two new records. For the first time, he looked at Luke and frowned. He turned back to Gwen and asked, "Where's Steven?"

"I left him in Santa Fe. He was being an asshole, plus he's old. I—"

"But rich."

"Yeah, but so am I."

Marco roared. "You're right. You're right." Abruptly, he again picked up his headphones, but this time he put them over both ears. "I'll see ya, baby." Without waiting for a response, he turned his attention back to the turntables.

"Great music," Luke yelled to Marco as he and Gwen turned to head back down the latticework.

"What?" Marco yelled back as he again removed his headphones, clearly annoyed at another interruption.

Luke already had both feet on the latticework, and it would be awkward to repeat his bland comment considering he'd have to go all the way back to the booth to be heard. But he didn't want Marco to think he'd said something rude. He ran back to the pissed off DJ and repeated his lame compliment.

Giving no response, Marco glared at Luke and then went back to his music.

Gwen led Luke to the middle of the pit and began to sway with her hands above her hung head. "Smurfette is feeling the X," she said, apparently to the ground. She drew in a very deep breath.

"So is Dreamy," Luke replied. He felt incredible. The drug had swarmed over him as soon as he had stepped into the sea of dancing bodies. It was as though the X had built up this inconceivable high while he was at the booth and had released it now that he had no distractions. The rush felt orgasmic, as exhilaration turned to euphoria.

Immediately, his thoughts focused solely on the drug's physical effects: the tingling in his toes and fingers, the elation sweeping through his chest and behind his eyelids, his neck's inability to keep itself erect. Offering less speed and more rapture than cocaine, the ecstasy tried to pull his body into itself—to compact its bulk—so it could economically reach out to all of his nerve endings.

"I've never had X so good," he groaned as he reached out blindly to Gwen. He no longer thought of her as an object of desire, but rather a companion in the high that dominated his senses. Gradually, his intoxication soared to another level and he absently pulled his forearm across his sweaty brow. "How much higher could we get?" he managed to ask Gwen between heavy breaths.

In response, he felt her forehead touch his and they swayed together, sealed by their moist faces. Obviously she could only manage curt dialogue as well, because he felt her draw in a deep breath as if she had a speech on the tip of her tongue, but she only whispered, "I don't know."

While the vivid strobe lights painted yellow, red and green on the inside of his closed eyelids, Luke's limited dancing consisted of a slow sway on unwieldy legs to the increasing tempo of the pounding music. Implausibly, he again felt the drug take his psyche to another level, rendering superfluous all motion and speech. He wanted to sit down, drop his chin to his chest and revel in the bliss.

Having forgotten Gwen's head attached to his, he made a move downward, but felt her wet skin soldered to his. Before, Luke was aware of nothing but the pulse of the music and his flying soul—even unaware of the hundreds of bodies that spun around him—but now the voltage between their skins took center stage in his mind.

Luke guided their heads down to waist level, then lost his balance. Though his eyes remained closed, he felt his head separate from hers. He landed on his back, as if he fell from the sky. But in a moment he again felt her connection as her hand reached up his jeans' leg and grabbed his bare calf. He curled his body to meet her hand, and an electric charge shot through his arm when their palms met and wet fingers intertwined. The drive to have her surged in his chest and limbs and crotch, and he pulled her to him. The crook he created in his arm as he turned on his side served as her headrest.

Even though he could've opened his eyes and seen her in the flesh, he kept them closed and imagined her body rising out of the spring in Santa Fe. The image of her wet hair pulled back in a thick cable was so lucid in his mind that he was surprised when he reached for her head and felt a dry clump. He grabbed it anyway and pulled it back so her face met his, his tongue diving and swirling into her receptive mouth. She returned his passion, and together they stayed sealed by their yawning mouths, pausing only when their bodies—in need of air—forced them apart.

Overcome with a paradoxical desire to devour her entire, round body and let it envelop him, Luke reached under her shirt and found her breasts with both hands. Still ravaging the inside of her mouth, he kneaded them, feeling the perfect pulp he remembered from the spring. He tore his lips from hers to lean down and take one breast in his mouth, then the other, circling her nipples one at a time. Then, opening his mouth wider, he sucked in each as deep as his jaw would allow.

He drove his right hand down the front of her pants, and she, in tandem, did the same to him, working him with her creamy palm. He froze with his hand cupped on her round pubis—her touch was like her breast, the perfect equilibrium of smoothness and tension. Exhilarated and unable to tame his craving for all of her, Luke wanted Gwen to feel the same. He found the top of her folded skin with his middle finger and mimicked the circular dance his tongue performed on her nipple. She moaned and flexed her hips upwards, grinding herself into his stirring hand.

They grew frantic as each blindly reached for the other's pants, but suddenly and wordlessly they recognized the inefficiency of their arrangement, and they turned their attention to their own clothes. After yanking down their pants and moving together, neither was satisfied with the shirts that still separated them. They pulled them off, unconcerned with the crowd that noisily twirled around them. Luke leaned his naked body onto hers, but she pressed back, wanting to roll on top of him.

After she flipped him, Gwen aligned herself on top of Luke and lifted her hips so that he could slide inside her. Luke complied, driving himself in as deep as he could. The damp warmth that enveloped him sent waves of heat rippling from his crotch through the rest of his body.

Gwen dropped her head onto his shoulder and began to roll her hips. Luke met her rhythm and force, thrusting fiercely, and she matched his ferocity, grinding down on him as he hoisted her body. They continued to pump and mill each other's loins, and Luke reached around her back, squeezing her as she continued to gyrate. Rocketing into her with abandon, only his shoulder blades and feet touched the ground.

The inside of her hot, wet body pumping and twisting became too much to bear; Luke felt the rising swell of orgasm. He stopped thrusting, but left himself deep inside her while she circled faster and faster, crushing into him.

He felt her muscles tighten around his member, and he could no longer remain still inside her. He fired into her, sending her leaning back. She put one hand on the ground and massaged his scrotum with the other. Her moans now came with every exhale, and Luke again grabbed her breasts so that he could milk each nipple as she came.

She froze for a long second, then exploded with a wail and vicious shake that, along with her tightening grip, sent shock waves through Luke's entire body. She leaned further back, and Luke's body clenched into a curl as he unloaded himself into her. For a moment they held their bodies in the impossible position. But finally, they could hold no longer and collapsed into a sweaty, heaving heap on the dirt floor. Even now, neither was aware of the rave around them and both sets of eyes remained closed.

The next morning, Luke woke up on a plaid couch inside a moldy mobile home. After a second of dread, his mind slowly slid into gear, and he eventually put together his location. He had no idea how the hell he ended up in the mobile home but recalled some of the night before and knew he was in the middle of federal land. He went to the back of the RV to look for Gwen, but when he passed the reeking refrigerator and opened the cheap plastic door he figured led to a bedroom, he found her not alone in bed. Marco clutched Gwen's naked body, covered only by a thin sheet. Luke went to her side of the bed and quietly pulled the sheet back to look at her pale, naked shape.

He stood there in no hurry to move but felt conflicted. Should he wake her up or just walk out? He wanted to see her green eyes once more.

A flurry of pictures passed through his mind: he and Gwen returning to Texas to meet his mother, having kids, sharing drinks and kisses into their eighties. In fact, he realized he wanted to see not only her green eyes but also her perfect body—the sum of extraordinary round parts—for the rest of his life. For that instant he felt he could be anywhere or nowhere, doing anything or nothing, as long as he'd be with Gwen. He started to lean down to her ear to rouse her, to tell her about his imaginings and the simple, contented life they could lead, but then he saw the whites of Marco's eyes. "What the fuck you doin'?"

Luke straightened. "Nothing," he said slowly, surprised at his conviction. Marco's rough voice and rancid breath slammed reality back into Luke's head, and his image of perpetual pleasure with Gwen vanished as fast as it had appeared. "Good luck," he said to Marco. He flipped the sheet back over her and slowly walked out, cursing himself for ever imagining a meeting between Gwen and his mother.

His heart raced when he returned to the tree where he remembered leaving his motorcycle and found nothing. Most of the cars in the lot were gone, and in the light of day, he realized how wide the field was and what little sense he had of where he or his motorcycle was. He turned a 360. *Jesus. Where's my bike!* In the distance he spotted a glimmer of chrome under a tree branch heavy with dew. He hustled over to his bike and petted it thanks for making itself known. He dug in his saddlebag for his map, remembering that the back road leading to the farm fed into Route 60. He found it on the map, and from there he could keep going west through Arizona or jump north into Utah.

Hopefully, one or the other would urge him into its territory, offering him answers, for it certainly wasn't with Gwen. He was foolish to think, even for a moment, that he could ever have a legitimate future with some girl who fucked him without thought, then jumped into bed with another man. How would she have helped him?

He tucked the map into his belt and climbed on his bike. Leaning it upright, he reached down to the bike's left side and inserted the key. He hit the start button, kicked it into gear, brought his feet up, and headed out of the makeshift parking lot.

Part 2

"I would for you, Kate ... "
Jane's Addiction

13

My girlfriend came home with me," Luke said to Alex, trying to connect with his sullen brother. Luke, an eighth grader, had brought home a date after school. The girl sat talking with Mrs. Stahl in the kitchen. Luke nodded that way. "She's in with mom."

It had been almost two years since Alex ruined his ankle and failed out of A&M, and he'd spent most of that time watching TV. Today was no different. His back to Luke, he sat motionless on the couch, his ankle elevated on the table. He said, "Oh yeah? What's her name?"

"Heather. Heather Loon."

Alex turned to look at his brother. "Have I ever met her?"

His brother's short questions predicted one of his outbursts. Aggression that used to be foreign to Alex's character was now commonplace. A part of Luke wanted to leave the room, but he stayed. "No," he said. Alex looked back at the TV and changed channels with the remote. Luke said, "I really like her."

His brother stared at the hazy picture on the screen. "Hook up with her then."

Luke winced. He shouldn't have brought her up. He should've stayed in the kitchen and talked about school with Heather and his mother. "No."

"Why not?"

"She's not like that."

"Last girl was."

Stung, Luke didn't know how to respond to his new brother, so he spoke in kind. "She was a whore."

Alex sighed and nodded to the kitchen. "And this one's not?"

"No."

"Why did you bring her here?"

Luke couldn't believe what he heard. "Because you told me to!"

Alex looked skeptical.

"You said Mom likes it."

Alex shrugged. "I'm glad for you." He flipped the channel. "I hope it works out and you have fifteen kids and live in Lubbock." Without looking up, he pointed the remote at the neighbor's house. "You can live right next door."

Mrs. Stahl walked in with Heather. The young girl wore rouge and red lipstick, put on too thick. She had on a jean skirt, a little short, with plastic studs like diamonds along the hem. Even with her misguided attempts at mature fashion, the young girl added a fresh light to the dark den. Her lips spread into a smile when she saw Alex on the couch. "Hi," she said. "I'm Heather." She extended her hand to Alex. Without turning around, Alex raised his backwards, but instead of shaking hers, he pressed the remote and changed the channel.

Mrs Stahl's face flushed. "Alex! Say hello."

Turning to glare at his mother, Alex said, "Hello." His eyes stayed on her for a moment, then he turned to the TV.

Nervously, Luke watched Heather who, undaunted, kept up her smile. "I remember you. My father took me to your games when I was little. I didn't really watch, but he said you were the best."

Alex's head flinched at the mention of high school. Heather, letting her smile fall, looked at Luke. Mrs. Stahl put her hand on Alex's shoulder and spoke up again. "Alex!" she said. "Heather's speaking to you."

Alex twisted again. "Luke tells me you're no whore. But I'm not so sure." He looked at her chest, then her thin legs. "If it walks like a duck and quacks like a duck."

Mrs. Stahl drew in a quick breath. She took her hand from Alex's shoulder and smacked the back of his head, snapping it forward. Heather put her hands to her mouth and turned to run through the kitchen door.

Luke stood, startled by both his mother's strange violence and his own wish to hit his brother.

Then his wits came to him as Alex, hobbled by his injury, tried to turn for his mother who'd stepped away. Luke snatched his brother's extended hand and threw it into his lap. "Don't you dare," he said. His mother left the room, both her hands, like Heather's, covering her mouth.

Luke yelled at his brother, "Just because you get kicked out of school and sit here like a pile of shit , you think you can make everyone else miserable?"

Alex dropped his chin to his chest and shook his head, but said nothing. Luke wanted to yell more, scream for his real brother to return, shake out the alien that had invaded Alex's body, but he couldn't bring himself to say a thing, for Alex had begun to cry.

14

For the little time he had spent driving on I-40, its roaring noise and wounding dirt trampled Luke, so he swung back onto the lonesome two lanes of Route 60. Then he rode Route 260 for the better part of four hours. He liked the solitude of the smaller highway, but it definitely slowed his pace, and his weary body cried out for rest. He hadn't seen a town worthy of stopping in until he drove by a sign that contained icons of gas pumps, utensils and beds. It read, "Camp Verde—10 Miles." Not that Camp Verde sounded like the stuff of riders' lore, but its relatively big name on the map promised a bed.

He needed a bed. He still felt like shit. The sleeplessness had caught up to him, and the hole he felt in his gut was no smaller. Banging some whore wasn't the answer. Maybe a girl was, but certainly not some sleaze. From now on, he promised himself he'd limit his attention to girls worth his heart and not just his dick.

He listened to his hungry stomach over his drowsy head and committed to pulling over at the next restaurant—hopefully before the city limits. After a good meal, he'd feel rejuvenated for the final ten miles to Camp Verde and his search for a motel.

Soon, a ragged sign tacked high on a telephone pole pulled Luke off 260. It was a piece of cardboard that looked like it was ripped from the back of a refrigerator's package, and above huge handwritten scrawl that read "Phil's Roadside Eats" it held a hand-drawn arrow pointing down the battered gray road next to the pole.

For a moment, the abused road seemed like a kind of frontage road that paralleled the highway, but it soon branched off on its own. In not so much as a mile, thick sand carpeted the ancient asphalt, and to Luke's left there appeared a small river bed with a steep embankment. Luke slowed on the dangerous sand, and as he did, glanced at the wisps of dying, yellow shrubs in the dry river bed.

Not only were the shrubs dying and the sand absent of tracks, but there was no sound of bird or creature. The last few miles seemed to take him to the middle of nowhere. It gave him chills.

The seclusion triggered the memory of his brother. In the past days, he'd repeatedly done what would've disappointed Alex, but he could think of no other way to address his pain. He felt frustrated that he kept making poor choices, but he had to go with what felt good, even briefly.

As Luke turned through a bend in the road, all of a sudden, the top of a little girl's head, followed by a set of glistening eyes, crested the river bank thirty yards ahead of him. After a slight pause, the girl's face continued its steady rise over the horizon. When it was in his full view Luke saw that it held the roundness of a young child, maybe eight or nine. She peered at him for a moment, then hopped up onto the side of the road, squatting motionless like a frog. Unsure of her curious conduct, Luke slowed to give her a good look, thinking his shiny bike and its low rumble impressed her.

Then, the girl stood erect—taller and slimmer than her chubby face had suggested—and sprinted toward Luke. Petrified of the little girl, her feral eyes and her random behavior, he seized his front brake with his hand and stomped on the back with his foot.

Both tires locked up on the sand and Luke went down with his bike, both meeting the sandy blacktop with an evil squeal and heavy thud.

The slow speed made for a minor crash, like a child's unwieldy fall on a heavy bicycle. The left foot peg sustained most of the shock. Luke wasn't injured. Nonetheless, he was disoriented, dazed by his instantaneous change in fortune. One minute he had quietly rewarded himself for a good day's voyage, and the next he bounced his ass off the hard road, impossibly frightened by a silent, sketchy little girl.

He had no time to consider his predicament because the fast little girl reached him in a second, squatted next to him, and stared at his face. When his eyes met hers Luke realized why he had seen her eyes glistening, even from a distance—she was crying.

Her scent caught up a moment after her rushed arrival to Luke's flat body, and he had to turn his head from the stink—she reeked of the mucus and saliva that buttered her face and clumped in her stringy hair. When she noticed Luke's wonder at her condition, she tried to clean her face off with the hem of her soiled pink T-shirt, only adding the shirt's brown dirt to the mix on her face. Without breaking her stare, she gave up on her cleaning and jammed a set of dirty fingers in her mouth, all the while examining him through her thick, streaming tears.

Luke noticed her examination of him wasn't one of concern; it was clearly an attempt to get something from him. In fact, nothing about her presence suggested that she'd noticed he had just crashed a motorcycle.

After waiting with an expectant expression, Luke saw that he would have to initiate the conversation, so he tried to shake his head clean of the crash as best he could. "What's wrong?"

She pulled her mucky hand out of her mouth and stuttered, "I … I … I … "

Still lying next to his bike, Luke tried to sound soothing. "OK. It's OK. Are you alone?"

"N … N … N … " She gestured back to where she had come over the rise.

Luke had never seen such a pitiful creature. He had no idea what to do. He knew he was OK to walk, and the bike would be safe in the middle of the unused road, but the entire scene freaked him out. There was part of him that wanted to right his bike and take off, but he knew he couldn't. If it was a man or woman who needed his help, he would have surrendered to this cowardly part of himself and bolted like a thief in the night, but he couldn't ignore a child like this.

"Do you want me to look?" he asked.

She nodded, turned, and ran back to the place in the bank over which she had jumped.

Before he was directly over the embankment Luke could see only a pair of yellow rubber flip-flops—the thong disappearing in the seam between the owner's swollen toes. But once there he looked down to see a body lying in a carved-out cave, under the lip of the steep river bank. He assumed it was the girl's mother. His position didn't allow him to see the mother's head or neck under the lip, but he could see that she lay on her side under a ratty blanket and had balled herself up to take advantage of the shade. Yet she couldn't bring her legs into her body to enjoy the same benefit. She didn't move when Luke jumped over her into the bank.

It took a moment for his eyes to adjust to the shade of the small cave, but he soon realized that what had looked like a pillow pulled close to her chest was actually a baby. From both faces and sets of hands grew layers of oozing sores. It looked as though any body part would burst and heave out its contents if pricked by a pin.

Speechless, Luke looked for some sign of what to do from the little girl who still stood on the road. When she offered him nothing but post-sob heaves and slobbers, an upsurge of anger swelled in him: *Why the fuck did I get put into this?* He considered himself recently experienced in the underworld, but this was, by far, the most unnatural scene he had ever witnessed. He not only felt irritated by his helplessness, but also, irrationally, by the nine-year-old girl's. He looked up at her, but she only jammed the index and middle fingers of both hands into her mouth. Now that she had gotten him to where she needed him to be, she avoided his eyes.

"Why did you bring me here? What can *I* do?"

She looked back at him. By now her eyes had dried. She yanked one hand out of her mouth and vaguely pointed from where Luke had come and said, "M ... M ... M ... "

"What do you want me to do?" Luke yelled.

At the sound of his yell, the turgid sack of skin above the mother's shoulders shifted. Luke thought the two were dead, but the clear sign of vitality threw another wrinkle into the bizarre circumstance. Again he addressed the girl and asked, "What's wrong with them?" The absurdity of the fact that he looked for guidance from this pitiful girl was not lost on him, but he blamed her for pulling him in—and wanted her to get him out. She said nothing in response, and he dropped his head into his massaging hands, attempting to knead out an answer.

The whir of an engine forced Luke to lift his head and look toward the road where he'd left his bike. A speeding Gremlin, followed by a cloud of dust, whipped around the turn. "Shit!" he screamed. He ran up the bank and jumped over the lip, but was too late to do anything except stare and hope that the careening Gremlin would miss his motorcycle.

Just before impact, the car swerved on a blanket of sand, barely skidding by the motorcycle. It came to a stop in a blur of swirling dust on the other side of the road. Luke glanced at the girl, whose vacant look and lollipop fingers remained unchanged.

The Gremlin's door cracked open and rocked back and forth, as if the driver tried to fan away the dust that surrounded his car. A short man in tattered fatigues jumped out, and just like the dirty little girl, ran directly at Luke, stopping five feet short. He had extraordinarily greasy hair; it clustered together in quasi dreadlocks around his face, and as he ran it swayed like beads in a palm reader's doorway. It was the filth in his hair, not on his body, that Luke thought he smelled first. Then the smell of the man's accumulated odors—sweat, blood, shit, grease, and smoke—hit him in the face like the back of a shovel.

Though strong odors usually woke him up, this stench took the edge off Luke's reality. He suddenly felt as if he was dreaming. In this state, he was surprised, but not shocked or worried, when the man wordlessly drew out a switch blade. Luke's consciousness remained in its semi-cognizant state, and when the man clicked the blade open, Luke's focus went not to the dangerous dagger but to the aggressor's extraordinary fingernails.

Their bottoms were intensely white—they glowed in contrast to the black dirt that covered the backs of his hands and fingers, each of the long tips packed with crud. Unlike the black grease or mud in a mechanic or landscaper's fingernails, this was light brown gunk. The crispness of the lines among the three colors made his hands look like a carefully drawn color-by-number project. God only knows into what orifices he had been shoving his fingers—whether his or someone else's—but the imagined smell combined with the real reek of the man made Luke wobble on the side of the river bed.

The man looked at Luke and then at the girl, a little statue with her hands in her mouth. "Where's your mama?" he asked the girl. She gestured to the place over which she had clambered minutes earlier. He snorted and turned to Luke. "Who the fuck are you?" he barked, pointing the blade at Luke's stomach.

Hearing the first voice besides his own since the entire nightmare began, the reality of his position sprung into Luke's consciousness, and his waking dream ended. The freak in front of him was more unpredictable than his little girl, and Luke had no idea what kind of response to offer. It was his turn to stutter, "I ... I ... "

"That your bike?" His small, gray eyes beat into Luke's.

"Yeah."

"Why the fuck you ride that rice burner? You some kinda nip?"

The abruptness and stupidity of his question helped Luke regain his perspective. Though he had a knife, the man was small and seemed out of sorts, especially if he mistook the Harley for a Japanese knock-off. Narrowing his eyes and nodding toward the bank, Luke said, "That your family?"

The man gave only a slight, skeptical nod in response.

"Shouldn't you take them to a doctor?"

The man's eyes widened and he stood staring at Luke, clearly overwhelmed by Luke's audacity. Finally, he said, "You want what me and her got?" He pointed his knife toward his wife. He paused for a response, but Luke casually shifted his weight onto his left leg, stunned into silent contemplation of the man's haphazard threat. He wasn't scared, more baffled by the small freak who waited for an answer as if his question wasn't rhetorical.

Everything Luke said or did made the man pause; his brain seemed to work slowly. Luke's daring clearly threw the man for a loop, and he made faces as he processed these complicated thoughts. After a while he tilted his head and scrunched his face, apparently to turn the conversation again. "Where the fuck you come from?" Again, he waited for a response, leaving his face in its squeeze.

Luke stayed quiet.

The man's face then fell out of its crunch as he appeared to come to his own conclusion, and with the knife pointed at Luke, he made a slow stab with his arm. Luke leaned back, away from the minor threat. He was almost giddy at the incredible play he participated in; it was like interacting with the missing link.

Not prepared for Luke's movement, the man planned what to do next. His face contorted a second time behind the greasy tubes of hair. At last, he extended his black left hand and flipped it over to reveal an unnaturally pink palm covered in boils. Silently, he extended his right hand to place the knife's sharp edge six inches above his exposed palm. As he shifted the blade to bring it downward, it briefly caught the sun, but the luminescence disappeared when he plunged it into the base of his pointer finger. He then drew the knife diagonally across his palm and up his wrist and arm.

The two witnesses and perpetrator stood silent, unmoving, looking at the man's palm. There was a faint, pink streak running from the base of his finger to the rolled cuff of his fatigue shirt below his elbow. The man didn't take his eyes off the slice in his skin. "You want what I got?" he repeated loudly.

All at once, the line widened and grew dark red. As he stretched his fingers, staring at them like they had just been transplanted onto his wrist, the blood surged out and down the sides of his hand and arm, running like hot grease into the absorbent sand.

Panic flew into each of the three faces, then each, respectively, turned into something else. The little girl's into horror, Luke's into disbelief and the man's into cold fear.

When Luke was thirteen and went to camp with older kids for the first time, he remembered when a guy who looked too old to go to the camp offered the same surprised look after he lit up a cigarette on the bus. His age, and his label-less black jeans and T-shirt, conjured up the quiet aura of a tough guy who needed the camp for some sort of remediation. He parted his hair down the center and feathered it, something Luke and his friends would have taunted him for, had he not been so intimidating. All of this, plus the fact that no one knew him and he sat in isolation, put him into the forefront of every bus rider's mind; even so, they tried not to stare, and instead chatted to each other about impending sleeping arrangements. After the rebel's smoke reached the front of the bus, the driver went to the back to tell him to put out his cigarette. With all eyes turned to gauge his reaction, and knowing that if he wanted to maintain his image he'd have to do something unexpected—even dangerous—he lifted his palm parallel with his face. He extinguished his cigarette into it. For a moment, he had Luke and his friends rapt with fear and awe, but then the pain hit. He started to shake his hand and jump up and down in his seat, while searching for a place to throw out the butt without further offending the bus driver. The act, which at first bolstered his image, dissipated into nothing more than raw stupidity when his face showed the excruciating pain.

And so it was with the grimy man in front of Luke. Once a threat, he was now only the pathetic victim of his own idiocy. Luke had no sympathy for the animal in front of him. He probably would have done the same thing to his daughter or wife had their palms been more accessible. But the pity Luke felt for the rest of the family urged him to pick up his fallen motorcycle and look for help.

As he left the scene, Luke looked back to make sure the man hadn't gone after his little girl. He was on his knees—completely unaware of Luke—frantically wrapping his hand and arm in the fatigue shirt he had stripped off. It wasn't clear whether the man's naked torso was sheet-white because of lack of blood or sun, but Luke knew he needed to find help quickly or the man would die.

15

When Alex first moved back, after failing out of school, the Stahls still ate dinner to-gether. But to Luke, the meals were so painful it felt like they'd been served broken glass.

One night, Mr. Stahl broke the silence. "Steak's a lot better on that Weber." No one responded. Then he spoke to Alex. "Central kicked our asses last night. Did you see?"

Alex blew on his full soup spoon. It looked tiny in his hands. "No."

"No defense. They let that nigger run all over them."

"Steven!"

"Sorry. Hundred and seventy yards." He elbowed Alex's shoulder. "We needed the Marauder back, huh? You would've put him in the hospital."

Luke watched Alex close his eyes. His massive body clenched.

Mr. Stahl nodded to his wife who got up and fetched him a beer. "Probably don't know that I remember this, but the highest yard total ever run against you was sixty-eight. Did you know that Luke?"

Caught unaware by his father's attention, Luke looked up and shook his head.

"Sixty-eight. And I—"

Alex interrupted his father, "Can we not talk about this?"

"Yes," Mrs. Stahl added, "let's talk about something else." She turned to Luke. "How was your day?"

Before Luke could speak, his father cleared his throat and pushed away from the table. "Well, sorry. I just thought the boy would like to know I remembered. I mean, my father didn't remember shit I did." He folded his arms, then looked from Alex to his wife and back. "All I'm saying is it would've been great to have you back. You would've—"

Alex got up from the table and left the room.

Luke and his mother looked at each other.

Mr. Stahl slammed his fist on the table and bellowed, "What? At least I'm doing something while you two sit here exchanging looks. Jesus Christ!" He stood and pointed at Luke, then Mrs. Stahl. "I'm trying to help and you two do nothing. He's been sitting here doing nothing. Nothing! I try to bring back a little fond memory, and you don't do shit."

Luke's mother looked into her hands and folded her napkin.

Luke spoke up, but directed his voice to his bowl. "Every time you bring it up, he leaves the room." Luke didn't know if he or his father was more surprised by his boldness.

His father asked, "Excuse me?"

Luke picked his head up and looked his father in the eye. "Every time you bring up high school or football, he leaves the room. Just let it go."

"Look here, Luke. I see you sit in there with him all day, silent. Not talking, just sitting. You think that helps him out? No. What's going to help him out is to get off his ass. Bringing up his success—his potential—will motivate him. Not sitting around with you all day."

Luke mumbled, "Hasn't helped yet."

Mr. Stahl rose from his chair. "Speak up, boy. You got something to say then say it. But don't mumble like some faggot."

Luke looked at his mother, who still focused on her hands. He stood. For the first time, Luke realized he was almost as tall as his father. "I said, it hasn't helped yet. Nothing you do has helped!"

"Don't stand up to me in my house, boy." He chuckled. "I like seeing some guts finally, but don't stand up to me."

His father's laugh fanned Luke's ire. Breathing hard, he said through clenched teeth, "Promise you won't bring up his past and I'll sit down."

Mrs. Stahl also stood. She grabbed her son's and then her husband's wrist. She pleaded with them, "Sit down, please. Both of you just sit down."

"I'll do whatever I want in my house, boy. And you will sit down if I have to throw you back into that chair!"

"Don't bring up his past, it's that easy."

Mr. Stahl reached across the table and grabbed Luke's collar. Luke felt the man's power. Though he wasn't much taller, his father was incredibly strong. He threw Luke backward into the corner cabinet, rattling the china inside. Mrs. Stahl wailed and ran out of the room. Then Mr. Stahl walked around the table to his son.

Inside, Luke raged with fury, terror and fear. Part of him wanted to ball his fist and throw it as hard as he could at his father, but the rest of him was too scared. He put up his hands as his father neared him.

"Get your ass in that chair!" his father yelled, again grabbing his son by the collar. Trying to throw Luke into his chair, Mr. Stahl sent him flying into the table. Luke's nose bashed the wooden surface, his hands too late to protect him.

Next to Luke's left hand lay his mother's knife. For a second he considered picking it up, but he didn't have time. His father's hands were on him again. From behind, his father whispered in Luke's ear, his breath reeking of alcohol and rage, "You better get your ass into that chair, boy, or you'll never sit down at my table again."

The inferno inside Luke leapt into his voice, and he yelled the only thing that came to mind—what he wanted to yell at his father countless times, what he felt summed up their entire coexistence, "No!"

His father still whispered. "Yes."

Before he knew it, Luke's shoulder absorbed what felt like a concrete block dropped from above, and he fell to the floor, his head landing by the baseboard. Though his ears rang, he heard his brother's voice say calmly, "Get off him." Luke looked up in time to see his brother's immense hands push his father, sending the older man flying against the corner cabinet.

This time, the shelves collapsed and the china shattered.

16

Phil's Roadside Eats was not much farther up the road, and in Luke's haste, he almost sped by it. He nearly spilled again trying to turn into the diner's parking lot. The cook behind the counter, wearing the same greasy white shirt and rolled hat as Mel from "Alice," fried a mound of bacon and sang "The Wheel in the Sky" along with the prehistoric Wurlitzer. Luke ran up to the counter and told him about what he had witnessed, to which the cook, presumably Phil, shrugged, flipped his bacon and slowly wiped his hands on his apron. Still singing along with Journey, he took off his apron, folded it and finally reached for the phone.

"Charlie?" the man asked into the receiver. "Phil. Young man just walked in and told me 'bout a pretty grisly scene. Probably should have one of your boys check it out." He waited. "Huh? Right down from me." He looked at Luke and asked, "How far back?"

Luke said, "No more than two miles."

Phil spoke into the receiver. "Two miles," he repeated. "OK, sounds good. Say hi to Cheryl." He hung up, then said to Luke, "Sheriff's boys'll be there in no time."

"Thank you," Luke said. "Do you have a bathroom?"

"In the corner." Phil went back to his bacon.

Luke turned and for the first time saw another patron. A young woman, about Luke's age, sat at a table sucking a Sugar Daddy. She looked at Luke, clearly relishing his story. She had pale blonde hair thrown in a hasty bun and she rested tan, strong arms next to a pack of cigarettes on the table. She smiled. Luke nodded to her and went in the bathroom to fill his nose.

He flushed the toilet when he snorted to muffle the sound. Then he ran the water to do the same again. He looked at himself in the mirror. Was that girl not begging him with her eyes? His mother had admonished him repeatedly for seeing only what he wanted in every situation, yet he was certain he saw a flash in that girl's eyes.

His parents' infiltration into his mind didn't stop with a rebuke. Luke heard his father's voice repeat what Luke had often heard as they sat at the dinner table. His father would recount a bland story about some deal he had managed to close in spite of the idiot on the other side. Typically, he would finish the story and take a pull of his mostly scotch and barely soda, then look at Luke and say, "You can't sit back, Luke. You can define the moment or let the moment define you."

Luke felt briefly inclined to reach again for the baggie in his pocket, but he thought better of it. Surely more coke would make him chatty, and he didn't want to overwhelm.

He walked out of the bathroom. The girl was gone. *Shit*, he thought. He turned to leave when he saw her leaning on the jukebox in the corner. She wore a loose, purple T-shirt and tight, stringy jean shorts that looked as though they had been cut by a saw. Out of her shorts emerged tan, lithe legs—the kind men dream of and boys foolishly overlook in deference to breasts. Clear ridges outlined her calves and hamstrings.

Like everyone, Luke had his moments of self-consciousness—like his introduction to Gwen—but throughout his life he had always felt like an insider, no matter what the situation. Whether he was in creative writing, freebasing cocaine in some beat up bungalow in Austin, or at a Beta house spring formal, he felt as though he could swing it. He reveled in a perverted pride that he was the only one who could fit in all situations. Rarely was he the lead entertainer, but he could hold his own in any circus. He drew on this pride as he cleared his throat. She turned.

He said, "Anything besides Journey?"

She took the candy out of her mouth, her long bicep swelling with the motion. She smiled. Her white teeth gleamed against the backdrop of Phil's dirty walls. "Just about anything from 'Freedom Rock.'" Her back arched, as if she wanted to move closer to him, but some invisible wire kept her linked to the jukebox behind.

"Well, turn it up!" Luke mimicked the hippie from the album's ad.

She laughed, then her face turned stern. "What happened back there?" she asked.

"If I can bum one of those cigarettes I'll tell you." They sat down in a booth, each taking a cigarette. Luke repeated his story.

"My God. Why?" she asked.

"What?"

"Why do those kids have to suffer like that?"

"I know. If life was so hellish for that guy and his family, why didn't he just split? He'd have saved everyone a lot of pain."

She recoiled.

"You don't think?"

"My father left my mother and me."

Luke looked at the table. "I'm sorry."

"He left when I was two. I didn't even know him."

"You think you're better off?" Luke was surprised at how quickly the conversation had turned personal. They hadn't even exchanged names.

She hesitated. "Probably. My mom, no. Me, yes. I guess if he was going to leave I'm glad he did before I knew him—at least that's what I tell myself."

She pulled another cigarette. Luke helped himself.

He asked, "Where you from?"

"Baltimore. You?"

"Lubbock."

"Where's that?"

"West Texas." She nodded. Luke asked, "Where you going?"

"I don't really know. I hitched here and you're the first person I've seen. You?"

Camp Verde didn't have the fabled feel Luke was going for, so he said, "Grand Canyon. Ever been?"

"No."

"You know how far it is?"

"No."

"I got an extra seat. You want to come?"

She smiled. "I think I would. Thank you."

"How much stuff do you have?"

"Nothing but this backpack."

Luke stood up. "My bike's right out front." He led her out the door.

Luke untied the rolled up sleeping bag he'd secured behind him on the back seat. Before he took it off, he looked at her and grinned. "I've been leaning against this thing for quite a while. It's made my trip a lot more comfortable. If you take its place, you may have to support me."

"Deal," she said.

He secured the sleeping bag and her backpack on the back fender. Without looking back at Phil's, the girl swung her strong, left leg over the back of Luke's motorcycle.

"Watch your leg," he said, pointing to the exhaust pipe under her exposed left ankle. "That sucker gets real hot." As he brought up the kickstand he said, "I'm Luke."

She leaned forward and said, "I'm Kate." Her voice felt native in his ear. Such an immediate, emotional connection felt incredible. It couldn't have been mere coincidence that they'd met after what Luke had just seen. They'd intimately shared themselves before they even knew each other's names. Maybe it was fate.

Was he lured to the desert to find her? Was she the remedy for his grief?

With Kate on the back of his bike, Luke headed back out toward Route 260. He had a good feeling Phil's call had cleared up the mess down the road. He was right. There was no one left at the gruesome scene, though he did slow to look down at a maroon patch in the dust—the only remnants of the man and his family, who were now nowhere to be seen.

Reaching Route 260, Luke turned and headed west again. A set of tracks supporting a chugging freight train eased in from the north to parallel the road so that the two stretched in tandem into the hazy horizon. Luke tried to match speed with the sluggish freight train, which was so long he couldn't see either its engine or caboose. He slowed to a crawl, enjoying the sensation of stillness next to the seemingly stationary train.

Riding between the endless freight cars to the left and endless fence posts to the right, he considered how worthless the land was that the fence was protecting— terrifically yellow and barren of anything more then the crisp wild grass that stood stiff at an angle from the ground. He wondered if the family who worked the land had finally given up or if they continued to press on in the face of such challenge, such endless disappointment. Maybe an exceptional father led the family to reassurance.

A romantic image of a hard working, wholesome farm family came to his mind, and he saw them at the dinner table, discussing their plan in the face of ruin. The father clearly ran the discussion, but he wanted to hear everyone's input, even the younger children's. To the father's surprise the kids wanted to keep trying, and the wife, heartened by her children's determination, agreed. Soberly, the father decided to call the bank and see what he could do, even though he knew full well he would be taking on most of the drudgery and heartache. With his decision, his kids and wife jumped up and down and kissed and hugged him, and they all decided to celebrate with homemade ice cream. Each took a turn cranking the ancient contraption until the sweet cream was ready. The family ate, knowing in their hearts that everything would be OK.

So they could make better time to the distant destination, Luke opted for I-17 North, even though he usually didn't like all the commotion. But he buoyed his spirits against the spewing gravel and swerving autos by imagining the picture he and Kate painted for the interstate's large audience. He knew people in the cars they passed looked at them and wondered about the young man driving the massive bike and the striking girl on the back. She wasn't the typical, battered biker chick. Luke grew dangerously aroused as he imagined the men in their other cars thinking about the tight legs that wrapped around his body and the thick, blonde hair that created a stunning white tail for their steel horse.

The feel of Kate's inner thighs against his hips and glimpses of her gorgeous reflection in the windows of passing cars pushed Luke's mind into rare contemplation. Could he have a future with the quiet, strong, beautiful girl who threw herself into his world with little more than a second thought? His mind raced with the possibility, regardless of the few hours and fewer words they had shared. Their first encounter would make for a teary-eyed story, and her sensitivity reminded him of his mother. Didn't people say men fell for women like their mothers?

Women fell into two stringent categories for Luke: sex objects; or pure, innocent creatures who must not be blemished in any way. And his respective behavior varied as wildly as the disparity between the two categories. He focused only on having sex with the first, and behaved as he did with Gwen in Magdalena. Sure, he'd have fleeting thoughts of a life with one of these women, but they'd mean nothing. He knew the intimacy they shared early on would forever taint her.

To the other women, the pure, innocent creatures, he wanted to give himself up completely. With this type of woman—whom he'd label in a matter of moments based on how innocent she appearanced—his behavior bordered on what the Brady Bunch would think absurd. In no time, based on hand-holding at a football game, movie or coffee shop, Luke would want to throw away everything in his life in order to settle down. Casual, too-early sex with such a woman would dirty not only her image, but also the future he'd concocted in his own head.

Three "pure" women besides Heather Loon had come through Luke's life, and inexplicably, he got immediately serious with each one—only to rise up months later alone, mumbling something about her not being the one. Yet his vision of the perfect mate seemed to remain the same: simple, wholesome, blonde and athletic, usually with big, white teeth.

Here he was again, sitting in between Kate's thighs, dreaming of their children, hoping her purity would somehow sanitize him. After hours of indecision on whether to press into Kate, Luke slowly leaned back, just a little. He sensed the gesture may be too much, but he had been dying to do it ever since she climbed on. He cautiously leaned further, leaving his weight in her lap. To his delight, she received his weight with her legs, willing to take it on as her own.

17

The south rim of the Grand Canyon was packed: families and couples, cameras and straps, strollers and bikes, Winnebagos and Fiats, babies screaming, parents shrieking, all baking under the Arizona sun. It was a hot mess.

Luke sat down next to Kate on a bench they were lucky to find unclaimed. "Peaceful, huh?"

"Really," she said.

"I got these," he said, revealing some sandwiches. "And these," he added, handing her a water bottle. "Ranger said we need to drink a lot of it. We won't know until it's too late if we get dehydrated."

"Thanks." She took a sip, then a bite of her sandwich. "How much?"

"It's the least I could do for great company."

"I'll get the next one." Kate bit and sipped again. "What did she say about the ride down?"

"All the mules are reserved—have been for months. Guess my idea was premature."

"Maybe we could hike down?"

"Maybe." Luke didn't like that idea. "She said three couples haven't signed in yet. If they don't show we can get their mules. But she said they don't start until the evening when it's cooler, so they may show."

Kate asked, "Why mules and not horses?"

"No idea. They've been doing it forever, though. My parents did it a long time ago. Said it was fun."

Kate nodded.

"Ever been on one?"

"No. You?"

"Not even a horse."

"And from Texas?" she asked, feigning shock. "I thought everybody rode horses out there."

And their conversation went this way, like old companions. For a swift hour they shared observations. Easy, free, comfortable.

At one point Luke asked, "What brought you out West?"

Kate shrugged. "I graduated from Maryland early. My mom had saved up some money for me to go to school, but I got a scholarship and finished a semester early. So I took the money and started heading west with a friend."

"What happened to her—or him?"

"We hitched to New Orleans and she stayed."

"Why?"

"She won a lot of money on one of the boats."

"No way."

Kate nodded. "She thought she could keep it up."

"And you left?"

"I've only got one chance at something like this trip. I didn't want to spend it on a casino boat."

"Have you talked to her?"

"No. She wasn't really that good a friend. We were economics majors—two of only a few girls. We both graduated early and had a semester off, so we went together. But I'm glad it worked out like this. It's been better on my own."

Luke felt encouraged he was the first she had opted to spend time with. He finished his water. "How long have you been on the road?"

"Since January. I left Baltimore and went south for some warmth, then headed out here. I've never been out here. Never been anywhere, really." She paused. "But I have to go home soon I think. I'm running out of money. I was staying at KOAs for a while, but I haven't found any, so I've had to go to hotels."

"Alone?"

She laughed to herself. "Yes."

"Your mom's not nervous?"

"Haven't told her. But she'd probably be proud."

"Why?"

Kate shrugged again. "She doesn't want me to rely on anyone."

"Doesn't sound like you have."

She smiled. "True. But that's kind of why I'm dreading going home. She wants me to find a career right away. It's annoying—she never says job, always career."

"My mom wants the same for me, I think."

"Really?"

"I think. She's been a teacher for twenty-five years. Longevity's important to her. She loves it, plus we have to deal with my dad who hates his job. She thinks I need to find something I'd love to throw myself into."

"Did you graduate?"

Flattered, Luke said, "No. I'll be a junior."

"What do you want to do?"

"I don't know. I'm an English major. I haven't done very well in school, though." Luke sighed. He said the next thing that came to his mind. "Maybe I'll teach."

"I could never do what my mom does."

"What's that?"

"She works for a bank."

"Pretty serious."

"Not really, she's in human resources. Actually started as a secretary."

"Now what does she do?"

"She's a vice president."

"That's impressive."

Behind them, a child screamed and dropped in a tantrum. Luke and Kate turned to see the toddler writhing on the ground behind their bench. The mother yelled, "Shut up!" The father picked the child up, who went stiff as a board, arms and legs pitched out.

He held the child at arm's length and said to the mother, "Don't tell her to shut up. It's a hundred goddamn degrees out here. What do you expect?" The parents walked to the shade of a kiosk, the shrieking child still rigid in her father's hands.

Kate and Luke turned around, sharing a look of concern for the little girl. Kate said, "But God, did my mother work hard. That's why she's so focused on me finding a career. When my dad left she wasn't qualified to do anything. She wants to make sure I don't ever have to start as a secretary, eating other people's dirt on the way up."

"And that's why she wants you to have a career."

"She calls it 'fuck you insurance.'"

"What?"

Kate looked at her bare knees. "She doesn't want me to get left holding the bag like she did. She says if something like that ever happens to me then I'll have my own career. My own life."

Silenced by her confession, Luke nodded. Then he said, "That's a heavy burden."

"It is and it isn't. A part of me thinks she's right. But at the same time I'm already ahead of where she was. She never went to college or anything. I feel like I've got options. I just don't know if I want to go home and work eighty hours a week as an analyst."

"You already have a job?"

"I got one at Jones Brothers in Washington before I left. I'm supposed to start in August, but I don't know." She finished her water. "I don't know if it's what I want."

Luke had never met such a qualified young person. Most of his friends didn't plan beyond the next kegger. Yet she wasn't conceited.

And she smelled so good. Faintly like orange peels. Luke's head started to spin with affection. Could this honest, articulate, thoughtful young woman have really jumped on the back of his motorcycle? He reminded himself that she too was unsure. Maybe in a way, she was looking to him for answers. It was almost too perfect to consider.

Luke said, "I'm going to check in with the ranger again. Maybe she'll know something." He stood.

"Thanks," Kate said.

"Sure."

"I mean for listening. I haven't talked like that to anyone in I don't know how long."

Looking into her eyes, he said encouragingly, "It was easy, wasn't it?"

"I know—so easy."

Luke felt his face flush. To distract himself he threw his thumb over his shoulder. "Want anything?"

Kate smiled, "No thanks." A playful curve touched her lips. "Don't take too long."

Luke's earlier ride on the soft, smooth motorcycle seat while leaning into Kate's firm thighs was the antithesis of the wicked mule ride they took into the Grand Canyon. To avoid the overpowering heat, they ventured in the evening with a small group of tourists they met on the south rim. Per the ranger's suggestion they would camp for the night and come back up the next morning.

The quixotic tale his father had spun about a mule ride to the Canyon's floor could not have been further from the misery Luke endured. He now remembered the party during which his father exaggerated the tale of his and Luke's mother's descent into the canyon. "Just an incredible time," he'd said. "Terrific. And the ranger said it would take longer than we'd expect, but they never know what they're talking about." He sipped his drink, grinning and scanning his guests. "It only took us a couple hours."

Already pissed that he had spent good money on this demonic transportation, Luke's anger swelled with every step as the mule's depraved body shot a bolt of anguish through his back and neck. Each time he looked back to Kate, she smiled. She didn't seem to mind her ride or the unbearable, relentless sun. For a while, Luke tried to feign comfort when their eyes met, but soon he could only focus on lifting his weary body's weight onto his hands to minimize the hammer blows to his spine. Stupidly, he thought the ten or so miles would go quickly on a mule, but the switchbacks were never ending, and he could focus on nothing but the engrossing pain and the sun's extraordinary heat, literally baking the desert floor.

However, for a brief time during his descent, as the sun's fever began to fade and the canyon's descending bands of red limestone glowed, Luke did have a moment of balanced perspective. He cursed himself for being such a grouch and not relishing the magnificent scene. But after a moment of taking in the view, he kept his eyes on the path ahead in search of uneven ground that would bring a violent jolt from the beast's haunches.

The group reached the bottom only minutes before darkness. Clopping along the canyon floor, Luke took solace in the fact that he made it to the bottom, and he puffed himself up for Kate. He eased himself off the miserable beast and leaned over, trying to stretch out his butt and lower back. The relief of his dismount was unimaginable, but he was still a little annoyed that the bottom of the canyon wasn't cooler; he couldn't sleep in this heat, and more than anything he wanted to get a good night's sleep next to Kate.

Kate hopped off her mule as though she had just gotten off the merry-go-round and wanted a ticket for another ride.

Luke took her hand when she met him. He said, "Beautiful, wasn't it?"

"Awesome." Her eyes shone even in the moonlight.

Luke had an urge to tell her how incredible he thought she was and how lucky he was to have found her, but he caught himself before he said anything. Luke had to hold back. He wanted to pour out his soul to her right there at the bottom of the Grand Canyon.

He decided to say something, and as if Kate wouldn't notice, he decided to lower the tone in his voice. "That was incredible," he said. Kate gave him a suspicious look—apparently the constant abuse to his balls had a surprising effect on his tone. Her quizzical look made him consider ending his lucid commentary, but he couldn't help himself. He continued in his new voice. "Weren't the colors of the different rocks amazing?"

"They were." She wiped a drop of sweat off her brow, the only sign of exertion she'd showed. She looked no worse for wear than when he picked her up earlier that day, while Luke felt like someone had bent him over a sawhorse and pounded a sledgehammer into his rear for eight hours. "These guys over there," she continued, "said they've been down before and know a great place to camp for the night. They said they want to show us what they missed the first time they came."

Though Luke had imagined a thick steak and a night of holding Kate's body while planning their future in the comfort of a warm bed, he was in no position to protest. "What are we going to eat? And sleep on?" He couldn't imagine sleeping on the packed earth.

"They said we can stop at the ranch to get some sandwiches and we can use one of their mats. It's too hot for sleeping bags anyway, and the night's clear. We really don't need anything." She paused and looked him up and down. "But you look like you could use a mat." Surprised by her comprehensive response and her tenderness for his backside, he relented. He straightened his impossibly sore body and fell in behind Kate and the two other young men. Both carried all the latest hiking gear, and neither turned around to introduce himself to Luke.

On the valley floor, the four of them followed the deafening Colorado River; no one tried to speak over the roar of the water. Surprisingly, the first part of the walk felt good after the ride on Satan's minion, and Luke could finally enjoy the Canyon's magnificence. But after a half-mile, his back was on fire and he felt ruined. He yelled up ahead, "This is good. I think we'll just stay here."

Kate turned around. She smiled at him, clearly tickled by his frailty.

Luke walked up to her. Though he tried to sound collected, he whined, "Did these guys tell you where they're going?"

"They told me they knew of a spot to make camp, that's it. I'm sure it's just a bit further." She looked into his eyes and smiled. He couldn't decide if her lips were more kissable like this or when parted. "They've got all that gear. I'm sure they know what they're doing."

"OK," he said. In the dark, he held her arm for a moment. "You know, I've never done anything like this before. I love being with you."

"Me too, Luke. It's like—I don't know."

"Go on."

"Something special, connected. I feel like I can sense you behind me. I feel protected."

Luke's heart thundered. He kissed her on the cheek, and she smiled. "I liked that," he said.

"Me too," she said. She leaned into him and pressed her lips to his. Passively, Luke accepted her warm mouth. She took his bottom lip between hers. Behind Luke's eyelids appeared masses of lights, flashing with his passion. He wished he could bring his entire self into his small bottom lip and stay locked between hers forever. He sighed.

She pulled away. "I feel the same."

"How do you know what I feel like?"

"I just do. I feel the same."

The innocent kiss replenished his spirit. "Let's catch up with them. The sooner we get there the sooner we can make camp and get cozy for the night."

She smiled. Playfully turning away, she hurried a few steps ahead.

18

*M*rs. Stahl dropped her bundle of essays on the kitchen table. Luke was eating a bowl of cereal. "Whew," she said and wiped her forehead. "I don't know how I'm going to get these exams graded." Looking at the mound of blue books on the table, she shook her head.

"You always say that." Luke slurped milk from his spoon.

"I do?"

Luke nodded. "You'll get it done."

"I guess you're right." She rubbed his cheek with the back of her finger, then looked around. "Is your father home?"

Luke shook his head.

As if his father's absence relaxed her, his mother sat down next to him. "How'd your first exam go?"

"Fine."

"I can't believe you're already taking exams." She stared at him like she wanted him to be five again.

"Mom!"

"I'm sorry. It's just I can't believe it—you with exams and Alex in college."

Luke didn't know what to say. He shrugged.

Mrs. Stahl went to the refrigerator and poured herself a glass of milk. "You're right, I know. You have to grow up." She took a sip from her glass. "Was there an essay question?"

"Whose fault was it that Old Yeller died."

She frowned. "Kind of a ho-hum question."

"It was lame, but easy. I'm sure I did well." He put his bowl in the dishwasher.

"How'd Sarah do?"

"Fine, I think. She hated the story, but I'm sure she did fine."

"Why did she hate it? I thought all kids loved 'Old Yeller.'"

"Too sad." Luke returned to the table. "She's coming over to study math later. You can talk to her then."

"Good." Mrs. Stahl paused and looked into Luke's eyes. "It's nice to have two kids in the house again. More cheerful."

Luke heard the garage door open. In a moment, Luke's father walked in the kitchen door. He threw his briefcase on the table. "What are you two looking at?"

"Nothing, Steven. Nothing." Mrs. Stahl went back to the refrigerator, pulling Mr. Stahl's attention away from the table and Luke. She asked, "How'd your day go?"

"Awful. I can't get the goddamn treasurer to sit down with me, so I spent the day tied up in his office getting shit on by his secretary." He went to the liquor cabinet. In one fluid motion, he poured a drink, threw it back and poured another.

"At least you're home now," Mrs. Stahl said.

"After that crap, anything seems like heaven."

Luke stood to leave the kitchen, but his mother put her hand on his shoulder. "Luke had his first exam today."

"In what?"

Luke spoke up, "English."

"He did well," his mother added.

His father grunted. "When's the important stuff?"

Luke didn't know how to answer. "Math?"

"Sure."

"Tomorrow."

"Make sure you do well on that." His father spoke loudly, like Luke was in the next room. "Listen to me, boy. English will get you nowhere fast. Listen to a lawyer who made that mistake, I can tell you—stick to math, it's cut and dry. Where the money is." He turned to his wife. "Alex call? They're ending spring workouts this week."

Luke looked at his mother for her response. Her eyes were closed. "No. He didn't call."

Mr. Stahl shrugged. He drank what remained in his glass and filled another. Without saying anything more, he went up to his room.

Simultaneously, Luke and his mother drew in deep breaths. Picking up her *head and offering Luke a false smile, Mrs. Stahl said, "I look forward to seeing Sarah. When did you say she's coming over?"*

Though dispirited, Luke tried to match his mother's counterfeit cheer. He jumped to the phone. "I don't know. I'll call her."

"Good," his mother said. "Good."

19

Once Kate was safely ahead, Luke checked the baggie in his pocket. He had put a barely-noticeable dent in its bulk, but it was still twenty times more coke than he'd ever had. Genuinely conflicted between his two selves, Luke stared at the baggie as he continued to shuffle behind the glimmer of their leaders' flashlights.

He quickly untied the wire closure, dipped his key into the powder, and raised a bump to his left nostril. He tried to do it while walking in the dark, but in spite of the huge supply it was too frustrating to let any fall to the ground. He stopped to fill his left and right nostril, and repeated the process four more times on their hike.

By the time they got to the campsite, the cocaine had untied Luke's voice. "Man, this looks great! By the way, I'm Luke," he semi-shouted at the two bearded young men. Each meekly shook Luke's hand without giving his name. "God, this is unbelievable! I mean, we're in the middle of the Grand fucking Canyon." He took a deep breath. "Jesus, this is amazing."

Kate's eyes expanded, and her jaw dropped. The bearded leaders nodded a quiet, puzzled assent and turned to unpack their gear.

"Where do you want to camp?" Luke asked Kate.

"Right here. Why, did you want to keep going?"

"No. No. This'll be great. God, I can't tell you how incredible it is to be here with you. I mean it's *so* intense. You, me, the Grand Canyon. Whew!" He looked up again. "How old do you think this is? Do you know what has to happen for something like this to form? And this river cutting all the way through this? Holy shit. I feel great! It's like this Canyon breathes life into you." He brought his face back down to look at

Kate's; her expression of wonder hadn't changed. Luke realized he was talking too much, and he pursed his lips to shut himself up.

"Are you OK?" she asked.

"Yeah, yeah, I'm fine. And you?"

The stupidity of the redirect caught Kate unaware. "Of course. It's just you seem different all of a sudden."

Luke found his low, slow voice again. "Me? No. I'm cool."

They unrolled their mats and began to unpack their sandwiches. Luke felt the telltale dryness in his throat and inadvertent shrugging of his shoulders—he was coming down. "Uh … I've got to go to the bathroom. I'll be right back."

"OK," Kate said without looking up from the plastic-wrapped food. "I'll see if they want to eat with us."

"Great," Luke shouted over his shoulder as he scampered off into the shrubs and reached into his pocket. Annoyed at the prospect of spending more time with their two guides, he went through another cycle of bumps, and as he looked into the bag, he felt a pang. The seemingly endless supply appeared to be diminishing.

The fresh cocaine in his nose brought an unusually bold idea: he thought briefly about offering some to Kate. Dreams of extraordinary revelation and lovemaking spun through his mind. But he checked himself for such a ridiculous thought. He put the baggie away and swore that would be the end of it. "C'mon. Make *her* your drug," he thought out loud.

When he returned to their makeshift camp, the three stood in a triangle, passing around a smoking pipe. Kate looked up and offered Luke a hit. He took it and reintroduced himself to Mike and Ron who, again, were disinterested in anything he had to say. As harmless as they looked, the two bearded, thin men exuded a certain power. Luke sensed that they thought this was their world—and guys like Luke should take a back seat to their expertise. Luke returned the pipe.

Ron cleared the silence and spoke to Kate and Mike. "The sunset's so cool down here. I love all the trippy colors that reflect off the river. I'm bummed we missed it, but we didn't walk as fast as I thought we would." He looked at Luke.

I didn't slow us down. We got to the bottom when it was fuckin' dark! Aloud, Luke said, "Yeah, I bet it is. I've never been here, but I bet it's sweet—" He cut himself off for fear of sounding like a wuss by trying to curry favor. "Kate," he said, "you want to go for a walk?"

"Yes." She looked at Luke, relieved. "I'll just grab some water." She left the three young men standing in the circle. Ron handed the pipe to Mike, then looked at Luke.

"So, where are you guys heading?" Luke asked.

"What do you mean? We're here," Ron said, shaking his head at Mike with a look like 'get a load of this guy.'

"I mean," Luke tried again, "are you traveling around, or did you just want to come to the Grand Canyon?"

"You ask a lot of questions," Mike said.

The bearded clam's aggressiveness surprised Luke; he couldn't imagine what Kate saw in these two druids. Just then, she returned holding a bottle of water. "Ready," she said, looking at him encouragingly.

Luke opened his eyes to see Kate's face, barely lit by the dying fire, looking down on him. With her middle fingers, she stroked his eyebrows from the inside out. Luke was shocked that she had sat by him while he slept.

"What time is it?" he asked softly.

"You've been asleep for an hour." She stopped rubbing his face, but her newfound intimacy woke Luke up. "It's about two-thirty."

"Where are Ron and Mike?"

"They're in their tent. I heard them rolling around and sighing," she said matter-of-factly. "I think they're gay. I'm sorry I suggested we follow them. They were fine with me, but they're clearly intimidated by you."

Luke couldn't tell if she was disgusted, disappointed or both, and he didn't know how to answer. He decided to be light. "Maybe they think I'm cute."

"I don't think so."

"No?"

"I think they came to get away. To be alone. And a guy like you—or how they perceive you—is what they're trying to leave."

Luke shimmied on the ground. "Gay guys have always liked me. Sometimes ask me out."

"Really?"

"Yeah. I don't know why. Maybe because I'm tall and thin."

She laughed. "Maybe. It doesn't bother you?"

"It's kind of flattering."

She nodded, her eyes clear with esteem. He desperately wanted her to touch him again—this time while he was awake so he could enjoy it. He sat up and a blast of pain drove through the top of his back and shot out his shoulder blades. "Ow," he groaned. "My back is killing me."

"You weakling. That ride killed you, didn't it?"

"No. Well, yes. I'm not used to it."

"You freshen this fire, and I'll see what I can do."

"I'll get some more wood." He scurried off into the darkness.

She lay on her side, glowing in the firelight when he returned. "I'm so glad you woke me up," he said.

Remembering how Kate's fingertips felt on his brow made Luke want to bury his body inside her. All it took was her slightest touch, and his heart galloped and mind filled with dreams of eternal contentment.

He sat at her feet, reaching out to play with the string hanging from her cut-offs, inching his way to the inside of her smooth thigh. Her skin was as soft as a baby's. Again, he had to resist an urge—this time to put his lips to her leg.

Luke tried to send her signals so that she would touch him again. Asking her to touch him, even though he figured she would, was a painful consolation compared to her own initiation. But it was better than the alternative. "You think you could rub my back now?"

"Sure, you baby," she said.

Luke took off his shirt and rolled onto his stomach. Kate positioned herself on top of him and leaned into his back with her palms. She pressed on his lower back, letting her palms slide up the muscles on either side of his spine, out his shoulder blades, then down the back of his arms. She repeated the circular motion.

Convinced that Kate needed to hear his story, Luke allowed her hands to bring out the words he had wanted to say for so long. "I had an older brother. He was a football coach in Lubbock. A bit outside of Lubbock, where I grew up. In West Texas." The words came easily, as if her rhythmic massage pushed his story out. "It gets really windy there, especially in the spring, but sometimes in the fall. If you don't watch yourself, things can happen you'd never expect. Crazy things. Things I swear you wouldn't believe. Roofs ripped clean off houses, carports ending up in the neighbor's yard, people getting blown over. The amazing thing about the wind is that it can come out of nowhere and die again just as quickly. Or you can be somewhere and almost get blown out of your shoes, while someone just a little bit away wouldn't feel anything at all. People talk about the wind all the time; it's kind of what West Texas is known for."

Luke told Kate about Alex's death.

"Luke, I'm so sorry." Kate leaned forward and lay on Luke's back.

Never had Luke spoken in such detail about his brother's death. He thought he'd keep going and tell her everything. Everything that's happened since—with him, his mother, his father. But he stopped talking because, for a moment, he felt literally weightless. Drained of his burden. He sat quietly, adoring the emptiness.

Luke closed his eyes and felt her soft cheek against his. He reached into his sock and handed her Alex's picture. "This is him."

Simply, earnestly, she repeated, "I'm so sorry."

20

Luke sat with his brother in silence. His father approached them. "You need to get up off that couch, son. Do something," he said to Alex.

Alex had his bad ankle elevated on the table in front of the couch. He didn't look away from the TV. "Like what?"

"Don't look at the Samsung—look at me when you speak."

Luke looked at the ground, petrified of his father. Alex turned his head and met his father's glare. "Like what?"

"That's up to you. But you have to quit this lying around like some woman feeling sorry for herself." He left the room.

For the first time in weeks, Luke looked at his brother and spoke. "Coach Limbech quit."

"Who?"

"Limbech, the assistant. I think he worked with the special teams or something. But he quit. Maybe you could get his job."

Alex shrugged.

"Tomorrow I can talk to Migs, see if he can ask Coach Stims if he needs someone. He'd love for you to work with the team. Most of the guys remember you."

Alex shrugged again but didn't say no.

Later that fall, Alex joined the team as the defensive coordinator. For Alex's first game as coach, Luke sat bundled in the bleachers with his mother on a bracing Friday night. Mr. Stahl stood next to the fence beside the field, like he had when Alex played. Luke nodded to other freshmen in the stands, some he could tell were drunk. He was glad he sat with his mother. Even at fourteen, he felt a certain comfort under the blanket with her. No pressure *to hang out with older kids or do pre-game shots at some party. Everyone left him alone because they knew he sat with his mother at football games.*

The other team received the kickoff, and Alex's defense trotted onto the field.

"Is that Heather?" Luke's mother asked him.

He followed the direction of her finger. He nodded.

"I feel awful about what that poor girl endured in our house. Just awful."

"She's all right."

"You ever see her?"

"Sometimes. We don't really talk."

"I bet."

Mrs. Stahl shook her head and turned her eyes back to the game. Luke followed her eyes to Alex. Though he had limped up and down the sideline before kickoff, he was now crouched in ready position, as if he was about to go in. Then, in a flash, he straightened and torqued his body as his defense tried to make the first tackle of the game.

Looking onto the field, his mother said, "Looks good, doesn't he?"

Luke smiled. "He does."

"You should be proud, Luke."

"Why?"

She turned to him. "You gave this to him."

Though he knew he'd helped his brother, Luke had never thought of it in those terms. For the rest of the night, a small fire glowed in him. That he could give his brother something, let alone a second chance, warmed his chest more than anything he'd known.

21

Hi, Mom ... I'm fine. I'm fine ... Don't. There's no need to worry. I'm fine ... Mom, listen ... I'm *fine* ... He doesn't need to. How is he? ... I'm sorry, but there was no other way. He hasn't reported it, has he? ... It's not like he needs it ... Jesus, Mom, I know. I'm not doing this *to you*, I'm doing it *for me*. You said you understood ... You did! You said you felt like it, too. Sometimes ... That's what you said. You said you felt like you needed to run, sometimes ... Well, I'm sorry, then. But that's what I thought ... Because I hate that car. The motorcycle's fine. Tell Dad it's fine ... I know. That's one of the reasons I called—I didn't realize what today's date was until this afternoon. I can't believe he would've been twenty-eight. How are you doing? ... I wish I was, too. But right now I think this is best for me. For all of us. How's Dad? ... Nothing will happen to his bike....Mom, I'm thinking of him, too ... I am, Mom. I'm thinking of him. It's why I called. In fact, listen, Mom... Mom, listen. I met this girl ... On the road. She's incredible. I told her all about Alex. She's the first person I've told ... I told her everything ... You'd love her, Mom ... I met her in a restaurant. She was just there waiting. It was like she was waiting for me. She had these huge eyes that followed me. She—No. Listen, I mean we only met yesterday, but it's like we're meant for each other ... I know, I know, but it's true. I can't believe it. She's different. So different. I can't wait for you to meet her ... No, no. She was just in this restaurant ... Maryland. Baltimore ... She graduated early and she's traveling around before she goes back to work. ... She's alone ... I don't know. I didn't meet them. I mean, her mom. She lives with her mom ... Yes, she'll call her, I'm sure ... Look, Mom, I know this is a brutal time, but I'll be home soon. And I'm bringing Kate with me ... I don't know yet. We'll figure it out when I get back. I'll go back to school. Tell Dad. And this time I'll do well. Tell him I promise. And I miss him. I miss you, too, Mom. I've really been thinking about you. This is tough, but it's getting better. It's definitely getting better. Don't you think? … We'll be OK... I love you. I'll be home in a couple days … I promise … Yes, a couple days … I don't know—a couple days … Somewhere in Arizona. Near the Grand Canyon. We just left … Fine … Don't worry. I'll be fine. Tell Dad I miss him and not to worry about the motorcycle … Thank you, Mom. I love you.

The inner tubes Kate pulled from the bin at Hairy Hal's Rental Shop looked dreadfully misshapen, but she assured Luke they'd be perfect for their ride down the quiet little stretch of river, visible through Hal's window. Luke let the screen door of the shop slam behind him, meeting Kate on the wash of sand outside the shop. They hooked their bloated hula-hoops under their arms and crossed the slight beach to the river.

After Luke's call to his mother, Kate had begged to check out the Havasu. Luke didn't look forward to more outdoor recreation, but he had melted when Kate grabbed his arm and whispered in his ear, "It'll be fun."

Now she said, "I've always wanted to tube. I've seen people do it on the Gunpowder, but I never did."

"What's the Gunpowder?"

"A river near my house."

Luke wanted to hear more about her home, but she said no more. Suddenly, she dropped her tube, dropped her white shorts, and kicked them at Luke. "I don't want to get these wet. They're the only ones I've got," she said. Her immodesty in front of the floating audience caught him by surprise, but he delighted in her playfulness. He put her shorts on his head so that the legs looked like demented antlers.

"Check it out!" he shouted. He jumped up and down with her shorts bouncing on his head and his tube around his ankles, howling like a dog. As he pranced, the shorts slipped over his head, and Luke inhaled. Kate's scent set off an unusual, visceral urge in him, and he instantly wished the trace of femininity would transform into something edible; something he could swallow and knit to his body's constitution. Though he couldn't imagine what form the victuals would take, he *felt* the hunger in his throat—a most unusual sensation. But as quickly as it grew, the desire died, and Luke shrugged off the urge. He took the shorts off his head, realizing Kate had paid him no attention.

Feeling foolish, he busied himself with preparations. To keep her shorts and his shirt dry as they floated the river, Luke put them in a trash bag they had taken from the rental shop. For the plunge into the water, he tucked his butt into his tube and held the bag to his stomach.

He didn't jump right in, for he caught sight of Kate, motionless at the river's edge. She watched tubers and rafters glide by, listlessly turning themselves in circles or lying back with a hand dipped in the water.

A family of five splashed past in three tubes and a small raft, yelling and hooting. As they floated by, Luke went to Kate. Awkwardly, he put his arm and plastic bag around her and tried to catch her eyes. She was lost in the family's world. Soon Luke, too, grew mesmerized by the slow-moving parade and pulled her closer as they watched.

After a long silence, she spoke. "I missed out on that. All that," she said, pointing to the family.

"Really?" Luke let his arm fall and turned to look at her. "Sometimes mine would go rafting. We'd go on vacation when my dad could get off work. We'd usually travel to some kind of water. A few times we went on the Colorado. I wonder if we ever looked like that," he said, nodding toward the boisterous family. "Actually, one time we went river rafting in West Virginia. It was incredible. We—"

Her eyelids sagged and for a second she was a world away. "I meant the family." Quickly, she brightened and returned.

"You'll make it up."

She turned to him, clearly enlivened by the idea. "That's exactly what I'm going to do. It's funny you said that—I feel like you read my mind."

"You should do what you want, regardless of your mom's plans."

Kate shrugged, then put her foot in the water.

Not wanting to push too hard, he asked, "Cold?"

"No," she said softly. Then she raised her face and looked at Luke. With more certainty, she said, "Well, yeah, it is. But we'll get used to it."

Yet, her energy only lasted a moment, and her voice softened again as she looked back into the water and asked, "So what kind of stuff did you do?"

"What do you mean?"

"You said your family traveled a lot."

"Oh." Not wanting her new gloom to cast a shadow over their day, Luke playfully kicked water at her. "I'll tell you *all* my stories once we're in."

Ass first, and still clutching his plastic bag, he launched himself into the river while looking back at Kate. Unfortunately, he had failed to gauge the depth of the water, and with one hand around the tube and the other holding the bag to his stomach, his ass crashed unprotected into the river's rocky floor.

"Shiiit!" he wailed. The pain from the mule ride reloaded and shot through his spine and neck. "Fuuuck!"

Kate looked at him and didn't try to stifle her laugh. He waited for her to ask if he was all right, but she didn't. "Nice one."

The water had held the tube up for Luke's ass to slide right through, so his legs were pinned to his chest and his arms flew up at a clumsy angle as he sat in the foot-deep water. "Come on in. It's very comfortable."

Cautiously, Kate proceeded into the river, tube in hand, testing each step. Luke quickly forgot the pain in his backside, for her unpredictability kept him rapt: one minute she shamelessly kicked off her shorts and the next she cautiously and grace-fully approached the cool water. In each situation, her actions were effortless. She was like no one he had known. "C'mon!" he yelled. "Just jump in. It's great. You're the one who said it's fine."

Ignoring Luke, she glided her shapely butt into the tube and began backing beyond him, into a deeper part of the river. She tripped on a rock and splashed into the cool water, soaking her body up to her chest. Her eyes widened and she lost her breath with the chill. "Whooh! It's cold!" she whooped as she clambered back onto her tube.

Luke bellowed, "That was terrific! Can you do it again?" Kate said nothing in response and set herself rigid on the tube, trying to lift her body out of the water by lying flat across its opening. Dying to touch her body, Luke tried to push himself over to her, but his ass was too fine an anchor in the shallow water. Disengaging himself from his ludicrous position proved a serious challenge, and Kate's floating away made his efforts all the more frenetic. After five serious hip thrusts, he finally popped his ass out of the tube, waded over to the deeper water and frantically paddled over to her.

The two floated quietly and easily in the river's steady pull while Luke talked about his family's travels. Kate was captivated by his lavish descriptions of California, New York and Chicago. He began to recount a story about going to the top of the Hancock building. He reached across their tubes and took her hand.

"You could see the entire city in all directions from the top. Really, it was so high you could see across the lake to Michigan. Once, when I was up there in the winter the wind blew so hard the entire building swayed."

"No way."

"Yeah. They're made to flex. If they built them stiff, they'd snap in the wind just like that." He snapped his fingers for emphasis.

"I'd love to go to Chicago. My aunt and uncle say it's the best city in America. Except for the winters."

"You pretty tight with them?"

She nodded. "They live right behind me. Honestly, I don't think my mom and I would've made it without them." She laughed at herself.

"What?"

"It's ironic they saved us. They're like the perfect family. They've got two great kids, and they all get along so well. They're happy and loving and trusting. They're like the ideal family—and there they are backed up to us."

"Doesn't sound ironic. It sounds like you're lucky."

"We ate dinner over there every night when I was little, and my aunt never complained. They'd take me in when my mom had to travel. My uncle came to all the daddy/daughter dinner dances."

Luke laughed. "Daddy/daughter dinner dances?"

"I know. It's hokey. But who knows when you're seven? When you're little and fatherless it's awful. It seemed like six months of preparation went into that goddamn dance. And the girls! They'd shop and talk and plan what they were going to wear—and where their dads were taking them for dinner. It was torture." She paused. "All I wanted was to be the same. And you know what? My uncle came to every one."

"He sounds like a hero."

"He is. Sometimes I dream of becoming my aunt, married to a perfect man like him and having a family." She shook her head. "My mom would shit if she heard that."

"You can do whatever you want. You said it before, you've got more choices than your mom did. One of them is having a family when you want it. It's as legitimate as any other choice."

"I know. Part of me thinks this trip has had the opposite effect than I would've guessed. I thought I'd travel, see the country and want to get back to work so I could make my mark. But the more I see, the more I think I may just want to be my aunt."

Luke's heart blazed with possibility. "You could always come back to Texas with me." He tried to sound joking, but it came out genuine.

"You're sweet." She added nothing and looked skyward.

Was she seriously considering it or brushing him off? The potential was immense, but her denial would crush him, so he didn't investigate her vague response. Instead, he squeezed her hand and tried to feel satisfied with her urge to start a family.

He felt puzzled, however, by a new impulse to swallow Kate, similar to the one that flared earlier. The feeling had surfaced a number of times. It wasn't a violent, controlling, devouring need for consumption; rather, it was that he wanted literally to ingest parts of her. Especially after his divulgence about Alex, his need for her seemed to manifest in this peculiar appetite. With the backdrop of the gleaming water, her hand in his looked delectable, and as he kissed it, he imagined unhinging his jaw like a boa constrictor and working her arm down his throat, inches at a time.

He pulled his lips from her skin and said, "Do you ever want to, kind of . . . like, eat someone?"

"That's disgusting!" Kate swiftly pulled her hand from his.

"No, not like cannibalism. It's as if you like someone so much you want to swallow them. You want to get so close to them, but feel like you can't get close enough, so you want to drink them."

"Not really," she said. But soon, surprisingly, the idea seemed to intrigue her. "I can see, though, if you loved someone so much, how you'd want to do it." She reached back out and grabbed his hand so that his tube spun, and the top of his foot slid into hers. In that position they entered a thin part of the river and the symmetry of their touching forms matched the canopy of trees above.

"You can?"

"I can see that."

Floored by her understanding, Luke had to restrain himself from flopping out of his tube and throwing his body onto hers. He delighted in their connection, and he allowed a composed quiet to take over the conversation for the rest of their float. *She was it,* he thought. *She'd fill in.*

They laid back on the dark water, under the light sky, until they saw Hairy Hal's son, equally woolly, waiting at the pull-out by a considerable bend in the river.

22

Alex put his truck in reverse to back out of the parking space, then reconsidered. He put it in neutral and pulled up the emergency break, then turned to Luke. "Why did you take off like that?"

"Because I hate him."

"He takes you out to play and you hate him?"

"He didn't talk to me."

"Didn't he ask you what you wanted for lunch?"

Luke glared at his older brother. "You know what I mean. Four hours, and he didn't talk to me."

Alex looked out the windshield. "Luke, I'm not defending him. Trust me. But, I think it's hard for him. With me, it just comes, you know, easy. We—"

"Easy? All he did was talk about your great shots and how you kept killing the ball. I had great shots, too." Luke pulled his seatbelt's shoulder strap away from his neck and flipped it over his head.

"I know. I know. But I tried to tell you how good—"

"You always tell me. Mom tells me, too."

"Well, I think he has a tough time."

"Why?"

"Honestly?"

"Yes."

Alex took a deep breath. "He thinks you're smarter than he is. And I think he feels like you're always . . . gauging him. Look, it's hard for you to understand, but sometimes adults can be intimidated by kids. He's proud of you, Luke. He is. But even when it comes to something as easy as this," he pointed to the clubhouse beyond the parking lot, "he feels . . . I don't know, edgy."

"That's crazy. You're a better football player than he could've ever been—and he loves you for it."

"He knows it. He knows football. And he knows the law. That's what he knows. But when you and mom talk about books and reading and what you both like, he feels like he can't contribute."

"But we're not talking about books or school or anything. We're playing golf!"

"I hate it, too. I see what he's doing to you, but the only thing I can do is try to make it easier for you." Alex released the brake once again and put his truck in reverse. "He's given us a good life, Luke," he said. "And he's tried to make it better. Give him some credit—he quit drinking."

Luke shrugged. His father had quit drinking before. He knew Alex was reaching.

Then, putting his arm behind Luke's seat and looking over his shoulder as he backed out of the space, he added, "And if he can't give you everything, well . . . maybe I can fill in."

23

For their return to the rental shop, Kate had wanted to ride in the back of the young man's battered pickup. As they rode, the bumps, which the pickup's rusted shocks wildly exacerbated, drove Luke crazy; they seemed to encourage Kate to speak.

"Where are we going next?" she asked, her voice bouncing, expelling its sounds like the rat-a-tat-tat of a machine gun.

"I don't know. Where do you want to go?"

She said, "California."

Luke laughed. "I thought you meant after we get back to the shop."

"I meant, where do you want to head to next?"

"I thought when we finished here, we'd start heading back east."

Kate's face dropped. "You're not going home already, are you?"

"I was thinking about it. My decision to come out here was a little less planned than yours."

"What do you mean?"

Luke explained the circumstances of his departure. He added, "I can't stay away forever."

He had wanted to broach his ideas for their future, and though he didn't imagine the back of a rusty pickup to be the setting for it, he took the opportunity to grab hold of the truck's roll bar and lean into Kate to tell her his idea. "I thought it'd be nice for you to meet my family. You could come back to Texas with me."

"I've never been."

"You'd like it. Maybe not Lubbock, but you'd love Austin."

"That's where UT is, right?"

"Yes." Luke decided to pursue what he had left earlier. "You could come back if you want. Austin's a great town, with tons of young people working and going to school. You'd fit in."

She appeared to consider his idea. "What would I do there?"

"Unfortunately, I don't think there are a lot of investment banks. But you don't have to do that right away, do you?"

"You mean defer the offer?" Kate, too, clutched the roll bar.

"Sure. I'm positive they want you so badly, they'd wait forever."

"What makes you so sure?" A massive bump punctuated her question and sent both of them flying back to the truck's gate. They crawled back to their chosen spot behind the cab.

"I would."

He waited for her reaction to his avowal. She didn't pull away as he thought she might. But she didn't throw her arms around him either. She seemed to weigh the heft of his proclamation.

He couldn't stand the silence, so he filled it. "We'd be good together."

"We are good together."

His gasp was audible. Even though he brought it up, the earnest possibility forced him to joke. "And we do *look* good together."

"That's true. When we met in that grungy restaurant, then took off on your motorcycle, I bet we looked like something out of a movie. I thought the same thing—we look good."

Luke couldn't believe their shared zest. "I kind of pictured us too. I mean, I've imagined myself in the movies sometimes, or, like, what I look like from the outside." Their mutual tendency excited him and he spoke quickly. "I do that all the time—imagine how I look when I do things." He again reached for the roll bar and pulled himself into her. "I also thought about it when I picked you up. Not like vain or anything, just interested in how we look—the picture we made."

She picked her head back up and looked at him. "I do that, too. I always think about how we look to other cars when we're on the bike … or even when I was waiting in that restaurant. I imagined how I looked sitting there."

"You looked gorgeous."

"We *should* go to Austin."

"Think so?" Kate's zeal whisked Luke away. She patted his hand as he spoke of the possibility. "I mean, I'm not being naïve. I know how young we are. But, it's like we fit. Not just each other, but each other's plan. How many college kids do you know talk about having a family?"

"Not many. But I don't know, Luke. It's so much right away."

A sudden flash of reality swirled through the back of the pickup and Luke shook his head. He put his other hand over Kate's and said, "You're right. Let's not get ahead of ourselves. First, I've got to go home and make good with my family."

Riding the motorcycle back to Flagstaff gave Luke a chance for uninterrupted thought. Kate's revelation had washed relief over Luke, and he inhaled the thin, dry air that lashed his face. The cool breeze allowed him to enjoy the waves of heat reflected off the blacktop.

Luke's thoughts drifted to his mother. Lately, he couldn't get the picture of her vacant face out of his mind, and he imagined the light resetting in her eyes when he returned home with Kate, a young woman who'd offer his family its missing fourth.

He also knew his mother let his excursion continue unchecked; she kept his father at bay with her own quietly suggestive style. She could have let his father report the motorcycle stolen or cancel the ATM card—or she could have pleaded with Luke to come home, knowing he would give in. Yet she did none of these things.

Luke rolled on his throttle and steered his bike into the left lane to pass a pickup in front of them. The truck expelled nauseating black smoke and had a bumper sticker that read, *My Kid Beat Up Your Honor Roll Student*. Once he passed it, Luke let his mind slip back to his parents, and he imagined the two of them in their living room: his dad pacing and raising his voice in disgust with Luke's selfishness, and his mom sitting with her hands in her lap, only speaking when he had fully vented.

"Steven, we have to let him live. No matter how much it may hurt us." Then she'd quietly cry. She'd always done everything noiselessly except recently, when she prepared meals, she'd begun to slam utensils and bang pots as if the crashes served to confirm her own existence. "When he gets back," she would say, "he'll be different … " she'd search for the right word, "older. And you watch—he'll go back to school." His father would offer no response except to drop his chin on his chest in defeat. "Besides," she would say, "he's coming home soon. He has no interest in staying away for long."

Luke reached back with his left hand to stroke Kate's bare calf. *God*, he thought, *she'd love Kate.* And not just her natural peace, but everything she represented. Kate would bring stability to Luke's life. His mom would sense her own nature in

Kate's presence and be refreshed by her focus. She'd see a glimmer of her younger self. And Kate's serenity would calm her family in ways not known since Alex.

Luke decided to splurge on a room at an upscale inn, The Dakota. He had seen it when they had first passed through Flagstaff on their way to the Grand Canyon. He knew Kate would love the place, but he wanted to make it a surprise so he kept quiet, leading her into the lobby.

At the front desk, Luke noticed the wood paneling and plush red chairs that surrounded the lobby, and he enjoyed the symmetry of the old home, whose grand front hall now housed the reception area and a mammoth Y-shaped staircase. It went up half a floor, then split, leading to the two sides of the inn. The smiling woman behind the counter waited patiently for the computer to accept Luke's parents' credit card, then offered him a key. He took it, said thank you, and led a stunned Kate to the staircase.

The dining room, an open-aired, refurbished library to the left of the stairs, allowed ascending guests to view the tables below. A few of the younger, well-outfitted guests drank at the tables, while a contingent of older guests sat eating their late lunches, all staring at Kate and Luke as they skipped up the stairs.

Unaffected by the guests' gazes, Kate leaned over the banister as she turned left and stepped up the side of the staircase. "I can't believe you can look down and watch the people eat!"

Luke gently took Kate's hand off the banister in an effort to hurry her. "Come on. We'll see it all again on our way back down."

The key to the room was a massive old chunk of brass, and Luke had difficulty unlocking the door. Once inside, Kate darted into the room and crisscrossed to every corner like a child. She turned on the TV and tested the remote, then went to the writing desk at the far corner of the room and picked up each piece of the hotel's complimentary correspondence. Next, she pulled the antique lamp's switch on and off, and kicked the wooden wastebasket beside the desk. She howled with delight when, upon opening the bathroom door, she saw the gratis bathroom products. She went in to inspect the loot.

"Ohhh. Look at this." She came prancing out of the bathroom with the shower cap stuck on her blonde head. "My Nanna wears one of these to bed every night."

"Maybe you should wear that out tonight," Luke said, adjusting himself comfortably on the bed. Though he tried to act composed, he was impressed with the accommodations. In spite of himself, he let out a pleasurable sigh when he sunk into the comforter.

"This is such a cool place." She added, "It must be wonderful for your dad to give this kind of experience to your family."

"I guess it is."

Kate looked pensive.

"What's wrong?" Luke asked.

"Nothing." She took the cap off and began turning it in her hands. "It's just that—it would be nice."

Luke sensed that she was protecting him and became frightened. "What are you thinking about?"

"My job."

"What do you mean?"

"My mom could never take me to a place like this. All her money went to my college. We ate eggs for dinner to save. Even my aunt and uncle couldn't do this." She put down the cap. "I want to do it."

Luke couldn't tell why she'd offered her wish as a contention. "And you will," he said. "So will I."

Kate looked as if she wanted to speak, but instead she grabbed his hand. He felt her look to be one given to a foolish child. He winced.

She said, "You're right." Then she kissed him on the cheek.

Unsure of how to take her response, Luke lifted the remote. He flipped through a few channels. "You want to take a shower or should I?"

"I'll go. A long, hot shower'll feel awesome." She returned to the bathroom.

Though her propensity for the word awesome irritated Luke, he tried to push his discomfort away. He turned down the TV so he could hear the running shower. Without warning, his mind rushed to Kate's nakedness behind the door. In Luke's outlook, Kate had changed. Though not a sex object per se, she was definitely sexy, and Luke could no longer look past it. Before, when he had dated pure women, the relationship would reach a point where consummation was natural. At some point with each of these women, the sexual part of him would emerge through the protective layer he had constructed and confirm the time for making love had come. Once he broke the threshold, he saw his partner in all her desirableness, and categorized his feelings not as lust, but as natural passion. Even so, each pure relationship would soon fall apart after this barrier had come down, so he had to be careful.

With these thoughts running through his head, he decided to take a test run.

He imagined Kate in the shower, and he focused on the moist, white rings of skin that encircled her red nipples. He leaned back and let his eye drift from the whiteness around her breasts, to her tan chest, then back again. In his mind, she turned away from him, and he saw the same whiteness on her tight bottom, barely quivering, as she shifted to let the shower's spray dance off her back. The image of the curve of her lower back and her compact ass ushered Luke's hand to unzip his pants and relieve the pressure rammed against his zipper.

He let his head drop and imagined Kate turning her soapy body to face him. She threw her head back, teasing him by thrusting out her hips and sliding both her hands up her flat stomach to cup and squeeze her wet breasts, taking each nipple in between her thumbs and forefingers. Then she raised her head so her eyes met his. Silently, she encouraged him over to the shower with a wag of her finger. Luke complied, and Kate reached her soapy hand into his jeans. She squeezed and worked him up and down. With a tight fist, up and down, circling her thumb on the underside and around the rim. Rubbing it up and down.

Luke moaned and finished.

With his cock springing out of his jeans, he jumped up and frantically scampered across the room to the box of tissues that rested on the writing desk. Just as he reached the desk, his jeans' zipper pinched the exposed skin on the bottom of his dick and he doubled over in reflex. But the edge of the desk found his plunging forehead. The vicious crash caused the antique lamp to wobble. Luke picked up his head to see a hazy outline of the trembling lamp, which he saw—even through his clouded vision—to have an expensive-looking, green glass shade, one he was in no mood to pay for. He dove to catch it.

Luke's sight was not the only casualty of the incredible blow to his head. He found that, as he instructed his legs in the direction of the lamp, his equilibrium was fouled up enough so that his legs propelled him well left of his target and he drilled his head—the same spot as before—on the wooden wastebasket. As though the second crack to his head wasn't enough, his zipper grabbed tighter on the thread of skin it ensnared and the lamp fell, glass shade first onto his chest.

"Shit!"

Frenzied because Kate had surely heard the commotion, Luke pushed the lamp off his chest. Still on the ground, he steadied himself with one hand on the desk. With the other, he reached up for few the tissues. Then he gave a fierce tug on his jeans, unlatching the underside of his half-hard dick to check for blood. Though he found none, his wooziness and pain made for a sloppy and slow cleanup job. He tossed the balled-up tissue into the basket. It made a thud.

Luke looked down to check for blood again. It felt like a jungle cat had taken a swipe at his cock.

"What are you doing?" Kate stood over him, patting dry her hair.

"Uh … "

"Why are you down there?"

"Uh … "

"Why is your … " she pointed, "out?"

"Uh … "

She waited.

"The light's better down here, from this angle." The pain began to subside.

She folded her arms.

"I was checking to see if—"

"Yes?"

He went for broke. "I jerked off and my dick got caught in my pants."

Kate scrunched her nose. "I don't buy it."

Her distrust was a relief. "OK … but I'm really embarrassed to say this."

She smiled, obviously enjoying his discomfort.

"I was measuring it."

"When it was soft?"

"I was getting prepared for measurement."

"Why now?"

"I do it every month. Just to see."

"Any changes?"

"Not since I was fifteen. But no sense quitting now."

"What do you use to measure?"

This was getting absurd. "I eyeball it. I can tell."

She walked closer to him. "Don't let me intrude."

He was in too deep to stop now. And things were getting spicy. Plus, he was certainly ready for a long go that would satisfy any partner. He asked, "Maybe you could help me get ready."

"Don't push your luck." His request broke the mood. She stepped away, but didn't leave. "Go ahead," she said. Then she sat on the edge of the bed to watch.

Totally under her control, and with no alternative, Luke began again. After some steady work, his boy began to respond.

Kate smirked. "I'm impressed," she said. She got up from the bed as if she'd seen enough. She went back into the bathroom, but before she closed the door she turned. "That may serve you well," she said, nodding to his crotch. "Good luck with the measurement."

Cleaned up and back in bed, Luke turned up the TV to watch a talk show. With the short, vile host by her side, a gigantic woman in a tiny white camisole and cut off jean shorts cried over her man, Dean, who had had sex with her sister. As she continued to reveal her sad story, it became clear that Dean was the Don Juan of their mobile home park in, of all places, Mobile, Alabama.

After the woman finished to the sympathetic oh's and ah's of the audience, the host patted her plump hand and jumped up to prep the audience for Dean's entrance. Not quite as fat as his girlfriend and donning similar cutoffs—though he wore an Oakland Raiders jersey with a huge number eighty emblazoned on the front—Dean stuck out his chin, saluting the crowd with two middle fingers raised defiantly in the air. The crowd showered a deafening chorus of boos on him. Then he went over to his woman and gave her a deep, open mouth kiss that she accepted, and even lengthened, by clutching his back with her puffy arms. The audience screamed "Nooo!"

"Jesus," Luke said.

"What?" Kate asked, as she walked out of the bathroom.

"These hicks are unbelievable. This scumbag has been with every woman in the mobile home park, including this girl and her sister. Can you imagine *that guy* being a hot item?"

"He's not that bad."

"He's wearing cutoffs and a freaking jersey!"

"So."

"*So?*"

"So?"

With great effort, Luke straightened his furrowed brow and made another attempt at connection. "It's creepy that these morons get up there and do this to themselves in front of the whole world. It's awful." He paused, but Kate said nothing. "You know why Europeans think we're idiots? Because of these shows. This," he said, pointing to the screen that was now filled with a melee amongst the guests and bald bodyguards, "is America to them."

"What are they going to do? This is their one chance."

"What?" Luke sat up in bed and faced Kate. "Those people are set up to look like fools, and they do it willingly. I read that the producers of these shows actually tell the guests to play it up so the crowd goes nuts."

"I know. But can you imagine their lives? Calling them pitiful is like blaming homeless people for their joblessness."

"But *look*," Luke said, pointing at the ongoing brawl. He was desperate to prove his point. "These idiots rip each other apart in front of a camera for others' enjoyment. It's sick." Kate's perspective was even more irritating now that he had relieved himself.

Suddenly, she offered a plastic smile, as if the past minute had never occurred. "Where do you want to go tonight?"

She was clearly adept at avoidance. The ease with which she cut through the thick tension caught Luke off guard—he had never been privy to such a skill. He shook his head and could do nothing but answer honestly, "I hadn't really thought about it yet. We should go to dinner, then maybe a movie or something." He couldn't believe what came out of his mouth, like he was a drone under her control. He desperately wanted to regain the upper hand and retrieve the issue, but now too much time had passed. She had made it go away, and he, powerless, acquiesced.

"Great. I'll just get dressed and then you can have the bathroom." She kissed him on the cheek and added, "Tonight will be awesome."

24

O
K, that's enough. Let's go," Luke said to Kate who, after several Alabama Slamma drinks at the steakhouse, found it fascinating to lean over the banister of the inn's staircase to look at the guests finishing dessert. After a number of Jack and gingers, Luke's sole drive was to get Kate back to the hotel room.

Her giggles pulled the guests' attention up to them. Luke, embarrassed, grabbed her arm, and steadied her as she wobbled off the rail. At last he got her back to the room's door.

After Luke fooled with the lock for a good minute, the two spilled inside and onto the bed. Kate lay on her back and looked at the ceiling, while Luke lay on his side looking at her profile. He began to stroke the side of her face with the back of his index finger.

"You have a nice day?"

"I had an awesome day, Luke." Even following her overused adjective, Luke couldn't help the shiver that ripped through him when she used his name. "One of the best of my life."

"Really?"

"Honestly. I loved riding and talking with you and dinner and this place. It's like a dream."

Luke continued to rub her cheek. "For me, too." Her warm words had blunted his focus on having sex; he couldn't help trying to connect further. "I feel so free when I'm with you. I don't worry about anything. I can just be myself. That's why I talk so much, I think. Usually I don't talk as much as I've been talking to you, but I feel like it's natural."

Kate turned her head and smiled at him.

With nothing to pursue in her reticence, Luke gently kissed her lips. He pulled back and continued to rub and look her face. He tried to look as deeply into her eyes as he could, but in his mind, he weighed his options. He wanted desperately to be with her, and he felt they had reached a point where their passion would be appropriate, but he anticipated her resistance. He didn't know whether to be gentle and slow or aggressive, a side he had wanted to act on more and more over the last day. He shut his eyes and continued to kiss and stroke her, moving his hand over her tight breasts and stomach.

She kissed him back and didn't attempt to impede his searching hand. He opened his eyes, surprised to find her looking back. He said softly, "What?"

"What what?"

"Why did you open your eyes?"

"Same reason you did."

Luke wanted to say I love you, but he didn't. He pulled away and took off his shirt. "Why don't you take yours off, too? We can lie together." He paused. "With our bodies touching." He felt awkward using the same lines he had used on late nights with so many drunken girls, but he sensed the same protected willingness in Kate.

Kate sat up, quietly took off her shirt, and to Luke's pleasure, her bra. *My God*, Luke thought when he saw that the bra was merely a technicality: Kate's unyielding breasts didn't move. Without even returning to kiss her first, Luke took one of her breasts in his mouth. She made light sounds of contentment as he went back and forth from one perfect nipple to the other, licking each erect to the size of a small marshmallow. She caressed his head as he devoured her chest, but when he made an attempt to bring his lips up to meet hers, she gave an ever-so-slight push on the top of his head, insisting that he continue in his activity. Luke had been with other women who had sensitive breasts, but never had a woman garnered such pleasure from his suckling.

Kate continued to caress Luke's head as his hands swarmed over her body. Finally coming up for air, he kneeled on the bed and reached down to unbutton her pants. She lifted herself so that her pants easily slid off her hips. Luke paused, giving her a chance to do the same for him, but she just waited on her back. He took off his own jeans. He squeezed his hands between her back and the mattress, making her arch her body closer to him. Kate reached out blindly for Luke's head and pulled him to her, but as Luke brought his lips close to hers, she again pushed him down to meal on her breasts. As he forcefully sucked her nipples, Luke brought his hands to the small of her back, then slid them into her underpants, to her tight bottom, clutching her supple muscle with both hands.

Reaching with his fingers, Luke felt her wetness and moved his hands to the front of her thighs to part them. Kate gripped his hair as he started to lower from her breasts; her hands directed his mouth to stay where it was. Frustrated, but compliant with her strange fetish, Luke, with one move, rolled onto his back, pulled her to her side with his left arm, and slid his right hand down her flat stomach and into her underwear, all while feeding her fixation. Her sighs of bliss grew louder as she opened her legs to allow his hand into her secluded space.

In one part of Luke's mind, he knew Kate's behavior was not typical for the virgin he thought her to be, but in the part of his mind he controlled, he reveled in the mastery with which he brought this young girl into the sexualized world.

He rolled her over again onto her back to pull his face away from her chest, breathing in deeply the unrestricted air, then grabbed her underwear and yanked them off.

Though her eyes remained closed, he looked into her face and spoke gently. "Are you ready?"

She briefly opened her eyes, looking surprised at his question, then closed them again. Her hands pulled his head back to her breasts, and Luke, though even more perturbed by her need, gave her what she wanted. He adjusted his hips, pulled up her legs and entered her.

He expected a tougher go, and maybe a tiny cry of pain or look of discomfort, but Kate's expression of delight didn't change. She continued to hum her song of pleasure.

She felt incredible, a sodden grip milking his sex. Yet she didn't feel like he thought a virgin would; there was none of the famed tightness. As he began to thrust into her more forcefully, she accepted him and locked her ankles high around his body. The back of her taut legs made a fantastic, firm wall that he railed against as he penetrated her.

"Do you like it hard like that?"

"Go deeper."

Surprised by her answer, he pushed harder with each thrust, but she grabbed his butt and kept him deep inside, indicating that she wanted him only to make short jabs while resting his pelvis on hers. He left himself inside her and followed her order. Her voice deepened, her sighs dissolving into deep groans.

Luke buried his head in her hair, relishing the pleasure of connection. The discussion about money and her uncertain future sprung to Luke's mind. He pushed them out just as quickly, focusing on their present union. If they could stay here, with him inside her, they could do nothing but embrace their extraordinary bond. He never wanted to move. Finally, he felt what he had given lip service to earlier—he felt real and wholly human again.

This young woman that he could give to, hold, pleasure, teach and learn from became his drug. He didn't need or want anything else if he could have her forever—not even the baggie that was tucked safely in the side pocket of his saddlebag. This is what he'd searched for. This was his medicine. He felt good for the first time since Alex was alive.

The pain fled in short sobs. He tried to catch them in his throat, but Luke finally let go and cried desperately into her hair. An odd compulsion rose in him to complete his addiction transfer and retrieve the baggie to flush it down the toilet, but before he could give words to his discovery, Kate suddenly flipped him over.

Luke closed his eyes and arched his back. Then he reopened them, hoping she'd be looking back at him. He saw only the top of her head hanging from her propped-up body, swinging back and forth.

Breathing hard, she asked, "What's wrong?"

Luke wiped his eyes with both hands. "I feel like I'm whole again."

"Oh, Luke." She leaned forward and hugged him.

"It's unbelievable."

She put her mouth to his shoulder. "I know. It's amazing." But her words sounded scared.

"Why do you say it like that?"

"Like what?"

"Like you're grieving."

Kate brought her lips to his, linked for a long moment. She pulled away. "Luke, we've been talking and talking. And I've loved it. But now, for tonight, let's just feel. Let's be free. Do whatever we want. Not care about future or past. It's been a perfect day. Let's just finish it." She kissed him deeply, silencing any response.

He pushed himself into her.

She said, "Oh, yes." She grinded into him, her effort growing furious.

At first, Luke couldn't tell why she hung her head; he thought she was lost in her own world of pleasure, but then she moaned, "Oh, it looks so goood." Luke realized it was watching their physical connection that gave her so much pleasure.

"Oh, God, it looks so good!" she howled, clearly rising toward her finish. With her head still hung, she thrust her hips into the air and back down again over and over on Luke's crotch, shaking the bed with her force. She came in a torrent, her entire body quivering, beating the bed into the nightstand and sending the old-fashioned alarm clock clanging to the floor.

"Luke, that was incredible. Amazing." She took three deep breaths. "Like I was free."

Luke stroked her moist eyebrows.

She said, "Your turn. Do what you want. Anything."

Luke rolled on top of her. He put her arms behind her, and with their chests, stomachs, hips and legs touching, he slowly worked inside of her.

He said, "Hold me tight."

"Like that?"

"Tighter. With your legs."

Luke felt her compliance in her taught limbs. Quietly, with little more than a sigh, Luke came. "Keep holding," he said. And she did until they fell asleep.

25

For Alex's home game against arch-rival Texas, Luke and his parents sat underneath the huge 12th Man sign in A&M's stadium. Luke's mother sat between him and his father. The game used to be played on Thanksgiving Day, but it had been moved to the Friday after, swelling the stadium with overstuffed, rowdy fans.

On the other side of the field, Texas Longhorn fans, bathed in burnt orange, swayed like a wheat field. On Luke's side, A&M's fight song roared, finishing with "Texas AMU." Crew cut young men in green army uniforms slammed their drums, sending into the air the POP-POP-POPs of college football. Their female cohorts, also in uniform, waved white towels above their heads, encouraging the faithful to follow. And the fans fell into line, rocking the stadium's anchors.

The Stahls had arrived early to secure good seats, but to Mr. Stahl's visible annoyance, they sat in the midst of many black players' families. For a time, Luke had enjoyed his father's pre-game discomfort—stiffly shaking hands and bowing to the other fathers. Now, the impending kickoff drew Luke's attention to the field. On both sidelines, scores of mammoth young men bounced with excitement, bookending the width of the field like gigantic bobble-head dolls.

On the field, Alex wore number 40. Standing three players away from the tiny kicker, he rocked back and forth, anticipating the kick. The kicker raised his hand, signaling his readiness. One, two, three giant steps, and the kicker booted the ball as the crowd shrieked; the two teams flew at each other, each player blasting-off into the nearest foe.

The first wave of colliding helmets smacked in Luke's ears. Alex dipped between two would-be blockers at midfield, avoiding any contact. Sprinting, his arms pumping at his *sides, he lined up behind his wedge breaker—the human missile assigned to obliterate the wall of men in front of the Longhorn kick returner.*

And what a job the breaker did! The four-man wedge lined up shoulder to shoulder in front of the kick returner, and after looking back to make sure their teammate had the ball, they starting trotting, heads lowered to shield the returner from the Aggie defense. But the breaker heaved himself into the wedge, turning slightly in the air, catching one Longhorn with his shoulder and another with his hip. He landed neatly on top of both.

For a split second, a window opened in front of the hapless returner, and Alex was there. The returner instinctively stepped to the left, trying to avoid the crash, but only made himself more vulnerable. His heels locked into the grass. Slightly before his brother delivered his blow, even from hundreds of yards away, Luke thought he saw the whites of the Longhorn's eyes.

Alex, his elbows tucked in, leapt off his left foot, launching his rigid body into the enemy. The returner held up his thin arm, but Alex's body ripped though it, his shoulder pad colliding with the returner's face mask. The returner's head rode Alex's shoulder backward over his buckling legs, then slammed into the turf. The impact seemed to separate the returner's neck from his shoulders, his torso from his hips.

The crowd bellowed its sanction even as the victim's body lay awkwardly twisted on the ground like a wrung-out rag, his hips facing left, his head right. Alex scrambled up from the ground and leapt into the arms of his wedge breaker, pointing to the Aggie faithful.

The Longhorn trainers, first aid kits in hand, hustled onto the field.

Luke didn't move or make a sound—his mind replayed the collision over and over. But instead of Alex hitting a nameless Longhorn kick returner, Luke saw himself crushing his father.

133

26

Kate wanted to visit the park described in her guide as, "The Only Place in the U.S. Common to Four State Corners." Luke had agreed, seeing it was vaguely east, toward Texas. As the receptionist had suggested, Luke took 160 to the north on his way east, avoiding the Hopi Reservation but running through barren, desolate landscape. What people found beautiful about the desert Luke never knew. For a time, the arid air was refreshing compared to the soaking heat of Lubbock; but the bleak, brown setting offered no markers, no interest, and no life. The summer wasteland was parched and dead, and Luke wanted to get through it as fast as possible.

"I'm thirsty," he yelled over the motorcycle's rumble and the whipping wind.

Kate leaned forward and yelled back into his ear, "But we're almost there. Can't you wait?"

"I mean for a real drink."

She tapped OK on his shoulder. He leaned the motorcycle into the parking of wind-torn tavern, next to an abandoned gas station. A neon light over the open doorway flashed "Lunch."

The wind had picked up since morning, and it thrashed the tavern, its dead gas pumps, and its patrons' cars with pellets of grit and sand. Scraps of metal hung from the top of the old cashier's station and the canopy over the pumps.

By the appearance of the customers, the place survived thanks to people who had found Four Corners on a map and decided it was worth a look, but first needed a bite to eat. The aged patrons and gigantic RV's in the parking lot didn't match the rugged landscape of the desert or the derelict pub in which they sat. The old people hunched over their food in pairs, quietly gumming their lunch.

Along with his bourbon, Luke ordered Kate a gin and tonic from an old waitress who stood under a toxic silver beehive. She had a wicked smoker's cough and could only nod in response.

Kate's final words from the night before still haunted Luke. After a taste of his drink he took her hand. "Can I ask you something?"

She squeezed. "Of course."

"What did you mean last night when you said, 'for tonight?'"

"What?"

"When we were in bed, you said, 'for *tonight* let's just feel.'"

"I just meant for then. For that time." She squirmed in her seat.

Luke got to his point. "Do you even want to go back to Texas?"

"Sure I do."

"Now?"

"Now?"

He squinted at her—hoping she'd understand his knowing gesture. For some, alcohol dulls perception, but what poured from his glass and down his throat sharpened his new acuity. The alcohol tore down the remaining props Luke had built around Kate. In Hairy Hal's son's truck, when her face dropped at his suggestion to return to Texas, Luke felt his fantasy start to crack. Now it crumbled.

"I don't know, Luke. I don't think I'm ready."

"For what?"

"For Texas. For life. For you."

He took his hand away. "What does that mean?"

"I think I have to go home."

"What about all your talk about us being perfect for each other?"

"I think it's true, Luke. But not now. Part of me thinks we could do it—go to Texas. But the rest of me, the other me, thinks it's crazy. I've been confused, and you were so sweet, but—"

"But what? You've been stringing me along?"

"I haven't been. At all."

"You have. You told me you'd come home with me."

She turned stern. "No, I didn't. You just thought I would. I didn't know what I wanted."

"You have to come home with me, Kate. I need you."

"You've only known me for a few days. I'm sorry I got swept up in your dream, and I'm sorry I led you on. But I can't be what you want me to be. Not now."

Luke put his head in his hands.

Kate reached across the table and touched his wrist. "Why couldn't we have met in five years?"

"That's a cop out."

"It's the truth."

Kate had clearly realized she was unmasked, and now, as they quietly drank, she met his stare. When they first sat down, Luke thought he wanted to talk, but he grew satisfied with the staring contest they fell into. Quietly over a time, they drank many drinks, their hands repetitively bringing their glasses up and down, as though they powered a small, two-man train car.

Luke asked, "Well then, what do you want?"

Helplessly, she shrugged. She nodded across the room to the beehived waitress who stood waiting at the bar. The woman pulled a pencil out of her high hair, and she wrote the order on a pad, then handed the paper to the bartender. Luke watched the curious exchange, then ordered his own drink to see if they would repeat the same silent ritual. They did.

The waitress brought their drinks, hacking up something awful as she walked toward their table. She tried to cover her mouth as she cleared her lungs but she had a drink in either hand. The best she could do was turn her head and cough into her shoulder, which only aggravated matters. As she thumped the tumblers on the table, she also delivered a dense wad of yellow mucus, which hit and jiggled like a stray chunk of putrid Jello.

Neither she nor Kate seemed particularly troubled by the nasty addition, and its removal required Luke's gesture. The waitress seemed offended by the request, but wiped the offense off the table and onto the floor. The ball of scum never changed shape, and in fact, Luke thought he saw it bounce before coming to a rest next to his foot.

Kate asked, "What do we do?"

Luke was at a loss. He didn't know. Though he had a suspicion of her withdrawal, her words had stunned him nonetheless. He said, "I can take you to Lubbock. Can you get east from there?"

She spun her finger around the glass rim. "Any farther east would help."

All of a sudden she sounded like she was speaking to a friend of a friend instead of the man she had recently agreed was her perfect mate. What else could he say? He ordered another round as they sat in silence. The waitress put their fresh drinks on the table, this time with no phlegm.

Finally, Luke spoke. "Do you still want to go to Four Corners?" The extra time would allow him to figure out how he was going to make it home with her on the back.

Looking down, she said, "Sure."

Luke put his palms on the table. "Then I'm going to the bathroom."

In the bathroom stall Luke sat down on a stained toilet, propping his chin on his fist. He read the single line of graffiti on the side wall. *What are you looking here for? The joke's in your hand.* He raised his head.

Closing his eyes, he thought, *Was this it? A fizzle? A bland offer to go a bit farther east? How could it come to this?*

"Fuck you," was all he could say.

He was the one who needed change, not her. He couldn't change her. She was who she was. She had a plan, a future, a choice. And after a few days, it was clear to her that none of it included him—no matter how hard he tried.

Suddenly, Luke remembered what his mother often said to him and Alex when they had insisted on tying paper wings to a mouse and throwing it off the roof to watch it "fly," or persuading a boy who was barely five feet and less than a hundred pounds to try out for the football team: Leave it where Jesus flung it. He unhooked the makeshift lock, walked out of the stall and over to the sink. "Yeah, Luke," he said to himself in the mirror, "leave it where Jesus flung it."

He tried to turn his shock into apathy, but he kept staring at himself. In a moment, he recognized his forced indifference couldn't last. He watched his own eyes as unconcern hardened into despair. The misery he thought he had repelled turned again, pouncing on him.

27

The nondescript gatehouse, plopped in the middle of the desert, did not bode well for a scintillating experience at Four Corners. Luke paid the ranger to enter. The park was pitiful. There were a few Navajos selling turquoise jewelry in decrepit huts, a meek information center, three port-o-potties and a couple of signposts describing the history of the demarcation.

A thirty-foot Winnebago rested at the far end of the parking lot, opposite the information booth. Luke pulled next to it so his motorcycle could rest in its shade. Climbing off the bike, he squinted into the sun and looked over the park, trying to detect anything worthwhile in the area. Nothing doing. The total effect of the place was sad, and Luke let Kate know how dumb her idea was: "Maybe we're missing something. I'll see what they have in the info center." Kate said she'd stay with the bike.

Once inside he noticed a glass-doored refrigerator with sandwiches and sodas, and he grabbed two of each, along with a map. A gloomy female ranger with a nose ring and purple spiked hair waited indignantly for him at the register. He paid her for the map and overpriced food.

As he collected the purchases in his arms, a rush of grief spread through him. He realized he felt so close to an experience that he had often fantasized about: As an older man, he'd be traveling with his family and he'd gruffly, but happily carry hot dogs, churros, and Cokes to his waiting family in some national park's parking lot. His kids would joyously shout for the treats while his wife and he would decide what the family should do first. But when he collected the change that fell from the spiky-haired girl's greasy fingers, he knew that at that moment he was no closer to his future.

He walked out of the cool air conditioning and started to set up lunch at a concrete picnic table. He stopped, holding a turkey sandwich above the table. On the near side of the Winnebago, he saw Kate talking with a tall young man, clad from hat to sandals in bright orange and green, high-priced outdoor gear. He was sporting reflective blue sunglasses and had perfectly messy, long black hair that sprouted from underneath his canvas fly-fishing cap. Too far away to hear what they were saying, Luke peered at the couple to get a silent sense of their conversation.

Wearing her backpack, Kate moved closer to the young man as he leaned against a BMW that matched his sunglasses. Luke noticed the DC plates. A flash of desire gripped him when he saw Kate make yet a closer move, but only with her hips. Her feet stayed rooted to the ground and her shoulders didn't move. It was the same pose she'd struck when he met her at the jukebox—her pelvis thrust out, arms and head held back, her quadriceps flexed, with her breasts fighting to break free of her shirt.

As if moved by her challenging and provocative position, the young man stepped away and pulled his shirt over his head, revealing a ripped, symmetrical torso. He threw the T-shirt into the open sunroof of the car. Kate, just as she had done with Luke, let an enchanted expression cross her face, but held her body in its curved masquerade. He watched her execute her routine, reeling in the unsuspecting young man.

Even though he felt an instant pressure release, Luke felt betrayed. The break between them would be clean, but he still felt soiled.

The young man in blue sunglasses reached out and plucked an imaginary something off the bottom of Kate's shirt. She, accordingly, kicked her right foot behind her and rocked onto it. She lifted the bottom of her shirt to examine it, exposing her brown stomach. She laughed and leaned back onto her front foot, pushing a stray lock of blonde hair back behind her ear.

The young man leaned into the front seat of his car and started rustling with things on the seat. Simultaneously, as if Luke's stare was a bee buzzing around her, Kate picked up her head and looked around.

She finally looked across the parking lot. Luke smirked and cocked his head in contrived bewilderment, to which she made no response. Then he nodded to the marked intersection of the states' borders as if to say, 'Have you even stood on the authentic spot you wanted to see?' For a time, they held each other's stare, and a peace passed between them.

She quickly nodded to Luke, half smiled, and looked away before her new friend pulled his head from his car and revealed two cigarettes. She took one and accepted his light. Silently, Luke wished the poor sucker luck. Then he gave Kate the chance she needed—he walked demonstratively back into the information center.

In the air-conditioned cool Luke looked around until he settled in the rear of the shop, distracting himself with the meager rack of postcards. There were pictures of the plaque that denoted the cross of the borders, cards with six different pictures of the same turquoise ornament, and even a completely black postcard—except for a caption that read, *Four Corners At Night*.

He positioned himself so that he could look at the door as he pretended to peruse the different postcards, and for a few moments, even against all reason, he waited to see if Kate would come in. His heart seized each time a new customer entered the shop, but it was never a familiar face.

The ranger barked from her stool behind the register, "You gonna buy any pothcardth or juth heat the plathe up?"

Her lisp, combined with her hostility, was too much for Luke. "No," he said and walked outside.

The blue car, the young man with his matching sunglasses, and Kate were all gone. Luke jumped on his bike and drove out of the park on the dusty, one-lane access road. The motorcycle was noticeably lighter, and Luke despised its new maneuverability.

28

An old lime-green VW van lurched and swerved in front of Luke, sending billows of smoke from each of the windows with every shift. Without a safe chance to pass the erratic driver, Luke settled back to read the bumper stickers plastered all over the bus: *My Kid Sold Your Honor Roll Student Crack*; *Meat is Murder*; *Jesus is coming... Look Busy!*

Mechanically, Luke would speed up and brake, keeping ten yards between his front wheel and the erratic vehicle. Soon his mind started to wander.

Luke envisioned the driver ahead of him taking offense to something he had done in his rearview mirror. He imagined an aggressive, long-haired man flinging his middle finger out the window, then, unsatisfied, pulling over his bus, leaping from it and yelling something to Luke about keeping his space. He was clearly ready for a fight. But Luke beat him down efficiently.

The dream was not a new one. Frequently, violent images of pummeling an agitator flooded his mind, and the present one followed the same pattern: the perpetrator was always the aggressor, and Luke, the honorable one whose safety was threatened, had to respond forcefully. His brutal reaction would always be justified. In each of these visions, Luke remained silent, knowing that his quiet would only provoke his aggressor, while leaving him blameless. He'd wait for the antagonist to make his move. After the enemy threw his first punch or drew a weapon, Luke sprung into action and battered the unwary foe.

The imaginings were fleeting, but nonetheless, Luke felt the burn of violence in his hands and chest. He gleaned a gruesome satisfaction from the inevitable, imagined outcome with him on top, having heroically protected himself, his family or a kind stranger. The thoughts were odd, he knew, but they didn't bring him concern. Rather, he liked the world he created where right and wrong were clear and indisputable. His rank as the good guy beating back the bad instilled in him an odd, physical confidence that otherwise escaped him.

Soon, both he and the van arrived at the park's entrance that opened onto Route 160. His head ached, no longer filled with free-wheeling 70's rock ballads, but rather wracked with the image of his mother's sad, expectant face, which had grown clearer as the days stripped away.

Her vacant countenance, Luke had decided, was the worst residual from Alex's death, and her remote expression remained branded into his brain. He imagined his return home and having to look into his mother's blank eyes—something he had tried to avoid for the past year. She would look at him when he held her cold hand, and she would smile, but it wouldn't be her. She was gone. The real her, the whole her, was forever hollowed out.

This agonizing thought smashed Luke's heart, and in an uncontrolled reflex to save what felt like loose pieces floating in his body he clenched forward as he drove. The feeling slowly passed and he straightened, but his thoughts stayed with his mother. He recalled the first time he noticed her empty eyes: a gathering at their friend's home after Alex's funeral.

His mother sat, listening to people who thought their quiet words offered her consolation, but she was the one who consoled; even when she had just buried her son, she comforted friends who needed to hear her say thank you.

Early in the afternoon, jarred when her husband grabbed her hand to go, she got up and politely excused herself, thanked her host, and waved off any further offers of assistance. But the woman Luke saw on his father's arm, politely leaving the party, wasn't his mother. She'd died with Alex.

Instead of taking Route 160 to 64 and heading back to Texas, as he had planned, Luke took it north into Colorado. His craving for home, which had been so keen, vanished. The sting of Kate's rejection had deepened as he left the park, and going home would solve nothing. What would he do there? Feel sorry for himself and his mother? He didn't know what he needed, but he knew it wasn't a girl— and it wasn't at home either.

A sudden, chilling thought flew through his mind: for a moment he considered closing his eyes and letting go of the handlebars. *God*, he thought to himself, *is that my cure?*

But he kept both eyes open as panic assailed him like a squall. His palms and socks filled with sweat. His heartbeat rushed, thundering against his ribs. His left side tingled. Unconsciously, he lifted his chin with each ramming heartbeat.

Luke quickly pulled over to the side of the road and stopped, barely kicking out his kickstand. He couldn't get off the bike fast enough. He clawed at his collar, suffocated by its constraint. Dread washed through him. He felt like he was having a heart attack. Was he going to die? Right here on the side of the road? With nothing learned? Feeling wasted, deserted?

He stripped his shirt. He took three steps in a tight circle, trying to tame the demise he felt gurgling in his throat. Three more steps. Walking released a bit of the pressure, but he still couldn't take a deep breath. He walked in a straight line, his chin raised to the sky, trying to allow more air into his throat. He started to feel better, so he walked a quarter mile up the road and returned.

After he dug into his saddlebag, he remembered he had left the cocaine in his back pocket. He withdrew the flattened baggie. It looked like it had been through a war. Though an occasional car sped by him, he couldn't have cared less about them—or the high sun that spotlighted his activity to anyone on a slight rise within a mile. He went to the side of his bike opposite the kickstand and sat down against the warm engine, his heels hanging off the shoulder, two inches above the desert.

His sprawled legs were the only visible sign to oncoming cars that the motorcycle on the side of the road had not lost its owner, but the precariousness of the position didn't occur to him; he only focused on what lay in his palm.

He admonished himself: earlier he was too quick to discount the coke. It was his only constant, his only reliable source of diversion. What could he do? He felt like someone had inserted a huge syringe into him and withdrew his vigor. This clump of white powder was his salvation now.

"First things first," he said.

He needed more than just a key bump, but Luke found nothing that could serve as a tray until he remembered the chrome battery cover on the side of his bike, under the seat. He pulled it off and dumped a pile of cocaine into it, took out a dollar bill and his parents' credit card, covered the mound with the bill and stroked the card back and forth to break up the chunks. The process always brought to Luke's mind Mr. Miagi's admirable advice: Paint the fence, Daniel Son.

"Wax on, Wax off," Luke said as he cut the smooth pile into six lines. He tried to cheer himself, but he couldn't shake the pain.

Before rolling up the bill and dropping his nose to the first line, Luke put the cover on his lap and looked up. The warmth of the sun on his face and chest matched the warmth of the engine against which he rested. Yet it offered him no relief. Promptly, old pictures of his mother's open, caring face and Kate's blank expressions twirled together in his head. That he had believed the two had anything in common, that they were in the least bit similar, was foolishness. His parents were right—he made her up to be what he wanted, and it had, once again, ended in disaster.

"Help me, please!" Luke shouted to the sky. He didn't know if he yelled to Kate, to himself or to his parents, but he shouted it again, almost upsetting the drugs in his lap. He sat with his head thrown back against the seat of the motorcycle, the sun shining on his face, his body limp with exhaustion.

Luke cursed himself, "Jesus Christ." He looked into the chrome cover. His rational mind saw another dead end, just like his attempted affection with Kate: he knew the cocaine's effect, like Kate's interest, would be momentary. There was never enough of either, and he felt awful afterwards. He raised the cover to fling the stuff onto the shoulder of the road.

But he couldn't. He placed it back in his lap.

The irrational part of him that tried to fill his spirit's cavern with coke wouldn't be outdone. He hoped that this time, for whatever reason, things would be different. It was his only weapon against his pain. He looked up and down the empty road and dropped his head to the battery cover. Without looking up he inhaled all six lines.

Part 3

"Dusting Off Your Savior ... "
Red Hot Chili Peppers

29

The first time Luke's father quit drinking, he cleared the house of all liquor. One night after he'd been dry for a week, Luke's mother went to dinner with Alex. She offered to take Luke, but he declined. At five, he'd never remembered being alone with his father. He wanted to try.

Father and son hovered over slices of pizza, Luke measuring his dad. "What's wrong, Luke?"

Luke pushed a strand of hair away from his face and said, "Nothing. You?"

"Nothing."

"Did you see the Cowboys score?"

"No. Did you?"

Luke shook his head.

"Why did you ask then?"

"I don't know."

Mr. Stahl threw down his pizza. "For a smart kid, sometimes you say the dumbest things." He looked above Luke's head to the cabinet over the stove, or 'The True Temp,' as his dad called it. He stared at it for some time, seeming to forget Luke sat next to him. Then he went to the cabinet and pulled out some cooking wine. After reading the label he noticed Luke's stare. He froze as if caught stealing. "This looks like wine, but it isn't. It's—oil." He nodded to the basement. "Why don't you go downstairs and play your Nintendo?"

Luke pushed away from the table and hopped off his chair.

Later, Luke's father yelled down, "Luke! Come up here a second." Huffing away, Luke arrived at the top of the stairs after thirteen thumping steps. His father sat on the couch with the bottle in his hand. It was almost empty. He asked Luke, "Do you need anything else to eat?"

"No thanks," Luke said, surprised.

"No dessert?"

"I had animal crackers in the basement."

"I could run to McDonald's and get you some soft-serve."

"And leave me here?"

"It's only around the corner."

"I'm fine."

"All right, all right. Christ. Shows you what I get for trying to be nice." Laying back on the couch, his father put his arm over his face. "Go play your game." His voice sounded muffled through the flannel.

Soon, his father yelled again. "Luke! Come up here a sec."

He jumped the steps a second time. Huffing again, "Yeah?"

"I'm going out to get a soft-serve. I'll be back in a second. Don't pick up the phone. Don't answer the door. And don't worry, you'll be fine."

"Can't you wait 'til mom gets home?"

"No. I want to go now. You'll be fine. My dad left me when I was much younger than you, and I was fine. Your mother's over-worried. Don't let her get to you." Luke crossed one foot over the other. "It's not a big deal, Luke. It's good for you."

In an hour, Mr. Stahl returned, smelling like a bar. "Mom home yet?"

Luke had cried for the last twenty minutes. His voice was sticky. "No. The phone rang at 9:00. I thought it was her, but I didn't pick it up."

"Good. Sorry it took me so long. There was a line. Redwings started to hurt my feet." Mr. Stahl looked at his shoes. He started to wobble and steadied himself against the wall. "Have you been crying?"

Luke looked down. He shook his head.

Mr. Stahl said, "Don't tell your mother I went out." He pushed off the wall, then turned to walk upstairs.

30

The intense afternoon sun bore down on Luke, but surprisingly, with the cocaine's impressive force and the dry wind in his face, the heat seemed unusually liberating. Soon after he had taken the pit stop to refill his nose, his focus narrowed to the freedom of his motorcycle's new, relative weightlessness. With this new feeling came his conclusion that heading even slightly in the direction of home didn't feed his revitalized need for peace. With Kate, he felt close to his answer, but he realized he wouldn't find it in another. He had to stop distracting himself with such absurd conclusions. Now, he knew his answer lay inside him. But he needed more time to find it, and going home would only curb his exploration.

That he passed a phone booth without any inclination to call his mother only bolstered his determination—as if he had received a signal from some higher power. When he passed a road sign indicating Route 262 into Utah was only ten miles away he decided to take it. His prompt choice to seize the new possibility reinvigorated his high and constitution. So much so, that as he leaned his bike off 160 onto 262, Luke started singing the refrain from U2's "Bad" at the top of his lungs: "I'm wide awake ... I'm wide awake!"

Huge, sporadic raindrops began to crash into Luke—so big that his eye could follow an individual drop from twenty feet ahead, until it burst on his headlight. The drops that hit his uncovered hands and face felt like they pierced his skin, forcing him to slow his bike to a crawl.

Blackness suddenly spread in front of him, and Luke knew the fat, occasional drips were merely scouts for the army of water that was poised to descend onto southern Utah. He knew such storms from his home: they alert you with a few drops the size of large marbles until the sky opens and spews out a blinding spray. Certainly not the time to be on a motorcycle. Determined as he was to find himself in Utah, he still had the sense to get off the road.

He pulled into a log cabin-like motor lodge and headed for the covered entrance of the lodge's tiny office. At the counter he met a pile of hair, sprouting out of a XXX-large, white T-shirt covering a pair of sizable, androgynous breasts. Luke needed a moment to find the man, or woman's, eyes in the midst of the canopy of hair. Like staring into a computer-generated image in which a picture suddenly springs from seemingly meaningless dots, Luke recognized a pair of lips and a slight chin hiding behind the wall of curls. Only these shadows of facial features distinguished the person from a curly-haired Cousin It.

Luke leaned on the yellowing counter top and nodded. "Hello," he said. No answer from the hairy thing. Thinking it might be deaf as well as ugly, Luke raised his voice, "Hello!" The person across from him raised its hand in surrender, as if suffering from an evil headache. Luke still spoke loudly and slowly. "I need a room. Do you have a room?" No response. "For the night." The mop tilted its head to the left in apparent inspection, then righted itself. Luke thought the gesture was some sort of investigation into his wherewithal. He added, "I can pay." Why he said such a foolish thing he didn't know—of course he could pay. But the mop's bizarre silence freaked him out, and when he felt freaked he said stupid things.

The mop appeared to acquiesce as it leaned under the counter to reach for something. As it did, Luke caught a whiff of its dank fur and had to cover his lips and swallow the vomit in his throat. The smell further withdrew his already ebbing high; he could feel the growing emptiness in his chest.

Silently, they executed a transaction that required Luke to hand over his parents' credit card, while the mop furnished sheets and a towel in exchange. Even into the rain, most would've walked away from the situation before it had gone this far. Some would've run at the sight of the receptionist, others when they smelled its wet dog stench, and *all* rational customers would've hit the road after receiving the nasty linens, handed over by the barely visible beast under the pelt. But again needing to bow to the cocaine altar, Luke could only think of a dry and private room to do his bidding, so he took the towel and sheets. Carrying them, and his crashing psyche, he went to Room 7.

When he exited the office, he stopped under the enclosed entrance and briefly considered taking the motorcycle in the room with him, for safe keeping. It would be tight, but there was no rise between the sidewalk and the doorway, so it would be a simple procedure. But he had no interest in the delay presented by the transfer, nor in the gasoline smell that would surely fill the room. *Besides*, he thought, as he looked up into the unrelenting skies and out at the few cars in the lot, *no one will fuck with it.*

After throwing his saddlebags on the bed and turning on the TV, Luke inhaled a relatively conservative line. Then he went to the bathroom to turn on the shower before returning to the room. The tingling in his sinuses promised a better mood, and all he wanted was to clean his skin.

As he took off his crusty jeans, the phone rang.

"Hello." No one responded. "Hello?" Nothing.

Luke hung up. A moment later the phone rang again.

"Hello?"

When silence once more responded, his heart began to pound and he hung up. When it rang yet again he was helpless against it. He tried to sound more aggressive, in spite of his heartbeat in his ears. "Hello?"

"Is that your bike out front?" The voice was thick and measured.

"Yeah. Is this the front desk?"

"No, this ain't the front desk." The man hung up.

Luke threw on his pants, turned off the shower water, went outside, and looked up and down the length of the narrow sidewalk in front of the other rooms. There were vending machines at the far end of the lodge, but no sign of anyone—not even a sound besides the static of the unyielding rain. He darted back inside his room, grabbed his key off the table, and hustled out the door and down the sidewalk toward the machines. Out of the entrapment of the room, Luke felt a bit relieved.

The only way to get to the machines without getting soaked was to hug the inside of the walkway next to the large front windows of the other rooms. As he neared what he guessed to be Room 12, its door shut. When he passed the adjoining window, he noticed its blue shade waving back and forth, as if someone inside had just let it go.

Finally, at the machines Luke felt relieved to be distracted, if even for a moment. He was scared to death of what or who waited in Room 12. He punched the button for a Mountain Dew and walked back to his room. As he passed, a face in the far corner of the familiar window disappeared behind the shade. Luke began to trot down the sidewalk, his bare feet slapping the wet concrete.

As soon as he got into his room, the phone rang. He let it ring nine times, then finally picked it up.

"Hello?" He could feel his voice quake.

"Sure's a pretty bike you got."

Luke was petrified and his fear ripped away any shrewdness. He stumbled into childish honesty, "Thanks."

"Where'd you get it?"

"Uh, Texas." He knew this response to a presumable thug was crazy, but maybe, he thought, he simply misunderstood. Maybe the guy just wanted some information on the paint job or something.

"OK." He hung up.

Jesus. Oh, Jesus, Luke thought. His mind screamed at him to run, but his legs were pinned to the floor. The phone rang again.

He had no choice but to answer. Luke prayed the man would disclose something that made his surely-benign intentions clear. "Hello?"

"Want to talk to you about your bike. Just stay there."

"N-n-no. No." Luke hung up. He picked it back up and dialed 0, but the phone just rang and rang. Then he dialed 9, but a busy signal cut him off before he could dial 1-1. He slammed down the phone, upsetting a small sign that indicated he couldn't dial out.

He grabbed only his wallet and leather jacket, put on his shoes, and backed out of the room onto the sidewalk. Once outside, his mind whirred. Yet, guided by a curious inclination not to draw attention to himself, he slowly walked toward his bike. He knew at any moment a man would step out of room 12 behind him, so he concentrated on facing forward and keeping his eyes glued to his target.

After five steps, a short man with greasy hair tucked under a red, backward baseball hat and a black Skid Row T-shirt stepped sideways out of Room 4, facing Luke. His eyes were on Luke as he reached across his body with his right hand to pull his door closed, but he didn't shut it all the way.

As he moved toward Luke, the man's right arm swung with his first two steps, but his left arm stayed stiff at his side. Along with the unusual motion he had used to close the door, the man's stiff walk kicked Luke's mind into recognizing the true danger in his unusual affect: the man's left hand held a gun. Luke started back toward his room's door.

"Hey," the man yelled. "Want to talk to you." He picked up his pace, his boots clicking on the sidewalk. Luke turned and ran the other way, but Room 12's door opened and another redneck came out, pulling the door behind him. Irrationally, Luke felt trapped between the men and the wall of rain to his side. It took him a split second to realize the rain wasn't impenetrable. He darted between a rusted white van and Pinto into the wet parking lot and turned again to face the gunman. The rain's chill jolted Luke's guts and filled his depleted nerves. He stared directly at the gunman, who clearly didn't want to leave the shelter of the canopy. Once in the parking lot, the white van behind Luke cut the second aggressor out of sight, and Luke unconsciously put him out of mind; he waited to gauge the gunman's motives.

After a motionless stare, Luke dashed toward the office, and suddenly, like a tracking Doberman, the gunman sprinted into the rain at an angle of pursuit. Their respective speeds brought the two men together before Luke could think. Instinctively, Luke lowered his body, planted his left foot and drove the top of his forehead into the redneck's chin. Through his head's crown, Luke felt his enemy's teeth shatter as they smashed together. Though stunned by the collision, and surprised by the redneck's body density, Luke didn't collapse like his foe. Instead he sprinted to the office. He looked back only once to see the gunman still lying in the rain. His cohort backed away behind the white van, his right arm stiff at his side.

Luke yanked open the door to the office and yelled, "Call 911! Call 911!" No one was there. Luke screamed, "Help!" Still no response. He considered running behind the counter to see if the mop was present, but he realized the receptionist probably conspired with his assailants.

Without further search for his credit card, he ran out the door and jumped on his motorcycle. In the torrential rain, he risked his life at forty miles per hour, but the adrenalin surging through his body rolled the throttle as he peeled out of the parking lot and up the road. After riding for a half an hour with no one in his rearview, Luke slowed and pulled into one of the many, strikingly similar log cabin motor lodges that dotted 262.

It took Luke an hour of checking his new room's window every two minutes before he had the confidence to take the shower he so wanted. Once under the nozzle's spray, he only marginally cleaned himself. He was too scared of the shielding curtain and the possibility that the shower would drown out any suspicious noises.

After a few more checks of the window he was satisfied that no one had followed him. Yet he was unable to slow his racing heart or mind.

He picked up the phone and dialed.

"Mom! It's Luke ... I'm fine. I'm fine ... Mom, some guys. They just tried to take my bike. Dad's bike ... I don't know, one of them had a gun. I think the other did too ... I'm fine now, fine. They didn't follow me, but my stuff is still in the other place ... Some motor lodge. I'm using your guys' credit card. I had to use two, actually, because I just came to another place. Mom, I'm sorry ... For everything ... Look, if you get a call about the weird charges, you know why ... I'm so sorry. God, what am I doing? I know I'm scaring the hell out of you. It's so stupid. I know I'm way out of line, but it's pouring here, and I can't go back ... Not yet ... I'm OK, I'm OK ... I don't know *what* I'm doing. I'm just sorry. And you were right about that girl ... She was an idiot ... Oh, I thought you did. But she was, anyway. And now I got into this. And I called you? I'm sorry. It's just going to make you worry, I know. It's so selfish ... I'm so selfish ... I'm coming home. I really am. No more BS. I'm coming home tomorrow. ... No. I'll go back and get my stuff in the morning when it's light. It'll be fine ... Thank you, Mom. I feel better. I'm sorry I called. Everything will be fine ... Of course. I'll call you tomorrow ... I love you, too."

31

The sun had barely begun its early morning ascent, and the curtain in Room 4 hadn't moved for the full hour Luke had watched. He stood behind a metallic blue El Camino on the other side of the parking lot. Satisfied with the motionless curtain, he convinced himself that it was safe to retrieve his belongings, then get the hell out of the motel.

Earlier, when he had driven into the parking lot, Luke made a quick decision to recover his parents' credit card *after* rescuing his belongings. By putting off the angst of encountering the fur ball, he could focus solely on the duty of recovering his goods. Either way, he didn't feel exactly thrilled about the quest ahead. In spite of how shaken he had felt while discussing his experience with his mother the night before, he felt fairly sure of himself when he woke up. Yet, standing here for an hour, looking at the curtain and the white van and the office and the room numbers on the doors brought back the terror of the day before and vaporized his limited courage. In an effort to retrieve his bravery, he tried to relive the thrill of thumping the gunman's chin with the top of his head.

It didn't work. Imagining the scene revealed the fortune, rather than skill, that allowed his escape. He was lucky enough to have avoided the gunman's clutch; luckier still to drill him on the chin with his one shot.

Nonetheless, he knew he had no other option. He had to act, so with a deep breath, he left his bike behind the El Camino and trotted out a wide, circular approach to the front of the motel.

With a thump, he slammed his back into the wall between the office and Room 1. No one was around, and every motel guest clearly remained asleep. In fact, nothing stirred in the morning air, save the soft calls of a few birds in the withered tress behind the motel. Luke, back to the wall, crept along to Room 7. He squatted as he passed each room's window, as if he was point man on a Delta Force raid.

With tremendous care not to make a sound, he unlocked the door to his room and stepped inside. He was astonished to find all of his things in the exact places he had left them. He hadn't previously considered whether the assailants would've tried to break into his room, but once inside he was surprised they hadn't. Relieved, he quickly threw the few things he had unpacked back into his saddlebags, and he left the room as silently as he had entered.

The extra weight made the wall hugging difficult, but he managed to slip by all the rooms and into the office, determined to repossess his parents' card. He rang the bell on the counter. The attendant who appeared was not the beast from before, but a young, Native American girl with a mouthful of teeth.

"I want to check out," Luke said, looking over her shoulder to make sure she was alone.

"OK. What room?" the girl answered.

"Seven."

She flipped through cards in a plastic file box and said, "We don't have you checked in. Do you have the credit card you used to reserve the room?"

"Shit!" Luke pounded the counter. He spun and looked up at the ceiling. "Goddamnit!" The Indian girl cowered behind the counter. "You mean you don't have my credit card back there?"

"No," she squeaked. "W … Why would we?"

Even though he knew the girl had nothing to do with his duping, he turned and screamed again at her, "How the fuck did some asshole get in here to steal my credit card?"

"What? What are you talking about?"

He chucked his key onto the counter. "Last night somebody in here took my credit card."

"We only take an imprint of the card. We don't take it."

"Who worked here last night?"

The girl looked horrified. "Jeanne was supposed to, but she's off for the week." She paused. "We're understaffed and she got someone to fill in."

"Who filled in?"

"I don't know."

"Where's Jeanne?"

"Mexico."

"What?!"

The girl tried to help, "What did she look like?"

"She was—or he was—" Luke stopped, realizing the advantage of being unrecognizable. "Has anyone else who checked in last night checked out yet?"

"You're the first."

"Get ready to have a lot of pissed off people on your hands."

The girl started to panic. She began shaking both her hands like she'd burned them. "What do you mean?"

"Someone was behind this counter last night. I don't know if it was Jeanne's friend or not, but he—or she—took my credit card and split."

The girl's hands fell to her sides. She looked doubtful. "What did the person look like?"

"Totally unidentifiable. Just call the police. Call them now." He couldn't believe it. Why had he fallen for such shit?

Then he answered his own question: because he needed to hit his blow. That's why he was hasty. And now this girl was on the phone with the cops.

He said, "I gotta go."

She put her hand over the receiver. "Wait. I'm on hold. They'll want to talk to you."

Luke repeated, "I gotta go," leaving the bewildered attendant to deal with the problem.

He walked outside and back to his bike, noticing only in his unconscious mind that the white van from the day before had disappeared.

On his bike, Luke kicked his feet way out on the foot pegs and sped on Route 191. He wanted to motor south back through Utah and Arizona to catch I-40 East and hopefully save time on the interstate. Before he had checked out of the second hotel that morning he had called his mother again. Even though she had believed the story about the stolen credit card, he still felt depressed. Her soft voice had calmed him, but after he hung up, her tender questions still rang in his head. In the midst of all the worry he had subjected her to, his well-being remained her paramount concern. Her unselfishness laid bare his tremendous self-absorption, and the realization carried incredible guilt. This—plus a one-night education in true vulnerability—proved that introspection was no longer in order. Luke only wanted to get home as quickly as he could to reconcile with his mother and try to regain a sense of his former self.

After a time, Luke relaxed. Though he didn't let up on the throttle, he reclined deeply into his bundled-up sleeping bag. His position rendered his rearview mirrors useless—all he could see in them were the T-tops of telephone poles etched into the pale blue sky. With only bleak desert ahead, nothing distracted him from the images that poured through his mind. To Luke's exasperation, his homecoming segued into reminiscences of Kate's face, voice, hair and eyes. *How could I have thought she was the key?*

Luke grew desperate for someone or something else to focus on, and the empty desert offered no distraction. He would've given anything to be in a car, to turn on the radio, even to pick up the grimy hitchhiker he passed, simply to listen to his stories, his life. But his bike promised solitary, quiet reflection. He could only nod and wave as he sped by the smiling, bearded man on the road's shoulder.

He swung into the oncoming lane to pass a number of cars, unconcerned that his reclined position impaired his vision. After passing a tiny old lady navigating her lilac convertible Cadillac—using what must have been ESP, considering her eye level sat somewhat under the top of the steering wheel—Luke drilled a gigantic pothole the size of the Cadillac's backseat. The shock shot his ass forward onto his gas tank.

He needed to readjust, so he pulled himself up to a normal riding position. As he did, he caught a glimpse of a blue, flashing light in the road behind him. He bolted erect to see a police motorcycle, holding back at about fifty feet. Though he could have been pursuing Luke for a long time, the cop's driving wasn't frantic: if not for the blue flashing lights, it looked like he was simply following a friend. Yet he obviously followed Luke, who quickly grew anxious about the baggie's bulge in his left front pocket.

Luke rolled off his throttle and gradually slowed his bike, trying to save time so he could grind down the bulge with his hand. By the time he pulled over, his efforts had worked somewhat—he'd milled the knob into a small, subtle lump. Still, a knowledgeable cop would surely ask to see the contents in his pocket.

The officer that came to Luke's left side smiled genuinely, a good sign. "Morning, son," he said, as the Cadillac sped by, followed by the other cars Luke had passed earlier. Each extended Luke a greeting by hand, finger or horn.

Leaning forward, Luke had his palms placed conveniently on his pockets. He smiled up at the officer. The fact that he was a motorcycle cop meant one of two possibilities: either he liked a biker no matter what, or he would think Luke's erratic driving gave riders all over the world a bad name.

"Hello, officer," Luke said, trying to sound as cooperative as he could in two words. The less he talked, the better off he'd be.

"Could you step off your motorcycle?" Luke tried covertly to flatten his jeans as he stepped off the bike. "Know why I pulled you over?" the cop asked.

"No." Luke prayed the next words out of the officer's mouth included anything but "stolen." He had no idea how long his mother could hold off his father, and he knew if they wanted him home, all they'd have to do is call the police.

"Two things actually."

Luke's heart sank.

The cop continued, "Had some reports of you doin' some reckless drivin'. Back aways." He waited for Luke's reaction and Luke generated an appropriately shamed expression. "When I pulled you over, you were doin' 'round seventy-five."

Luke was puzzled. Though he had driven quickly, and passed a few slow cars, he didn't think he was out of control. Nonetheless, he tried to sound disgraced. "I'm sorry. Jeez." He shook his head. "I was just kind of cruising along, and I must have lost track of my speed." He paused to see if his act had any effect on the officer. "It's so cool out here," he added. "I'm just trying to take it all in. You probably know how that is."

"Sometimes," the officer said. "Also got a call about some stolen credit card back at the Logger motel. Girl gave a description of the guy who reported it and ran off—you fit."

Blindsided, Luke scrambled for words. "Oh. Well ... I got nervous."

"'Bout what?"

"The girl said she didn't know how long it was going to take."

"How long what was going to take?"

"For the cops to get there. I had just called my mom to cancel her credit card and wanted to go home."

The cop looked unconvinced. "Let me see your license."

Luke swallowed as he reached into his back pocket. He hated to draw any attention to his legs. But as he pulled out his wallet his stomach shrank with a new fear—he didn't have a motorcycle license. "Here." He cringed as he tried to prepare himself for what was sure to follow.

After taking the license, the cop made a move back toward his bike but halted and turned as he looked at the card. "You don't have a class M license, son. How come you're driving a motorcylce?"

"I got in a fight with my dad and just took a drive."

"From *Lubbock*?"

"Well, the drive kinda lasted a while. I just couldn't go home."

"Why you going home now?"

"The guys who stole my credit card wanted my bike. They attacked me."

"Attacked you?"

"Tried to. I escaped."

The cop took out his notepad. "What did they look like?"

Luke gave a description. He asked, "Did they get any other cards?"

"Just yours and another." He asked a number of follow-up questions about the credit card and Luke's trip and his plans.

Luke answered them all without sounding defensive.

The cop appeared satisfied. "You said they wanted your bike?" Luke nodded. "There's been a few stolen recently. But not this far east." The cop thought a moment. "Anything else you remember?"

"Actually, yes. There was a white van in the parking lot last night that was gone this morning."

"See the plates?"

"No."

The cop scribbled in his notebook, then he read over his notes. "Oh. What about this attendant last night? What did he look like?"

Luke described him. "I don't know if it was a he."

"Anything else?"

Luke shook his head.

The officer snapped shut his notepad and looked back at Luke's license. Then he looked at Luke. "You know, if I was your dad I'd be pretty worried about you. He's probably dyin' of worry right 'bout now. I'm gonna' go back to my bike and look at a few things." Again, he started to walk away and then turned back. "You don't have any guns on you, do you ... " he looked at the license, "Luke?"

The question was a surprise, but Luke felt relieved the officer was only asking about guns. "No, sir. I don't even own a gun." The chance for an honest answer relaxed the knot in his stomach.

"No drugs, right?"

The cop might as well have jabbed Luke in the abdomen. He did his best to stand still and absorb the punch. "Nooo, sir." The cop turned to leave.

As he looked in the rearview mirror, Luke saw the cop working at a small computer he had set up on the console between his handlebars. As if he had a nervous tick, Luke rubbed his palms down the front of his pants. He had two purposes in mind: he hoped to impress the cop with how anxious he behaved in the presence of such a noticeably stellar police officer, and he wanted to make the lump of cocaine invisible. "Please," he whispered to himself as he looked at the cop in the mirror and stroked his legs, "don't be in that computer."

After several minutes, the officer returned and gave Luke a stern warning. With a sympathetic tone he admonished Luke about the license. Luke's clean record must've put him in a favorable mood. He added, "I know how it is. I used to get into it pretty good with my old man, and sometimes all I could do was get on my bike and take off. Even before I had a license."

Luke welcomed his understanding. "It's not that bad. He was just giving me shit about not doing well in school and getting a job and all."

The cop nodded approvingly. "Well, you've gotten this far safe enough and you're not too far from home."

Luke groaned. "I can't wait."

"It's nice to get home and settle things."

"Yes, it is."

"I need to get back," the cop said, nodding to the blacktop. "Get a class M license as soon as you get home or you're toast. Understand?"

"Yes, sir!"

"Be careful."

"Thank you, officer."

That Luke had escaped the cop scot-free was incomprehensible. Looking in his rearview, Luke half expected the officer's back-up to arrive, but the cop only climbed back on his bike and, with a salute, motored by. Luke's incredible luck rekindled his spirits, but he wanted no more narrow escapes. Once the cop's motorcycle all but disappeared, he made a cuff in his jean's right leg, placed the baggie inside, and rolled both legs up. Even though it was an unusual look, he liked his idea for a hiding place. He made sure the drugs were secure by jumping up and down and shaking his leg. Then he resumed riding in his reclined position.

To his immense frustration, his mind soon went back to Kate, and she ruined his mood. He couldn't believe he was such a fool, and he wanted to kick himself for telling her about Alex, especially in such detail.

Yet, he still couldn't cleanse his mind of the fantasies he returned to often, and this time Kate took the lead role: From an A-framed farmhouse staged in front of a glorious sun, three blonde children ran squealing up to him as he returned home and stepped out of his car. He scooped each of them up, tugging them back to the house so he could kiss their mother hello. She waited at the door, patting her wet hands on her apron. The mother in Luke's scene had been ever changing, but typically she was the most recent object of Luke's affection. Sometimes she'd be a kind woman he'd ordered from in a restaurant or had met at a party. This time, though, he couldn't shake Kate's visage out of the picture.

32

Luke sensed someone followed him. He leaned forward to look in his rearview and saw a non-descript white van a quarter mile behind.

He took a deep breath and frantically tried to remember the last road sign he'd seen, anything that would give him some indication of a possible exit. But he remembered only one sign, miles back, indicating the Arizona line waited fifty miles ahead. There was no escape from the one-lane highway. Luke again looked into the rearview, praying the van was some wicked coincidence. But it was still behind him—and closing in fast. He leaned forward, rolling on the throttle to gain some distance from his pursuers. For a fleeting moment, he dreamed of finding the kind officer ahead, but he knew he was out of reach.

Soon, the van was on top of him. In his mirror, Luke could make out the greasy blonde hair and red, backward baseball cap on the passenger side.

Behind Luke, the van pulled into the left lane and yanked back to the right, then repeated the cycle. Luke could see the wide smiles and pumping fists of the hicks in the front seat as they swerved back and forth. When the van yanked back into its position behind Luke, his mind, maybe in a gesture of self-preservation, suddenly arrested.

For a moment he achieved a quiet peace with no regard for the menace behind. Even unaware of the wind in his ears, he heard only silence and saw only promise in the endless road in front of him. He relished the prospect of the white line and the road it bisected, which reached out into the infinite dust of the desert. The line seemed to lead him into his next life, his next world, away from the pain and memories and speculation and misunderstanding. The road's gift of possibility was even more monumental as he received it while engulfed in a ghostly silence.

Though the feeling lasted only until the van jerked back into the left lane behind him, it was the most profound, serene second of Luke's life, and he felt recharged by its promise. Without thought, Luke leaned on his back brake, feeling, irrationally, that if he stopped, everything would go away and his peace would be real. The road would take care of him by pulling the threat farther and farther away.

The van shot by on his left, then jolted back into the lane in front of him. Still in his irrational state of mind, Luke was buoyed by his new position behind the van, thinking it was some sort of advantage, yet he had no time to consider what to do with it; in an instant the van's bumper and red break lights seemed to lurch at him. Luke's hands and feet could not react quickly enough. All he could do was brace and curl himself as his body and bike crunched into the filthy back doors of the stationary van, the collision ringing like a twelve-gauge blast. Shocked that he could still stand after the crash, but seeing the middle and front doors open on the passenger side, Luke tried to run away.

He thought he had sprinted away from the scene, but as a car whizzed by he looked down to shield his eyes from the dust and saw remnants of his father's bike's headlight—he hadn't yet moved ten yards away from the spot of the impact. He realized that though his mind screamed at his legs to sprint, he moved at a snail's pace.

Horror gripped him when he turned around to see the same sight he had seen at the motor lodge: greasy hair waved back and forth from under the red hat as the gritty man walked toward Luke, and while his right hand swung freely his left hand stayed stiff against his body, wrapped around blue steel.

Oh Jesus, please let another car come by. Please.

But there was no one for miles. Luke could only crouch and raise his arms in defense as the stocky figure took him over. The man raised his left arm to the sky, then slammed the gun down against the side of Luke's head.

Luke attempted to straighten and run away, but like a wounded bird, he wobbled, spun, and collapsed to the asphalt. He tried to push his body off the ground, but only his arms would obey his mind. His legs were lifeless. Luke began to crawl on his right arm, dragging his legs behind.

A second man with a grim smile entered Luke's hazy vision. Neither attacker said a word as they flipped Luke onto his back, pulling him by his feet off the road and into the ditch beside it. As if he watched the beating from outside his body, Luke saw the attackers raise their arms and feet, smashing them down again and again on his body. But he didn't feel a thing.

Slowly, the men assaulting Luke slid out of his vision, and he turned his head to look toward the wavy horizon. A figure with a familiar gait walked toward where he lay, but Luke couldn't make out who it was. He tried to stand, to go to the person, to indicate his need of help, but he was pinned to the ground by some invisible force.

As the figure approached, Luke still couldn't make out his face, but he realized who it was; he knew it was Alex.

Alex's legs moved one in front of the other, but he came no closer to Luke. It was as though he had suddenly climbed onto a treadmill in the middle of the desert. The heat waves whipped the ground between the brothers, and Luke felt them lick at his face as he strained to push up from the molten asphalt.

"Alex! Alex!" he yelled. "I'm over here! Here!" His screams swelled his head with fluid, but they had worked: Alex started to come closer.

But then, all of a sudden, Alex seemed to board another treadmill. "No! No! Please Alex, just keep coming. Keep coming! I can't move!" Even though his screams drove unbearable pain through Luke's skull, he knew his shouts coaxed Alex closer. "Alex, please, please come to me! I'm right here!"

Again, Alex came closer, this time trying to sprint. His limp was distinct, like when he'd just returned home after his injury. He was close enough so Luke could see the purple crescents that hung under his eyes. His frame had diminished to look like Luke's: wide but thin. It was Alex, but it was Alex at his worst.

Luke reached his arms out to his brother, wanting to help him out of his wretchedness. Alex stopped ten yards from where he lay. Luke tried to yell, but his lungs had grown as useless as his legs. He could only whisper, "Come here. Please, come here. Where have you been? I knew you weren't gone. Mom told me you were gone, but I knew you weren't. Please—" But Luke stopped speaking.

Without warning, Alex's head began to jerk as if an unseen hammer smashed into the side of his face. "What's wrong, Alex? What's wrong with you? Alex? Answer me!"

Luke's brother said nothing and only absorbed the invisible blows.

"Are you OK? Jesus! What's wrong?"

Alex's head shook violently and then, in an instant, his neck snapped and his ear locked to his shoulder, leaving a gaping wound where his skin had torn from his collar. He collapsed into a lifeless pile.

"No!" Luke managed to reach out his right arm, but Alex's eyes closed. Luke's world went black.

Under the high, blazing sun, Luke awoke. For a moment, he thought he was in a healthy body in his own bed, but his immense pain punctured the dream. His realization became absolute: he was broken and alone, in the middle of the desert. He pushed his body into a sitting position and felt the sides of his face. Long, smooth pads formed ridges on either side, like a catcher's mitt. His mind shook to life and brought the memory of his assault into focus. Trying to stand, he looked down at his bloody arms and realized he didn't have his jacket; he dug in his pants in hopes of finding anything tangible, but he had nothing. Each movement told him he was badly beaten. He was lost in the middle of the desert with no water, no jacket, no money and no ID.

He tried to calm himself, but fear took hold. Starting to tremble, Luke unrolled his pant leg and pulled out the only thing he had left. To find the baggie's opening, he had to bring it across his face to his right eye, for when he drew it in front of his left eye it disappeared. Disregarding the fact that he was half-blind, and with incredible focus on his task, he opened the baggie and looked around for something to usher the drug into his nose. He found nothing. Dejected, he brought the entire bag up to his face and snorted.

Some dust flew into his right nostril, but he realized his left didn't work. He lifted his hand to where his left nostril should've been, but it wasn't there; it had collapsed, flush against his face. Panic washed over Luke as he imagined his dead body by the side of the road, the smashed left side of his face picked at by a ministry of vultures.

The only thing that would fend off insanity and death, he decided, was to try to keep moving and find some shelter from the sun. Closing the baggie, now covered with clumps of blood, he held it in his mouth. He pulled himself up the side of the ditch, over to where his father's motorcycle once lay. He picked up a shard of headlight and dropped the baggie into his other hand. After smoothing the edges of the glass against the asphalt, he dipped it into the bag and brought a heap of the bloody powder to his right nostril. Some of the powder found its way into his body and tapered his sense of physical doom, but his mind knew how bad off he was.

Besides the fact that he was alone in the middle of the desert, he had only about three grams of coke left. He knew the only way he was going to stay sane was to keep the drug coming. But three grams wouldn't appease his pain for long. He did feel more strength in his legs, however. To distract himself, he tried to stand, but he had to favor his right leg. There was a little blood on his left pant leg, but there was no outside indication of severe damage—no awkward angles or smashed components. Still, he knew enough not to pull his jeans up, for an inspection of his lower extremities would surely sling him further into depression. He took another snort and rerolled the baggie into his pant leg.

He hadn't seen a car since he came to, and with each breath, Luke began to drown in a sea of dread. The waves rocked him at every step, starting to fill his mouth and nose so that it was harder and harder to breathe. Nonetheless, he began to limp backward with his thumb out. But after only fifteen steps, Luke's body could no longer propel itself. He fell to his knees.

Then he saw a glimmer of speeding metal coming toward him. He mustered the strength to rise back to his feet and raise his thumb. The hazy shape turned into a black pickup truck. As it neared, Luke dropped his head to hide his pummeled face. The pickup slowed and pulled over.

Thank God.

Luke saw the driver, a nice-looking kid with a cowboy hat and the beginnings of a goatee, lean over his seat to open the passenger door. But when Luke lifted his face to accept the offer, the driver's eyes widened. Before he even shut his door, he pulled his truck back onto the road and sped off in a heap of dust.

Though he didn't know if it would be a curse or a plea, Luke wanted to yell, but he lacked the energy. He collapsed on the side of the road and could no longer stave off the rising sea. With the high swells came a swirl of faces around his head: his mother and father, Alex and Kate, and the image of his own distorted countenance, spinning like clouds around him as if he were tied to the top of a swaying mast.

On his stomach, he put his face in the crook of his arm. With the stench of tar, oil and blood in his nose, and the images of those he loved in his closed eyes, he called for death to come noiselessly and take him away.

33

Alex rolled down the window in his truck. He yelled into the speaker, *"Two number three meals, please. With Cokes."*

It seemed like an eternity since Luke sat in Alex's truck, ordering drive-thru with his brother. Alex was rarely home during his senior year in high school, and Luke's beloved excursions with his brother were infrequent.

As Alex turned, Luke looked up at his brother's strong neck, hoping someday that his muscles, too, would flex when he turned to pay through the window.

"One number three for you," Alex said, placing a Styrofoam box and a bag of fries on Luke's lap. *"And one for me."* Casually, he tossed his food on the dashboard and shoved a few fries in his mouth. *"Want to eat here?"*

Luke shrugged. Usually, he sat in quiet awe around his brother, and today was no different. He wanted to tell Alex he missed him, how he wished they could do this everyday, how he wanted Alex to take him to A&M, but the words wouldn't come. Instead, he watched with wide eyes as his brother jammed his truck into gear.

"I'm sorry we haven't been hanging around a lot, bro," Alex said between bites. *"I've been busy. With football and school and all this recruiting shit. It'll settle down in the spring."*

"But then you go."

"I know." He paused. *"You want to know something I've never told anyone?"*

Luke nodded vigorously. The pride that his brother would confide a secret in him was almost too much to bear.

"I think I can make it. All the way."

"Where?"

Alex frowned; Luke silently rebuked himself for disappointing his brother. Alex asked, "Remember Charlie? Charlie Gamble?"

"The black guy?"

"No. White kid. Played safety?"

"I don't remember him."

"Went to UT? Put some weight on and switched to linebacker? You remember, I used to point him out on TV?"

"Oh, yeah," Luke lied.

"He's on the Jets practice squad now." Alex looked Luke in the eye. "He wasn't even that good. Just fast." Hitting his steering wheel, he said, "I can make it!" He looked out the window, and as if to himself added, "I will make it."

Alex's disclosure, and the fact he'd trust Luke with such confidence, sent Luke into fraternal ecstasy.

"You gonna play safety?"

"Probably not. Wherever I go, they'll probably move me to linebacker, too. If I could add twenty pounds and keep my quickness, I could make it." Luke's brother looked at him. "And I'm taking you with me."

Luke's eyes widened.

"Wherever I get drafted." Alex spoke in a rush. Luke had never heard his brother speak quickly. "They'll set me up in a little house, maybe a condo. I'd be making great money, wouldn't need anybody's help. You could move in, go to school wherever I end up. Maybe even in Dallas." He paused. "I've thought it all out."

Luke bounced up and down. "I'd come to every game and sit in the box and wear your jersey!"

Luke's brother scrunched his nose and turned up the radio. Santana blared from the speakers. "You and me, bro." He started bobbing his head, making up his own lyrics, "Can't stop us. No! Going to Dallas—to the show!"

Luke mimicked his brother's dance and dipped his fries in a puddle of catsup in the Styrofoam. He held up the bundle like a microphone and repeated the verse, "Can't stop us. No! Going to Dallas—to the show!"

34

L uke woke to a nudging in the ribs. He could tell by the toe of the someone trying to turn him over that this person was checking to see if he was alive. Luke held up an aching hand to indicate that yes, he was alive, though he left his face in the crook of his arm.

"You all right?" a gruff voice asked Luke from above his shoulder.

He picked up his head and turned it to the side, away from the examiner. He tried to speak, but nothing came.

"Hello? You all right?"

Again, Luke tried to speak, but his throat felt packed with barbed wire, and his mind couldn't come up with words. The examiner walked around Luke's prone body. Luke heard the boot steps and picked up his head to see a pair of dark eyes, implanted in a brown, leathery face. "Whew," the man said in a long, quiet breath. "I guess you ain't all right."

Luke started putting his position into perspective. Lying closer to death than life, and looking every bit the part of a distorted monster, Luke realized that he was the kind of man mothers warned their children about: dirty, mangled, alone, incommunicative. If he were this examiner and saw a person in his state lying on the side of the road, he would have been terrified. Like he did with the lunatic who sliced his hand, Luke would've left the poor bastard, made a call to the police, and never given him much more thought.

But as gruff as it was, the man's voice held genuine concern, and this was enough to pump a billow of hope into Luke's half-dead body. Luke again raised his head and uncracked his eyelids. The setting sun allowed him to leave them open for longer than he expected.

"Can you talk?" the man shouted, figuring more volume would miraculously give Luke the gift of speech.

Luke closed his eyes again, and with great effort, shook his head. His mother's face at his brother's funeral invaded his mind again. Her admonishment to Luke rang in his head, "I can't lose you, too." For her sake, he tried to grab enough energy to give his potential rescuer a sign that he wanted to be saved. He heard hard boot steps once more walk around him and then fade.

The man was gone. Luke dropped his head and almost called again for death, but he heard tires slowly crackle over gravel and then the familiar boot steps.

"Here. I know this will probably hurt, but I'm gonna get you into the truck."

Luke's brain sent a message to his head to nod, but he couldn't tell if it got there. A boot came down on either side of his body, followed by a groan as the man bent down to slide a hand under each of Luke's arms. Though the man's movements were slow and tender, every time he adjusted Luke's body, fire shot through Luke's left side. As the man turned Luke onto his back, Luke heard a low whimper. Luke didn't know if the sound was his or the inspector's; it sounded like his voice, but he felt none of the vibration that comes with vocalization.

Once the man had Luke turned over, he dragged him to the passenger side of the pickup. He took a few clumsy attempts at propping Luke up while he unsuccessfully reached for the door handle. He cursed himself, then put Luke's body down in order to open the door. "Sorry partner, I should've done this before I brought you all the way over here." The fact that the man was the one apologizing in this situation caught Luke in his throat—his extraordinary selflessness reminded him of his mother.

With the man's assistance, Luke's hips painfully hit the seat of the truck, and the blood rushed out of his head. The door shut, he leaned against the window and passed out.

A hammer of pain pounded into the top of Luke's cranium and his eyes flung open. He sat up on a white gurney, encased by a pale sheet hanging from a metal rim. With much effort, he blinked a few times—in hopes that visual clarity would tell him where he was. Leaning forward, he tried to prop himself up on his left hand. The ensuing blaze of pain prompted a recall of his situation: he immediately knew where he was and why, and thanks to whom. Yet, his lack of temporal sense frightened him. He had no idea if he'd been in the hospital for a day, a week, or a year. This consideration brought down the hammer with even more force. He winced. The pain on the top of his skull started to crawl down to the base of his neck, and as it did, metamorphosed into a feeling of a sharpened crocheting needles probing into his muscle.

Fearing that nothing could distract him from his anguish, Luke cleared his throat in an attempt to get some attention. Relieved that the barbed wire in his gullet had gone, he knew he could speak. But when he inhaled deeply to test his voice the familiar inferno ran up and down his left side.

Painfully, he turned his head and looked down at the purple, black and yellow splotches on his left arm and leg. At least he could see out of both eyes again. He also noticed that the only machine hooked up to him was an IV needle in his right arm: the first good sign he'd seen. He closed his eyes again and tried to put together a timeline.

His plan came to no avail, and he panicked, thinking his parents had probably been waiting for him for half a year while he sat holed up in some hospital in Utah with no ID. Again he cleared his throat, though louder, and within a minute a massive man dressed in white pulled the curtain back and walked next to Luke's gurney.

"Well, hello there. How you feeling?"

"OK." His voice sounded foreign, crumpled.

"You sure have been through it." The breadth of the man's meaty shoulders spread at least three feet, and Luke had to concentrate to keep his focus on the nurse's cheerful eyes. "I'm glad you're awake."

"Thank you. How long have I been in here?" His voice got louder with each word, though it also became clearer it wasn't his.

"Two days. You've been in and out for most of the time, but the doctor has lessened the drip." He pointed to the IV. "It's helped you come to a little bit. How do you feel?"

"Like shit."

"Can you be a little more specific?"

"My left side is killing me, but I guess I can see why." He looked again at the wretched purple and black mosaic on his skin. "Does my voice sound weird?"

"Not to me, but it probably does to you. Part of your throat was crushed and we had to open it up again. Your voice may sound different for a while." He paused. "Mouth sore?"

"Yeah." Now that the attendant mentioned it, Luke felt the rawness in his mouth and throat. "Will my voice ever get back to normal?"

"May. I don't know. May not. Nonetheless, you should feel lucky. With the story the guy who brought you in here told, sounds like you could still be out in the desert getting eaten by scavengers."

"Christ." Luke rested his head back, but kept his eyes on the nurse. "Where is that guy? Did you get his name?"

"I don't have it, but they have it on record. He must be from somewhere around here 'cause he's been back to see you a couple of times. Real nice fella."

"You're telling me." Luke shook his head at the care he didn't deserve. "What else did you guys do to me?"

"You were beat up pretty bad, but it's all stuff you can't do much for—nothing broken except your throat. And your nose. Well, and a couple of your ribs were cracked, but that just takes rest. Three of 'em. On your left side, which I'm sure you could tell. You have a chip off your jawbone there," he added, indicating the right side of Luke's face. "Plus, you needed a couple sets of stitches. On your elbow and in your leg and cheek. Swelling looks good, though, especially in your face." He paused to let it sink in. "May take a long time to go down, but it will eventually."

"A month?"

The nurse remained stoic. "May take a year, or even two for it to go completely down, but it will." He shifted on his huge legs as he waited for Luke to respond to the severity of his last statement. Luke nodded. "What happened to you out there?"

"Some guys ran me off the road and stole my bike." He let out a sound of disgust. "Beat the shit out of me, too."

"Well, I'll get an officer in here so you can report your bike. Otherwise, just take it easy. You're gonna be hurtin', but you'll be OK." He paused and leaned over Luke, for the first time using his threatening heft. "*If you rest.*" After the warning he straightened. "You need something, just hit that button and I'll be over. Anything else you want right now?"

Luke thought about making a call home but decided against it. "No, thanks." The nurse stepped away, but Luke spoke up. "Actually, you have anything for my head? It's killing me."

"I bet. I can't give you anything without the doctor, and he's on rounds. But when he comes back, I'll see what he can do." The nurse laughed.

"What?"

"Sorry. It's just that you asked the same question when you came in here, 'Can you do something for the pain?' It was an unusual question."

"It hurt."

"Oh, I'm sure about that. But most people are moaning or yelling. You just asked politely, 'Can I get something for my pain?'"

Luke didn't see the humor. "Did you help me?"

"Sure we did. But we have a saying in here—treat the disease, not the symptom. Just giving you something for the pain wasn't enough."

"Sounds logical," Luke said, almost to himself.

"I think we did a pretty good job, too. You'll be up and at 'em in no time." He turned. "I'll find the doctor."

"Thank you," Luke said.

The nurse was right. Luke needed to treat his disease. But how? He didn't even know what it was. The refrain he shared with his brother about Dallas replayed in Luke's mind. Was he mad at Alex for not coming through? Sad that his brother's potential had been snuffed out? Disappointed that Alex became capable of abuse as well as generosity? He wished he could step out of himself to study his pain more objectively. Where did it come from?

But nothing worked. It was like trying to do jumping jacks in a phone booth.

All Luke wanted was to get out of there as soon as possible and arrive at home in one piece. No more phone calls—it needed to be in person the next time he spoke to his mother and father. He put his head back against the pillow and focused on the nail driving into the top of his head and the needles digging into his neck.

This approach had worked once before, Luke remembered. When he was six, he was swinging from a tree on a rope as his brother tried to pass leaves to him. A few times they were successful, but then they simultaneously held onto a leaf too long and Luke fell off the rope, headfirst into a root. Alex called to his mother inside, but never left Luke, cradling his head in his lap, looking down on him saying, "You'll be fine. You'll be fine." Without even noticing the blood, the throbbing felt like his brain shook inside his skull. But he focused completely on the pain and Alex's chocolate colored eyes, and he remembered how it nullified the suffering. Try to subvert the power of the pain by doing exactly what it doesn't want you to do— focus completely on it. He knew the pain wanted him to try to distract himself, but he closed his eyes and thought of nothing but the rhythm of the sledge that was going to come crashing through his head at any moment. He also peered into Alex's eyes that looked down on him. Soon, he felt regular beats in his swollen face and neck, pulsating in rhythm with the hammer.

Focusing on the pain did disembody it somewhat. Strangely, the pain felt like his voice: certainly his, but foreign at the same time.

He kept his eyes closed and pushed out the urge to make a plan. Instead he concentrated only on his pain and Alex's eyes until the rhythm of the throbbing grew slower and the doctor came to restart the mechanized, clicking release of the IV.

35

F eeling like he had died and been resurrected, though only halfway, Luke leaned against the broad window on the passenger
side of Carl's corroded Toyota Tundra. The pickup's bumpy ride shook Luke's
view of the surrounding desert. Not at the controls for the first time, Luke could
contemplate the land through which he sailed. He found himself dissonantly frightened of the quaking flatlands that encircled him. He peered into the bushes lining
Route 191, trying to discern any movement or sign of life struggling to prolong itself,
but the only motion was the bounce of the trampoline on which the desert seemed
to rest.

As they had traveled, Carl made it clear to Luke that he had not only saved his
life by taking him to the hospital in Moab, but he had also put off his own trip to
Colorado to wait for Luke's recovery. *Why*, Luke had thought as they left the hospital,
would this guy care about me?

His answer came when Carl continued his story. During Luke's hospital stupor
he had told Carl about his last week in fine detail. "There was no way I could leave
anybody in that position," Carl had said in his coarse voice. "And I figured waiting a
day or two extra before heading to my sister's in Chromo would give you a chance to
get closer to home." His gentleness in deed and word undermined his hunching,
hulking shoulders and hardy face.

Out of embarrassment not only for his need of assistance, but also for his swollen
face, Luke had tried to avoid eye contact with his redeemer. It was also clear that Carl
must not have had many talking partners, because he could've talked a tree to death.
Luke had earlier made the mistake of looking into Carl's eyes, and, trying to be polite,

nodding, which only sent Carl off on more random discussion. So when the lifeless desert no longer held his attention, Luke had to find something on his side of the truck to focus on. He looked to the passenger's side floorboard.

He saw drops of his own blood from days before, though he didn't remember ever being in the seat. The sight of his own blood made him break his silence. "I'm sure I've already said this, or I hope I've already said this, but thank you." He moved his feet around on the floor mat and examined the stains. "It looks like I made a bit of a mess in here."

"That's all right, truck's seen a lot worse." Carl smiled. "And, yes, you have said thank you a number of times." Carl paused, but then geared up for more talk, clearly encouraged by Luke's voice. "I knew you were a good kid, 'cause every time I did something, even in as bad as shape as you were in, you said thank you. It was funny, too, 'cause you always said thank you, never just thanks. I heard you say it to the doctors a bunch of times, too." Carl leaned forward in his seat. "Your Mama raised a good boy."

At the thought of his mother, Luke's chest tightened and his nose began to tingle. *Jesus Christ, hold it together.* "I guess she did." He sat quietly for a moment. "I need to get back to see her. She's going to be worried as hell." He continued to stare at the bloodstains on the floor. "I told my mom that I'd be home three days ago, but I don't want to call her. I can't call her. If I tell her what's happened over the phone, she'd lose her mind." He looked at Carl, measuring his reaction. "I think it's better to wait and see her tomorrow in person."

"Don't know." Carl shook his bulky head and leaned back into his seat. "As a parent myself, actually in a very similar situation as theirs, I'd want you to call home."

"My dad doesn't give a shit." The threat of his own vulnerability distracted Luke from the stains, and he shook his head in agony. "I can't believe I'll see him soon."

"You don't want to?"

"I'm dreading it." Quickly, Luke realized he didn't want to discuss his fear of returning to his father. Rather, he shifted to address Carl's comment. "What did you mean 'similar'?" He looked at Carl, who stared into the road.

"I lost a boy, too. My oldest," he said.

The blunt declaration stunned Luke and he gaped at Carl's scruffy face. But in Carl's countenance rested a temperate expression—he clearly hadn't meant to surprise Luke. He had only wanted to comfort him with shared misery.

They had been on the road for two hours, but it seemed like two days since their last stop at a filling station. Before he and Carl had left the hospital, Luke started himself on a cycle of cocaine out of the stash that had remained undetected in his jeans' rolled cuff. He had continued with it at each of the rest stops he said he needed. But with the thought of his mother, the talk of dead boys, his beating, and the view of endless desert, he plummeted.

Because he had sniffed and snorted and rubbed his nose all morning, he knew he could probably reach in his pocket and withdraw his baggie, lean back over the bench seat to pretend to look for something and, undetected by Carl, inhale a pinch. Yet even in his desperate state, he couldn't do it—the possibility that Carl would notice him was too keen.

Looking out the window, Carl didn't wait for Luke's response and continued in a softer voice, pausing between phrases as if each was an independent thought. "He was a courier, in New York. Actually, he was trying to act. You know, in plays and things. His mother didn't want him to go, thinking New York was too dangerous, but I said we gotta let him try it if that's what he wants. He was always into theater in high school. Damn good, too. He was in *Our Town* and *Oklahoma* his senior year." Carl trailed off and raised his chin as he focused ahead on the horizon.

Regardless of his discomfort, Luke couldn't dispel his intrigue with Carl's story. "He could sing, too?"

"Yeah. Pretty good set of lungs actually. My wife's a piano teacher. That's where he gets it."

"How'd he die?"

"Got hit by a cement truck on one of his deliveries." Again, Carl tipped up his chin as if he held back threatening tears. "Problem was, he got hit on 9/11 last year, so there weren't any EMTs around." It seemed to take Carl an extra breath to prepare for what was to come "Not that he would've definitely made it if there were, but it kills me every time I—" He sat there for a full minute trying to regain his composure. Luke could see his barrel chest rise and fall quickly, and he looked away out of respect.

He thought about the fact that he'd never seen his father cry and was touched by Carl's reaction. A part of Luke felt an eerie relief—at least some good fathers existed. The problem is, they're no more protected from tragedy than the bad ones.

Carl got himself under control and tried to finish his recollection. "It kills me to think of my boy lying bleeding on the ground and no one coming to help." He coughed out one, quick sob, hastily wiped his eyes and went silent.

Luke and Carl looked out of their respective windows onto the scraggy shrubs, Luke wondering why each, one involuntarily and the other deliberately, had to tell his story about death.

Carl pulled the pickup off the road and into a dusty parking lot. "This place has the best pie in Utah. I guarantee it. Come through here every time I visit my sister."

After three hours of ache and annoyance, the stop invigorated Luke enough to nod slightly at the offer, but his mind raced to think of a polite way to get himself to the bathroom—fast.

Carl must've noticed Luke's longing for an exit. "I'm sorry if you ain't feeling too well," he said, as he cut the engine and opened his door. On their way in, Carl added, "I thought we were stopping enough. Did the bumps get to you?"

Luke had limped in front of Carl toward the entrance, and he turned around to nod. "A little." He grabbed his stomach to enliven the drama.

Luke's appreciation of Carl was deep, yet once inside the restaurant, he needed to get into the bathroom before the conversation could continue. He turned left by the cash register and said over his shoulder, "I'm going to hit the head real quick. Just order me some pie and coffee. I'll be right out." He still heard the buzz in his voice and it scared him. He tried to put it out of his mind, reaching for his baggie as he walked to the bathroom. His broken soul and body screamed at him to take the edge off, but when he shook the bathroom's brass doorknob, a voice inside said, "Give me a minute."

Luke gasped and leaned over as if he just caught a foot in the gut. *Fuck.* He looked to his right out of the bathroom hall and saw no one in the main room return his glance, so he reached for the women's room doorknob.

He shut the door, dropped to his knees and closed the toilet seat in one motion. He pulled out the yellowing baggie. He was surprised: he had inhaled nearly the entire stash in a seven-day period. Actually only four days, he reminded himself, as he thought of his time in the hospital and his putrid line about Kate, "Make *her* your drug."

He cleared his throat, lifted the toilet seat, and spit out a wad of blood and bile that made him gag. Though he had no idea how much coke he needed to get him home, Luke figured he could lay out some lines. This was probably the last time he'd be undisturbed. He closed the toilet seat in front of him and hid the baggie in his front pocket. Then he rolled a dollar bill into a wide tube and inhaled the cocaine.

He shook his head as he leaned against the toilet seat, saddened by the feeling in his body that crept toward less pain, yet nowhere near pleasure. Luke walked out of the bathroom, to the seat Carl saved him at the counter. "Feelin' any better?" Carl asked.

"A little," Luke replied, looking at a half-empty bottle in front of him. He felt like the island of cigarette butts floating on the surface of the remaining Pepsi.

"Let's get that right out of here," Carl said, reaching for the bottle and sliding it to the other side of the counter. "I ordered you some pie. Cherry. My favorite."

Even with their shared tragedy and Carl's extraordinary generosity, Luke's affection for his saccharine character began to fade. He didn't feel like he was in any sort of shape to play this guy's long-lost son.

Carl must have read the new look of disdain in Luke's eyes, because he looked squarely at Luke. He dropped his voice an octave and said, "What you need to remember is what Sigmund Freud called the Reality Principal. Do you know who Sigmund Freud is?"

"Yes." Luke perked up at the first unexpected thing he'd heard in a while.

"Great man. People give him a lot of shit these days, but they're just narrow-minded. He was a great thinker, but he couldn't reconcile civilization's pain and civilization itself—they were part and parcel. He thought the outcome of civilization was convenience, but also pain, guilt and malaise, you know?" Luke carefully nodded. "One of the building blocks of his argument was that humans naturally go after what feels good. What's pleasurable." He laughed a wet laugh that reminded Luke of the cigarettes in the Pepsi bottle. "Of course, Freud thought that the true measure for happiness, and for everything, really, was sexual love. But regardless, he expressed the Reality Principal like this: you need to feel bad in order to know what good feels like."

Carl's choice of words surprised Luke. In that one statement, Luke saw how this salt-of-the-earth man from Utah could produce a son who wanted to go to New York to be an actor. His perspective encouraged Luke back into appreciation. "Yeah," Luke responded, "but didn't he also say that most people are so bombarded by misery that they spend their time trying to feel less miserable, as opposed to feeling truly happy?"

"Have you read Freud?"

"Not exactly. My mom has read everything, and she tells me about it."

"Well, she's right, and the good thing is you know that. So, you should pursue happiness, not simply the end of misery."

Luke felt like a new man had sat down and took the place of the simple, kind fellow who had helped him avoid certain death. Yet, he grew concerned that Carl knew a lot more than he let on, not only about the world, but also about Luke.

Luke said, "I know, and I've thought I've had it. Usually with girls. Even this girl I was just with. I thought we could really be happy."

Carl put down his cup and looked Luke in the eye. "It ain't gonna' be with girls. Or drugs." He emphasized his last word by widening his eyes. "Or anything else. It's gotta come from *you*."

The simple phrase struck Luke and he considered its meaning, but again he attempted to swipe away responsibility. "I mean, shit, I understand the pleasure principal and all, but I've been gettin' kicked in the balls for a year now."

"A year? A year's nothin'. Some people live an entire life of misery and think a five-day trip to Disney World makes it all worth it. They'll talk about Mickey and Goofy and the Small World ride, and even the monorail that ran through their hotel, but the misery that's pounded them for thirty-odd years never comes up. Consider yourself lucky." Carl let out a knowing sigh. "Look, I know you're young, but still, you can point to *one* bad year. I know it's been bad; I ain't denyin' your sufferin'. But your norm has been pleasure, it seems. Just think about all those people who are getting pulverized by life and all they do is talk about that trip to Disneyland in '95." Carl looked into his cup. "Life couldn't have been too bad for you growin' up: your mom reads Freud."

"I know, I know, but—"

"But nothing. You can't be waitin' for the good to come. You ask when's it gonna turn up? It's gonna turn up when you make it turn up. *You* need to be the one to change it." He sipped his coffee, shook his head vigorously, and signaled to the waitress to refresh his cup and bring the check. "Thank you," he said to her, smiling.

He swallowed his coffee and looked beyond the counter into the kitchen, which seemed to replace Luke as Carl's discursive partner. "Eros and Death," he said slowly. "That's what Freud said, Eros and Death."

"What about them?"

"He said humanity can be boiled down to the pull and push between the instincts of Eros and Death. The instinct to love and the instinct to destroy. It's a tug-of-war. Within each individual and civilization itself. For all his cynicism, he originally thought love could win out, but when Hitler's threat grew, he didn't know if love could do it."

"So, we've got to let love win?" Luke disbelieved such a simple conclusion.

"No," Carl said, and looked at Luke like he was an idiot. "You've got to *make* love win. Even with a dead brother. And a tough father. It's not the love of a girl, or all that other stuff, but love of what's within you." He paused again and looked back into the kitchen. "Most people can't do it. Like out here. Lot of miserable people out here.

Come to the desert 'cause they can see their souls."

Luke wondered if his own unconscious brought him to the flats.

Carl lifted a small pack of cigarettes out of his breast pocket and lit an unfiltered Camel. "Want one?"

"Sure." Luke reached in his pocket for his lighter and felt the baggie. He considered for a moment what it would be like to get high with Carl. Now that he knew of Carl's alternative personality, he figured the guy might even give it a shot. And then, a flash of realization blinded Luke. He knew Carl would never in a million years do cocaine. "Excuse me," Luke said, pushing himself from the counter, putting the cigarette down. "I need to make another pit stop before we get back on the road."

36

*L*ate on the Thanksgiving night following Alex's death, Luke raised his head off his pillow. He thought he heard a coyote's wail. He'd never heard one so close to the house, and it scared him. In his mind, he knew they were small, timid creatures, but he felt fearful nonetheless. He held his head up, waiting for the sound again. It came in two quick bursts, then subsided.

"Shit," he said, as he pulled himself out of bed.

He went to the window. As he scanned the dark yard below his room, he heard the wailing in repetitive bursts. "Howl. Howl. Howl." Looking out into the darkness, he saw nothing. Then he saw a shadow in the floodlight by the garage—was that an animal? Luke didn't know. He'd prefer to see a hungry tiger rather than fear some invisible threat, no matter how minor.

Then the noise changed. The wails continued, but sounded muffled, as though the coyote shrieked into a hole. He turned from the window and started to put on his shoes when he realized something. It was in the house.

Luke walked out of his bedroom, toward the stairs. On the way, he opened the hall closet, pulled out a nine iron and clutched it with both hands. He reached the bottom of the stairs. Taking a deep breath of courage, he leapt out into the living room, with the nine iron held above his head.

But he found no wild animal.

Instead he found his mother. In a white nightgown, she sat on the living room couch. She faced away from him. Frozen, Luke watched her. Without regularity, but not quite hysterically, she howled. "Howl. Howl. Howl."

She gripped the pillow next to her, then all of a sudden, seeming to realize her noise, *put the cushion to her face. "Howl. Howl. Howl."*

Luke lowered his nine iron but stood still, petrified of his mother. After his brother had died, Luke had seen his mother cry, but it wasn't a bawl, not even a sob. Now, she bayed like an animal made to bear vivisection. Luke gazed in horror.

"Mom?"

Without wiping her face or nose, his mother turned. She looked like she'd been run over by a train—her nightgown twisted around her body, her makeup ran like blood down her face, and her hair spun around her head. For the first time, his mother looked ugly to him. Almost disgusting.

She motioned to Luke to come to her. Scared as he was and stiff with wonderment, Luke went slowly to his mother and sat beside her on the couch. She reached out and clutched him. She smelled stale, musty.

Rocking with Luke at her breast she howled again. And again. "Luke!" she cried as if she searched in the dark.

"I'm right here."

"Don't leave me!"

They sat for many minutes, Luke's mother rocking him in her bosom. "There's a hole in my heart, Luke!" She moaned, "A hole. And I can't fill it. No matter what I do, I can't fill it."

After a time, it seemed as though clutching Luke had calmed her. Her howls turned to soft hums.

Then she spoke, but her voice was hollow, distant, like she spoke to Luke through a tube. "Be careful, Luke. Be careful."

Luke didn't understand his mother's general request, but he knew it was essential to her calm. He answered, "I will, Mom. I promise, I will."

"I can't lose you, too." She rocked him, then repeated, "I can't lose you too."

37

The grungy men's bathroom made the women's feel like a suite at the Ritz. Luke closed the door, which was merely a piece of plywood nailed to two dangling hinges. He turned his back to the gap between the door and its frame, took out the baggie, and held it to his right eye for close inspection. He leaned forward to position himself directly under the one hanging light bulb and began to examine the cocaine. It had flecks of accumulated dirt and grimy blood, and when he shook it, he saw a number of BB-sized clumps.

He pulled out one of the pebbles, which looked unappetizing—completely the opposite from his first sight of coke in the Beta attic. All the boys looked so cool as they passed the mirror, and Luke thought his invitation upstairs to partake meant that he had "arrived." His brother would've killed him for being up there, he remembered, but he relished the exclusivity of the attic. Gaining acceptance in the fraternity, he found out, wasn't the height of selectivity. There was another level to the elite: brothers' kegs, attic rendezvous and secret societies.

He dropped the pebble into the toilet, then another. Soon, only powder remained in the baggie.

"Almost done in there?" a voice boomed through the gap in the door.

"Just a minute." Luke dipped his index finger into the powder and brought it to his nose. He didn't inhale it. Rather, he tried to smell the familiar petrol in the cocaine but his sense of smell was poor. He swirled the tip of his finger with his thumb, and he watched as the powder sprinkled into the toilet. The water shifted subtly, but the drug itself disappeared.

Could he do it? Dump it all? Walk out and feel relieved?

He couldn't. The coke was the only thing that had made him last this long. What did Carl know? Luke felt like shit and the cocaine helped, even if only a little. Carl had his cigarettes and coffee. What's the difference? Luke needed it to get home, then he'd quit. He thought again, *It's the only reason I've gotten this far.*

Or, he thought, *it's the reason I fell so far.* Why he was in this situation in the first place.

Luke looked at his hands. Like the coke, his long fingers were spotted with blood and dirt, his nails packed with filth. He thought of Alex's thick, strong fingers. His brother had dug them into Luke's armpit to elicit laughs, and he'd dug them into the ground to sling himself into an opponent. Alex had used them to aim Luke into his future. He used them to withhold his father, comfort his mother. Alex was not perfect, but he used his hands for good.

Luke shut his eyes. What did *he* do with his hands? Nothing but usher drugs to his nose. He frowned at his weakness. The coke made nothing better. He'd used it to attack the symptom—and it had stopped treating even that.

With the most conviction he'd had since he left home, Luke turned the baggie upside down, and in a circular pattern, sprinkled the remainder of the powder into the water. He dropped the baggie in, rubbed his hands, and flushed the toilet.

Back on the road, Carl's concern for Luke was palpable. "You feelin' all right? You ain't lookin' so hot."

Luke's head felt filled with grout. The noble gesture in the bathroom now seemed like the worst thing he had ever done. Speaking made everything worse, but he knew he couldn't give into selfish rudeness. He pushed out a response. "I'm OK. My ribs are just starting to fire up." He looked out the window, hoping Carl would catch the hint of his minimal response.

But Carl was not one to stay quiet for long. "We've only got a couple more hours until we get to my sister's. Then you can rest all you want. It's really quite a place—I think you'll love it."

Carl's voice rattled Luke's head. He closed his eyes and prayed silently that Carl would stop speaking.

In order to gain some perspective on his misery, Luke tried to remember back to Santa Fe, and his awful drive to the hot springs. He didn't think he felt as bad then as he did now. With Carl he had more air and more room, but his body was battered. Plus, on his drive that day in New Mexico he had the contentment of a full baggie— a light at the end of the tunnel. He carried no such solace in Carl's Toyota.

A slight sound, reminiscent of air escaping a balloon, interrupted Luke's thoughts. He lifted his head to look at Carl, whose face stiffened and eyes shifted back and forth, feigning surprise at the sound. He rolled down his window, and before Luke could do the same, the smell of warm death penetrated his half-wrecked nose.

"Sorry," Carl said, still looking straight ahead. "Though I love that pie, there's something about it. May be all the coffee I drink 'long with it."

Holy Shit, Luke thought. He wanted to turn and scream at Carl, *How could you do this to me?*

Typically, Luke was a big fan of flatulence, especially one with force, but this was no such case. Luke had felt he'd rather be dead *before* smelling Carl's fart. Now, he wanted to open his car door and lean out, rolling to his demise filled with the smells of the road and his own blood instead of Carl's ass. Luke closed his eyes and redoubled his focus on the fresh air filling his nose.

Carl laughed nervously. "I could tell you 'bout what Freud says about body odor, too." The name of his recent obsession brought more confidence to his voice. "He sure was a crazy old coot. He thought that when humans started walking upright, using sight instead of smell as their primary sense, that everything strong in odor became an affront. Everything but our *own* smells. He says that's one reason we're so conflicted about sex: we're driven to it, but we don't like the smell." He waited for Luke's response, which Luke gave by putting a fist to his mouth and motioning to the side of the road.

"Whoa, now!" Carl shouted as he slammed on the brakes and yanked the truck onto the shoulder. He brought an imaginary walkie-talkie up to his mouth and yelled, "Houston, we've got a problem!"

Luke opened his door before Carl came to a stop. He leaned out, and hurled out his pie and coffee onto the road and the side of Carl's truck. As it stopped abruptly, the truck rocked back and forth, and Luke used the swaying energy to fling himself out and onto his knees.

For some reason, the art of reflection descended upon Luke as he continued to heave: here he was, yet again, in very bad shape on the side of a road in the Southwest.

He thought of his junior year in high school, when he studied *On the Road*—how drawn he was to the life of the rebel runner. But here he was, trying to escape his own demons, and he couldn't even get off the *side* of the road. This thought, along with the memory of Carl's vicious fart, brought another round of gagging. *Good, I deserve it.*

The vomit had had a cleansing effect on Luke's mind as well as his body. He started to see the humor in his ridiculous situation. His drug withdrawal, Carl's fart, the discussion on Freud. Maybe he'd write a book about his own pitiful journey, *On the Shoulder*. He stuck his finger down his throat to clear away any hidden junk, coughing up some God-awful yellow, tacky stuff. Then he wiped his mouth on his sleeve and climbed back into the truck.

After a few miles peeled away, Luke's humor and irritation with himself ebbed as his self-pity flowed. *Jesus, I want to be home.*

He wanted to settle with his mother. Tell her that he had done what he needed to do and that, yes, it was stupid, but now he'll be helpful this summer—and go back to school on a mission. He wanted to make her proud. He wanted to show her that he felt her pain, that he isn't always a selfish bastard, that he has grown, that she can rely on him. That's what it came down to—he wanted her to know that she could trust him to do right. He would be there for her. As awful as he felt physically, Luke sensed a glimmer of relief in his soul.

"Feelin' better?" Carl asked him.

Again overcome by the kindness of this man who had not only taken care of the undeserving, but had actually saved a life, Luke nodded. "I am. I think I'm gonna try and sleep a bit, if that's OK with you."

"Absolutely." Carl said and smiled at Luke. "We'll be there in no time."

"Thank you."

38

Luke and his new host, Alan, sat in uneasy quiet on Alan's wide porch. They had just finished a meal of peppered pork loin, potatoes and stuffing. Though the meal had mitigated Luke's withdrawal symptoms—his shakes, bone-dry mouth, and feeling of internal void were diminished—his body still cried out for a bed. But it wasn't yet time.

After the meal, Carl had turned to help his sister, Wendy, with the dishes. He had urged Alan to take Luke out to the porch, "To show 'em the backyard." Alan nodded in assent, as if exhibiting his backyard in the dark was perfectly normal. He opened the back door, gesturing for Luke to follow.

After his eyes adjusted, Luke saw that around the porch expanded a seamless lawn that came to a neat conclusion at a row of carefully planted, young pine trees. Alan flipped a switch, and along with a faint light on the porch, a high-strung light behind the trees flickered, casting a slight shadow onto the wet, emerald grass.

Alan cleared his throat, drawing Luke's attention away from the landscaping and to the remembrance of his earlier faux pas with his host. As soon as Luke and Carl had come into the house, Wendy showed them to the dinner table. Luke realized they were late. Clearly, Wendy had gone to a lot of trouble in preparing the full-sized meal, and she had fretted over whether everything would be cold. Alan's annoyance with their meal's delay was clear, and he leaned hungrily over his plate when the three others joined him.

After a prayer, all had gone silent at the table except the clashing of steel utensils and china—even Carl had grown strangely reticent. The quiet made Luke fidget in his chair. Alan smiled at Luke, which Luke figured to be a sign of forgiveness for putting off his meal. Thanks to the nap during their ride, Luke felt more energetic and grateful than he had in a while. He smiled back. Alan's gesture was something he could hold on to in the midst of the awkward silence. As this thought rested on Luke's mind, he noticed something was stuck to the side of Alan's chin, and felt he should return Alan's graciousness. After a short internal debate about the appropriateness of such a bold, albeit helpful, gesture to a man he barely knew, Luke decided to help out his host. He gave him a signal that a piece of food was stuck to his chin. With a dubious look, Alan reached up to his left side and swiped at his face, to which Luke responded by gesturing to the other side. Alan made an ever-so-slight move to his right, when he halted and stared at Luke before returning to his pork. Luke realized that what he had thought was a renegade piece of stuffing was, in fact, an unsightly mole on Alan's chin.

Thankfully, the seat on the porch Alan offered to Luke was to his left, so the source of both men's embarrassment was out of the way. Stuffed, they each sat in their rocking chairs and caressed cups of dark coffee. Luke sat still while Alan rocked and hummed quietly. Along with his blunder at dinner and its ensuing mortification, the fact that his entire left side, running from his toes to his face, still felt packed with cement intensified Luke's discomfort. Plus, he felt like he was again under some sort of microscope, behind which Carl and Alan had silently taken turns through dinner. And Carl's unusual suggestion that Luke and Alan share some quality time on the porch only sharpened Luke's apprehension. So there he sat, motionless, afraid to irritate his injuries or reveal anything to his host.

Finally, Alan said, "You been havin' fun with Carl?"

"Yeah," Luke said, relieved by the harmless comment. "He's a great guy. I can't believe he waited for me before coming down here to visit." Alan peered at him, his examination forcing out more of Luke's words. "You have no idea how much it helps me to get this much closer to home," he continued. "I'd've been lost without him."

Luke waited for Alan to put words to his dubious facial expression, but his features relaxed and he looked out to the young pines. He said, "Carl says you've seen the bad as well as the good of late."

Luke closed his eyes and shook his head. *Does this entire family need to get into my shit?* He appreciated Carl's ride, and Alan for the place to stay, but why couldn't they just talk about the Broncos?

However, like with Carl, Luke felt indebted to Alan for his generosity. He knew the only sort of payment he could make was conversation, which Alan drove. Luke said, "It's been a tough year, and I haven't done myself any favors these past couple days."

"Carl told us about what you've been through. And, you know, I figure if I got something I think can help, I'll say it. That may sound blunt, but I've seen too many kids at school who just need a little direction. They're in the spot you're in. They're at what we call a crossroads. The problem is no one tells them that there is a good choice and a bad one." He took a sip of his coffee.

As Alan spoke, an unusual affect grew in him. Before he talked, Alan would take a short breath, and between each phrase, he'd widen his eyes as if every sentence he uttered was an incredible thought that just occurred to him. "That's one of the reasons I became a social worker. I was headed down a bad road. Really, no different than the crossroads you face."

Indignant with Alan's assumption, Luke asked, "What do you mean?"

"My brother died, too. When I was about your age." Alan paused and looked at him for a response.

Luke nodded his head, trying to appear unconcerned, but his mind lurched. *Why does everybody want to talk about this?* Then he realized why. Carl hadn't had a plan to come on his own to visit Alan and Wendy. He trumped up the trip in order to get Luke right where he was: sitting on the porch with Alan the social worker, talking about death.

"Cancer," Alan said, then took another short breath. "Nothing they could do." Short breath. "Not back then. Today ... shoot, he'd be fine. Not back then. He was twelve; I was ten." Short breath. "What about you?"

Through clenched teeth, Luke said, "Twenty-seven and nineteen."

"Little different, but not much in the scheme of things." He paused again, but Luke remained silent. "Like I said, I was at a crossroads, and I was pissed off. I turned into quite a hellion. I even started sneaking off with my Daddy's bottles. Ten, eleven-years-old, and I was off with his bottles." He looked at the bright brown lacquer on his porch. "Man, did I give them hell. Whew." He took another sip of coffee and shook his head. Luke's cynicism took over—he tried to find flaws in what he thought was surely the same act and speech Alan gave all his charges to make them see he's one of them. "But you know, as bad as I was, they never gave up on me. They tried all different things: they thought lettin' me do what I wanted might work, but that just got me in a world of hurt, so then they didn't let me out of the house, which just caused me to sneak out and get in worse trouble." Again, he shook his head. "Before, when I'd look back on my behavior I'd be so angry with myself for bein' so selfish, but I realized I needed to be selfish." Now that his speech rolled, his short breaths ceased. But Luke couldn't tell if he spoke more smoothly because he was honest or practiced.

"I mean, I didn't have to behave like *such* a jerk, but I needed to be consumed with myself in order to deal with my problems."

He looked through the dim light into Luke's eyes, and whatever he saw encouraged him to keep talking. "Actually, I didn't really deal with them. That's when my parents, God bless 'em, did the right thing. They set me up with someone to talk to." He made his final point while he looked into the darkness.

Broaching the subject of parents spurred Luke's curiosity, overpowering his skepticism. "Who'd you talk to?"

"Back then, it was looked down on to see a psychiatrist, but they did it anyway. I think my Mama might have started seeing one, and she thought it worked for her. Actually, it was probably after I started causin' my trouble that she saw one. Even after my brother's death, I don't think she did. Not that I can recall. She and my Daddy got a lot of strength through church. They were close to the preacher and had powerful faith. It helped 'em through my brother's death, but not through the hell I caused 'em."

"You think that happens a lot?"

"Getting strength through faith?"

"No, I mean, when one brother—or someone—dies, the other loses it a little bit?"

"Yeah, I think it does. But there are people who can help. That's why I do what I do. I wanted to be like the guy who helped me." He sipped his coffee. "One of the groups I lead in school is called 'Rainmakers'. We name our student groups so that the kids don't feel too weird about comin'. It's made up of kids who've lost family members. There are more of 'em than you may think. And a lot lose their way."

Luke leaned forward in his chair. "What do you tell them?"

"There's not *one* thing to say. But it's interesting that a lot of the kids act the same way after the event. Usually, it takes a little while, but soon they start to cut themselves off. Very subtly. Not like they lock themselves in their room and never come out. Well, some do—but most don't." He turned to face Luke. "A lot turn all their own needs outward. All the care and help they need, they turn around and lavish onto other people, but they never take it." Luke looked into Alan's face. Alan nodded and smiled, then took the last swig of his coffee. "It's as though the kids need someone to protect, to hold. But they never want to be held themselves, even though it's exactly what they need."

Luke's heart started to rumble. He finally sat next to someone with answers. With his wide eyes, he begged Alan to continue. Alan said, "It takes a while for the kids to figure out that it's very healthy to let yourself be held. Not just for you, but for the person holding. You know how it is when someone you love is in extraordinary pain? You want to do *anything* to help. It's good to let those who love you help you. Sometimes letting someone hug you is a bigger gift than giving a hug."

"I know what you mean. My mom's doing that."

"Maybe." Alan sat quietly, seemingly waiting for Luke to speak, but Luke said nothing. Alan continued, "You can help her."

"I know. I've always thought of her as the giver." Luke paused. The drips of relief started to fall quickly. He relished the feeling. "I'm the one to help her," he added, satisfied.

"What about you?"

"What about me?"

"Seems like you need some help. At least to settle down."

"I will."

"Could be dangerous if you don't. I've seen it a lot. Kids just do what I call 'run and rip.' They can't sit still. They fidget. Literally, some can't sit in the same chair for more than a minute. Some can't ever stay in one place for long, always moving around in their house or school. Some just bolt. Just take off. Either way, they rip through everything. It's like if they rip through their dinner, or rip through girlfriends, or rip through each day it somehow eases their pain. Really, it's just another form of running. They're just putting it off."

Luke could only sit and gaze into the darkness as he reeled from the surgery Alan had performed on his psyche. The words spoken by another finally laid bare his problem. It was so simple, and yet he couldn't grasp it until someone else uttered it. Alan had probably said this a million times, but Luke couldn't get over the fact that in Alan's words he saw a perfect image of himself. He'd done exactly what he wanted to do, he ran away. But he realized he tried to elude inescapable demons that trailed him like a shadow. To make them vanish, he'd have to come to rest under shade.

Suddenly, Luke saw something move in the distance and he leaned forward to peer into the darkness. A coyote pranced across the lawn, looking this way and that, never stopping, constantly on the lookout. "You get them around here a lot?" Luke asked, gesturing toward the animal.

Alan shook his head. He, too, was leaning forward. "Not this close to the house."

Luke leaned back in his chair and began to rock. "So," he said slowly. "What if the kid lets somebody hold them, and stops running, but he doesn't feel any better?"

Alan joined Luke in his rocking. "That's not the way to feel better. It's just part of living a balanced life. I don't know the *one* way to feel better."

In a shot, Luke's hope that he had found a true sage collapsed. He didn't hide his annoyance. "So what the hell do you tell your kids?"

"I tell them different things. The best thing I can tell them is that when I was trying to deal with my own brother's death, I kept trying to fill the void by devouring everything in sight—girls, booze, food ... whatever. It was like pissin' in the ocean." Now he stopped rocking and leaned toward Luke, his entire face, mark and all, clear in the soft porch light. He raised his finger to the air and said, "The answer ain't on the outside. It ain't drugs or fights or sex. It's *you*," he said bringing his thick finger to Luke's arm. "Don't get me wrong. This ain't easy, but neither is your situation. Shit, your brother died. That's not like getting fired or losing a girlfriend. This is *hard*. It takes time, but time only helps if you're spending it trying to deal with your situation. If you put it off, then no matter how much time goes by, it'll still be there waiting. Look, there he goes back," he said, pointing at the coyote across the lawn. "I wonder what he's doin'?"

"Maybe she's getting food. Maybe it's a mother, bringing back some food."

The two men sat silently for a long time, watching the coyote dart across the lawn, then disappear into the yawning shadows of the trees.

"You know," Alan said, "I haven't gotten *over* my brother's death. Carl hasn't gotten *over* his boy's death. It's with you always. Sometimes the loss and ache come out of nowhere, and bam!" He looked into his empty coffee cup. "I'll be at the grocery store or at home listenin' to music, or—and this happens a lot—I'll be at a Rainmakers' meeting, and a kid'll say something about his or her brother or sister and a dagger cuts my heart. It's like I just found out he died all over again. You never get over it, you just try and deal with it."

Deal with it, Luke thought. *Alex is dead. Dad is unchangeable. Mom needs help. I need help. Deal with it.*

They shared another long silence. Luke's head swam with too many thoughts to organize, and for a moment he wanted more help from Alan. But soon his desire dissipated; he knew Alan had said enough. For the first time in as long as he could remember Luke grew calm in the night's silence.

Neither man looked at the other. Each simply continued to stare into the darkness. The coyote came out of the shadows again, and she followed the same path. Across the lawn and then back again, undoubtedly collecting for her family. She went twice more. Then, with only a nod, Luke and Alan agreed she was finished, and they went back inside to go to sleep.

39

Luke and his mother ate alone. His father didn't eat with the family during the post Labor Day rush at work, nor did Alex during football season. Often they spoke easily about the day's events but sometimes they shared comfortable quiet. Tonight, they ate without speaking. Even so, they anticipated each others' needs—passing the salt, refilling a glass.

Suddenly, the kitchen door swung open and Alex walked in. He sat down at the table. Luke and his mother stopped eating, each holding up a fork full of potatoes.

His mother asked, "Why aren't you at practice?"

"Coach let us out early because of morning workouts tomorrow." Alex looked down, rubbing his large hands together. He never entwined his fingers, but rather rubbed his palms as though he rolled an egg between his hands.

Puzzled by his brother's entrance, Luke tried to read Alex's bent face hidden behind his hair.

Mrs. Stahl asked, "What's wrong, Alex?"

Alex said, "I want to drop down in English." He stopped rubbing his hands but kept his head bent. "It's too hard."

"But you just started," she said. "How do you already know it's too difficult?"

"I can tell. The teacher's ancient and angry, and we have to read huge books. It's not for me."

"What happened today?"

"Nothing happened today. It's been a week. You told me I should try it, and I did. I don't like it—it's all the smart kids. You said I could drop down if I didn't like it."

Mrs. Stahl nodded but said nothing. She touched Alex's arm.

"It's just—well, Luke knows." He looked at the table.

His mother asked, *"What?"*

Alex mumbled something inaudible.

She repeated, *"What?"*

"Luke," he said. *"What's it like when some kid you know doesn't belong in your class is there because his parents pushed him in?"*

"I-I don't know. They just join and no one cares."

"Yeah, right. I see everyone whispering in class when I try to answer a question." He turned to his mother. *"It's not for me."*

Mrs. Stahl said, *"Alex, that's ridiculous. Are the boys on the team putting you up to this? If they want to think it's cool to be dumb, then let them. But you're smarter than that. You need a challenge."*

"I was challenged! In my normal class. What can I do, Mom? It's not for me."

"Have you had a paper yet?"

"No."

"A test?"

"No. But I know I'll fail it."

Mrs. Stahl threw her hands in the air. *"How do you know? You have to push yourself, Alex. You try so hard in football. You're never satisfied. Apply some of that will to English."*

"I've tried, Mom!" He looked at the floor and spoke in his usual slow pace. *"I'm not Luke. He's smart. He can read and write. I can't. It's not me."*

Luke suddenly felt ashamed. Alex's admission was matter-of-fact, but hearing his brother articulate his inferiority caught him off guard. He said, *"Mom's right. You try your butt off at football. That's why you've done well."*

"But it's what I'm good at. That's all I can do."

Mrs. Stahl spoke again, her voice dry, *"No, it's not."* As if she was about to fall out of her chair, she grabbed Luke's arm as well as Alex's. She sat in a silent debate while her two boys looked on. She seemed sure of what she wanted to say but uncertain of the timing. Finally, she said to Alex, *"You've helped me raise Luke."*

"I was just his brother," Alex said.

"You know you were more."

He shook his head.

His mother said, *"Alex, you're smart and caring and sensitive and thoughtful. Sure you're a great football player, but that's not all you are. The proof is sitting next to you. You may think I sound too much like a mother, but you can do anything you put your mind and spirit to. You didn't choose to help me with Luke, it was thrust upon you. But you invested yourself—and look at the outcome."*

"That's different than school, Mom. C'mon. I love Luke. Helping him was natural. English isn't. I'm not good at it. Why is that so tough for you to understand?"

Luke felt unprepared to see Alex's vulnerability. He said, almost pleading, "You can do well."

His mother added, "Just because no one else on the team is in honors doesn't mean you can't be."

"They'll break my balls."

His mom asked, "Who?"

"Everyone. They expect me to be—to be, I don't know. The Marauder. It's hard enough to be in Honors English. But what about when I flunk? What then?"

Luke's mother shifted in her seat, her eyes searching Alex's face for answers. Again she asked, "Who, honey?"

"Everyone. The team. The girls. The coaches. I'll look weak when I fail."

Mrs. Stahl said, "You're making no sense, Alex. You're not going to fail."

"How do you know? Everyone thinks I'm nice, I know. But they also think I'm tough. When I fail, they'll pity me. Poor Alex should've stuck to football, they'll say. I don't want to deal with that."

"Alex, no one's going to pity you. And no one's going to hurt you." She clutched his hand, which laid in hers like a bird's broken wing. She added, "My job as your mother— my most important job—is to protect you." She turned to Luke. "And you. I would never let anything happen to either of you. I would never put either of you in a position where you could be hurt. If that happens, I've failed. I've failed as your mother. You have to trust me, Alex. And you do too, Luke." She grabbed his hand as well. "I won't let anything happen to you."

40

With his foot resting uncomfortably on the massive wheel well of the Greyhound bus, Luke pushed his forehead to the cool, thick glass, trying to connect, even slightly, with the road that rolled by ten feet below. Though he mashed his head against the glass and turned it to either side, the road on which he sped was invisible, silent.

The poor view relegated his concentration to the telephone line that paralleled the road. Between the telephone poles, the wire bounded up and down, and when he forced himself to look directly out, not giving into the desire to look ahead, the wire looked alive—like a razor thin snake that sped alongside him, trying to keep up through the repetitive dips.

Beyond the poles, the tall grass laid down, beaten against the earth from the recent rain. Though still quite yellow, the base of the blades had taken on a greenish hue—they'd absorbed some of the torrent that had trapped Luke in the sights of his abusers a week before. After a time, the grass became more sparse as the urban concrete made further and further inroads. As much as he wanted to smell the stiff scent of the last few fields before the city, his position on the bus wouldn't allow it. The separation from the natural forced him to look closer in.

For five hours he'd been trying to keep himself busy. After his 2 a.m. departure out of Pueblo, he'd slept for three hours, but suddenly awoke to the squeals of a woman two rows behind. He turned to see her swipe at something that appeared to be invading the skin on her right arm. She dug her black fingernails into her skin as her mouth and eyes, both encircled by black makeup thick as tar, widened simultaneously. Through Luke's bleary vision, the girl looked like a rabid raccoon. She dug furiously into her arm, finally raising a tiny, bloody something into the air. She peered at it. Before he could see if what she held was moving, the girl smelled it, licked it, bit at it, then stowed it away in her black purse.

Luke couldn't fathom what troubled her. Would he ever escape these freaks? For some reason he knew he wouldn't. But he realized he could do nothing for them. Some people and some things you just can't change. There was so much he could do nothing about.

Once awake, and unable to close his eyes for fear of what the girl was capable of, he had kept his focus outside the bus. First, on the sky that began to glow red, then on the phone lines illuminated by the morning sun.

He transferred at 10:15 a.m. in Amarillo. Though the bus station was a haven for rancid deadbeats and homeless children, it felt good to rest his head on a plastic bench that, unlike the bouncing seat on the bus, allowed him motionless rest. But when he closed his eyes, Luke realized his mind wouldn't equal his inactive body; serene slumber was not a possibility, especially with the ever-nearer prospect of his return home.

As he dipped into sleep, Luke's dreams rushed to a picture of himself standing alone in a sea of gravel. Around him, bubbles surfaced and then popped, sending tiny pebbles into the air like drops of water. One huge bubble rose, but instead of propelling stones, the boil sent Luke's father's disembodied face levitating upward. His father's face rushed at him—eyes blood red, mouth opened in a silent scream. Swirling around him, its size and shape grew more distorted as Luke pleaded with him, "Dad! It's me. Stop, please. Stop!" But he didn't.

Then, slowly, as the face whipped like an electron around Luke, its skin started to melt, slipping and dripping onto the stones below. Luke held up his hands, each one clutching a swollen, black saddlebag to protect his face from his father's gruesome skull, but it continued its assault, nearer and nearer. Ultimately, his father's head swung out as if to get a head of steam for a decisive collision, but just before impact, Luke's mother rose out of the stones and deflected the threat. Luke shook out of his sleep.

The sound of a garbled voice pounded from the loudspeaker above him, jarring him out of his haze.

" … Canyon … Tulia … Plainview … Hale … Center … Abernathy … Lubbock … " Luke wiped the drool from the corner of his mouth and picked up his head. Hoisting himself out of the chair reignited the fire in his left side, but the echoing name of his hometown lifted him erect, and he limped to the terminal's exit.

He tried to forget the grisly portrait that had just invaded his sleep.

At least he knew what to make of the vision. Certainly, his mother needed his help. She'd protected Luke for as long as she could. Now he had to return the care. But for his father, Luke could do nothing. He would put up with him through college, and that would be it.

With nothing in his hands, he walked out of the terminal. Besides the clothes on his body and shoes on his feet, Luke carried home sixteen dollars and a piece of paper with Carl's address and the amount Luke owed him—$113.00. Along with tossing hoards of discarded McDonald's wrappers, torn tickets and empty Pepsi cups into the air, the familiar wind ushered him into his homebound bus.

Once they stopped in Abernathy, Lubbock was only thirty minutes away. But Luke felt none of the classic jubilation of return. No smile crossed his lips when he recognized New Deal's battered stores on Main Street, slouching away from I-27; no relief came with the anticipation of seeing his mother's anguish disappear; no fresh conviction with his promise to Alan that he'd talk to a psychologist; no hungry expectancy for the possibility of getting back to school and reregistering for Professor Stewart's writing class; no lightness in his chest at the chance to be home. Nothing. At least numbness, he reminded himself, is better than pain. He was moving in the right direction.

After maneuvering off of Buddy Holly onto Broadway, then left onto Avenue L, the bus swung under the terminal's canopy on 13th street, staggering to rest as its air brakes belched out their relief. Luke had thought he was beyond the point of puking, but when the bus staggered back and forth, the latrine smell of shit and piss and disinfectant evoked an image of the bus's swilling toilet basin. The taste of vomit rose in his throat. He lurched up and limped to the front of the bus, much to the chagrin of the degenerate passengers who probably thought he tried to secure pole position for the impending dispatch. In fact, he did exactly that and reached out for the handle next to the driver. The door opened, inviting his release before he threw up.

The floor in the backseat of the A1 cab housed a montage of spills and swipes that went from white to yellow to red, the responsible liquids having dried long ago. Luke had stared between his knees at the medley of colors since he stepped into the ancient cab, and he traced the stains' outlines for the entire ride home. The empty spaces of gray fabric between the blemishes looked like a series of unconnected islands, and when Luke let his eyes go fuzzy their borders would merge as if the islands drew together from some unyielding, gravitational pull. Luke focused and unfocused, smiling at the connection he could generate with only the slightest effort. The grin felt foreign on his swollen lips.

"OK," the cabbie grunted, making Luke pick up his head for the first time. He realized they had probably idled in his driveway for a while.

Swinging his leg out of the car, Luke felt the gravel's familiar crunch under his foot. The driveway was one of the few things his parents hadn't changed since they moved from Dallas, and he remembered well the times Alex had humored him and helped him build mini volcanoes that they'd then stomp flat.

He leaned forward to offer the cabbie his fare, then stepped out of the cab. Leaning on his right leg, Luke looked at his reflection on the glass that framed the oak doors to his house. The sun shone on him from ahead, painting his clear picture on the window. He stood still looking at his reflection, which showed his empty hands, his battered face, his favored leg, and his feet in the gravel, sinking just a bit as he shifted more weight to his right side.

The house inside was still. Quiet. Empty.

There was a shudder inside. A slender figure left the last step on the front stairs and walked toward the door. She was home. Living on. Waiting. Her only hope that he come home alive.

Luke alone, safe, would satisfy her.

Acknowledgements

I have many to thank who made this book possible: Elizabeth, Anthony, Greg, Brooks, Peter, and Merrill for the readings—I know it was painful; Dan for the laptop; and Courtney, Elaine, and Jonn for the counsel. You've helped more than you can imagine.

Printed in the United States
1113800002B/142-150